Royal ESCAPE

By JJ Knight
USA Today bestselling author of
Single Dad on Top
Big Pickle
Hot Pickle
Spicy Pickle
Royal Pickle
Royal Rebel
Royal Escape
Tasty Mango
Second Chance Santa
The Accidental Harem
Uncaged Love
Fight for Her
Reckless Attraction

Want to make sure you don't miss a release?
Join JJ's email or text list.

About the Royal Series

★★★★★ **The cutest laugh-out-loud rom com of the summer!** ~ *USA Today* bestselling author Blair Babylon

★ ★ ★ ★ ★ Quirky and charming but enchantingly heartfelt, **this regal read will be one of your very best rom-coms this year.** ~ BookAddict

★ ★ ★ ★ ★ **A fabulous royal romance read!** ~ The Dragon Den

★★★★★ This book delivered on the humor I love and come to expect when reading a JJ Knight rom com. **I gobbled this book** rather quickly because it's hard to put down. ~ Nicole's Book Musings

★★★★★ **A refreshing romantic comedy that will put you in a great mood!** ~ Sunny Shelly Reads

Royal Escape

The hot mess everyone knows as Princess Lili is falling in love with one man and having wild monkey business with another. Yeah, I mean me. I'm the hot mess.

Don't judge me. Not yet. There's some back story.

First, I ran away from my royal duties.

I escaped to America, party hopping as the wild, red-haired lifestyle influencer Indigo Flame. I peddle everything from blue eye shadow to flavored pickles to get by.

Don't judge me!

Then, I met the kind, sensitive artist Jesse Adams while looking like the real me — princess me. This is a problem. Huge. I can only see him in secret or the jig is up.

But then I discovered the Masked Man. I met him at a vampire ball dressed as Indigo. Within ten minutes, we were locking the door of the dressing room and things got *hot*.

I planned to lead a double life all along. I have to if I want to be free of my royal shackles.

But now I have a triple life? Quadruple?

All I know is that Jesse opens my heart, and the Masked Man opens ... everything else.

And if I don't get my act together, I'm going to lose everything.

———

Royal Escape is a hot, hot, hot romantic comedy about a princess pretending to be an influencer pretending to be a princess, a man who can't keep his hands off her (as long as he's wearing a mask), a meddling Pickle family who opens a castle in Colorado without realizing the pretend princess is a real princess, and a triple-double twist that everybody sees coming — except the donkeys.

This is the final book in the Royally Pickled trilogy, but can totally be read as a standalone. (Just don't tell Princess Lili's sister 'cause she'll be super mad if you skip her. Prince Leo? He'll be chill.)

Casey Shay Press
PO Box 160116
Austin, TX 78716
www.jjknight.com

Also available in paperback: ISBN 9781938150975

CHAPTER 1

Lili

I might be the only princess in history to stow away on her own private plane.

But here I am.

I crouch in the bottom of the suitcase closet, wishing I could cut off my legs.

Or maybe, I guess, cut a hole in the wall *for* my legs.

I've been curled up for close to eight hours in various pretzel positions.

And I'm about as flexible as a skillet.

Then, of course, we hit turbulence.

My head bangs against the back wall, and I clap my hand over my mouth to stifle a yelp. I can't let the flight attendant hear me.

The pilot doesn't speak over the intercom to calm the passengers. There aren't any. There's only him on board, plus Ruby, the flight attendant.

And, of course, me, hidden in the bottom of the closet.

I want to climb out of here and lie on the bed.

And pee.

No, no. Not on the bed.

There's a fancy bathroom at the back of the plane.

But Ruby will spot me, and she'll report me in an instant. Ferron, the pilot, would probably turn the plane around.

I have to be clever and careful. Because at some point, my parents, the King and Queen of Avalonia, are going to notice that their youngest princess is missing.

By then, I need to be buried deep in New York. My brother Leo, the Crown Prince, evaded the palace guard for almost a year.

It's my turn.

I check my phone. It's 6:58 a.m. New York time. We'll be descending soon. I switch screens to bring up my USA BUCKET LIST. It's everything I want to do while secretly in America.

1. Lose my virginity. This should be easy. I've watched dozens of American movies about dating and sex. I just need to look across a crowded room and spot the guy who will carry me into a romantic sunset.

2. Meet normal people. No one can know I'm the Princess. I want to live a regular life.

3. Have a killer 21st birthday. First one on my own. I have two weeks to make something happen.

Hopefully I won't get caught before then.

The sudden bounce of the landing gear makes me lose my grip on my phone. It clatters on the floor and I snatch it up, holding my breath.

But the plane taxis to a stop, and no one comes for me.

I ease the closet door open. There's a clear view of the cockpit.

Ruby's there, talking to Ferron. "How long are we stopping over?"

"Just long enough to fetch the rest of the Pickle family." Ferron tucks his cap under his arm. He's in full uniform even though there aren't any passengers.

They move toward the side of the plane with the exterior door. Several mechanical noises echo back, including the ka-chunk sound of the stairs dropping into place.

"Are we going into the city?" Ruby asks.

"We have a car coming," Ferron says. "I need to do post-flight."

The two of them return to the cockpit.

I place my knee on the carpeted floor. It's bliss to stretch out after eight hours tucked in a ball. For a moment, pins and needles shoot through my feet, but I manage to stand up, crouching low.

I wasn't able to bring much, just an overstuffed back-pack. I slide it onto my shoulder and pull my hood over my head.

As I tiptoe through the plane, Ruby and Ferron talk in the cockpit. I pass the dining table and duck behind a row of seats. Their backs are to me. The door is open. The stairs are down.

This is it.

I race for the exit, and my feet fly down the steps. I'm not sure which way to go. I can't be seen and the flat tarmac is endless.

I adjust my bag and walk swiftly away from the plane, opposite where Ruby and Ferron might spot me through the cockpit window. Maybe I can hide until their car takes them away.

I head toward the nearest outbuilding, but I'm spotted by two men on a four-wheeler.

Oh, no.

They zip toward me and squeal to a stop.

"Where did you come from?" one of them asks.

I wave vaguely at the small planes. "How do I get to the terminal?"

The man stares at me for a moment. He's older than my dad, wearing a cap and a bright yellow and orange vest. "Your pilot just left you out here?"

"Yeah. Told me I could walk, but I don't think that's allowed?"

"It's not." He frowns, then jerks a thumb at the seat behind him. "Hop on. We'll take you."

"Thank you." I don't waste a second climbing on board. The cool wind whips my hood as we race across the tarmac.

So far, so good.

When they drop me in front of the terminal, I sit on a bench and pull out a phone with a US SIM card. I acquired it by making a chirpy video on Instagram for the company.

I've been a secret social media influencer under the name Indigo Flame for over a year. I've been amassing gift cards, credits, and contacts, waiting for this moment.

Now I can finally use it all.

I load the first of my stack of Uber gift cards into the app, then call a ride to a small boutique hotel in Chelsea. It's owned by one of the biggest lifestyle influencers, and my personal hero, Monica Best. She has millions of YouTube, Instagram, and TikTok followers.

She set up the hotel as a center for the artists and influencers she finds interesting, and I've had an invitation for a week-long stay waiting for me for months. While there, I hope to meet other people in the biz, get leads on other hotels that will have me, and ride the wave as long as I can.

I have no choice, because even if I had access to royal bank accounts or credit cards, it would be too easy for the staff to track my movements.

I have to do this on my own.

The car ride is long, and I peer out the windows. I've been to New York before with my family, but this one will be so different. I can do anything I want!

We pull up to a three-story building. It's brick with tall windows lining each floor, the sashes painted in vivid orange, green, and red. It looks modern and bright.

I sling my backpack over my shoulder and head inside. The foyer repeats the exterior colors, an enormous painting filling a wall behind the check-in desk.

A young woman waits behind the counter. "Can I help you?"

I realize I should have put on my Indigo wig before entering. I look like me! I tug my hood low on my forehead and keep my chin down. "I'm Indigo Flame."

Her eyes light up. "Oh! Indigo! Do come down for a selfie when you're settled!"

"Sure." I'll be sure to look like Indigo then.

"I see Monica has comped you a week stay. Did you download the app for the hotel?"

"I did." I turn the phone screen to her.

She strikes one more key. "I see you! You're all checked in. Room 233. Your phone is your key. So excited to meet you."

I nod. "Thanks."

I head for the stairs. Each step is painted a different color, gradually shifting from green to orange to red like a mango.

The air smells of fresh citrus. Everything about the colored wallpaper, the asymmetrical mirrors, and the wildly patterned floor fills me with excitement.

I'm here! I made it!

And nobody knows who I am. Nobody expects me to produce an ID with my social media handle.

I couldn't have come up with a better scheme.

But I better get my wig on and apply my makeup. Then I'll log into the influencer Discord chat and let everyone know I'm here.

I can't believe I've done it! Leo will be so proud.

I sober for a moment. I left my brother behind right as his first baby was being born. There was no better moment, though. The entire castle was in upheaval, and the plane was empty, heading to the US to fetch more of his wife's American family.

I wave my phone at the door and the latch pops open. The interior is amazing, all cool greens and natural textures, like I'm inside a head of lettuce. In fact, the room smells faintly of fresh produce.

I drop my bag on the bed. Pee first! The bathroom is as bright and green as the main room, and utterly photo-genic. Monica knows how to maximize the Instagram potential of a space.

That taken care of, I open the curtains and realize I'm peering out the windows I saw from the street. Below, people walk the sidewalks. There's a flower vendor, a crepe shop, and two clothing boutiques. I can go anywhere, look at anything. No guards. No rules. No decorum to follow.

It's paradise.

I pause in front of an unexpected door in the center of the side wall. I'm used to suites. Does this room have another room?

I twist the deadbolt and try to open it, but it doesn't budge. I jerk and shake it, then realize there is another latch that drops into the floor. I bend down and lift it.

The door opens to reveal — another door. But this one doesn't have a knob. That's odd.

I run my hands along the edges. Did Monica build a puzzle in this room? I believe it. She'll do anything to get social media play. Maybe I have to figure out what to do to get to the bonus room.

This door rattles just like mine did when I pulled on it. Is this part of the puzzle? I press my ear against the wood to listen.

Then suddenly, the door flies open, and I fall onto the floor on the other side!

My face smashes into orange carpet. It smells like an orange, too. I lift my head. "What in thunder?"

There's a mandarin duvet on the bed. Orange walls, textured to look like the inside of a peel.

Then, right by my cheek, two feet.

Man feet. Square nails.

Pants, no cuffs. The hem lands exactly where it should, custom tailored.

I rise to my hands and knees, shaking off my fall as I lift my head. The pant legs are tapered and crisply ironed. The belt is Italian leather. The shirt is pale green, the cuffs rolled up to reveal strong, tan forearms.

The neck is unbuttoned.

Then I see his face.

Good Lord. He's gorgeous and blue-eyed with sandy hair. He must be a model, comped a stay by Monica. I'd comp him anything he asked for.

He stares at me with an odd expression of amusement. "Falling for me already?"

Worst opening line ever.

But yes, yes, I am.

CHAPTER 2

Jesse

I'm not used to strange women tumbling into my hotel room. I heard all the noise at the door between the two rooms and had to investigate.

This girl scrambles to her feet. She wears a gray hoodie and ripped jeans, like any twenty-something trying to be hip. This hotel is full of them.

But when she finally stands, there's something about her that's different. The way she holds herself. The lift of her chin. Her hair is shiny and golden brown, falling in soft waves to her shoulders. Everything about her is polished and expensive, from her skin to her nails to her eyebrows.

She sees me looking and brings the hood up, then changes her mind and drops it back down. Curious.

"So, hello?" I say.

Her eyes dart to her room, like she might make a run for it. But then she says, "Ha-lo."

That accent. I can't quite place it. I'm instantly

intrigued. This woman dresses like an American but talks like a European.

"I'm Jesse." I extend a hand.

She takes it, clearly unused to a good shake. Her fingers curl around mine awkwardly. She seems surprised when I lift them up and down. Even more curious.

"And you are?"

Her hazel gaze meets mine. She's hesitating.

I let her off the hook. "That's okay. I wouldn't tell me either." I release her hand. "Are you here by invitation or a regular tourist?"

She touches her hair as if it has the answer. "A tourist."

"First time in New York?"

"No. I came here before. Six months ago." Her eyes return to the safety of her room.

Damn. She's not into me. It happens.

"Well, I won't keep you. I'm sure you have places to video and people to selfie." Also lame. I'm not making a good impression.

But she tilts her head, her eyes back on me. "Are you an influencer? Or a model?"

That old thing again. "Neither."

"So you're at Monica's hotel as a regular tourist?" She pauses. "Too?"

Now I'm burning with questions. "I'm not sure regular tourists know about Monica or her connection to models and influencers." I lean against the door frame. "You ready to confess?"

She snorts in annoyance. "Scat diddly."

"Come again?" She's definitely not from around here.

Her eyes spark fire. "It's another word for shit. I've

been resurrecting old curse words."

Oh. I get it. I like this side of her. A lot. "That would explain the 'what in thunder' when you fell."

"I have a lot of them."

"And 'what in thunder' comes from…"

She smiles, her soft lips drawing my attention like a perfect strawberry. "I borrowed an old phrase and coined a new one."

My mouth has gone dry, but I manage to say, "Ah. Nice. For your followers?"

She crosses her arms over the front of her hoodie. "Maybe."

"You know you want to tell me how many you have."

Her eyes pierce mine like a challenge. I love it.

"Two-point-two million."

Oh. She's serious then. "That's impressive. Should I know you?"

An expression like fear crosses her face. "No."

"With two-point-two million—"

She ducks past me into her own room. "I have to go."

"I can't get your Insta handle?"

Her side of the door slams in my face.

Oh, I like that, too. She's everything I love about New York. People with secrets. Double identities. Celebrity that doesn't like to be seen without its face on.

I'm so fascinated that it takes everything I've got not to knock on the door again.

But I leave my side open. If my neighbor wants to drop in, she can do that any time.

I certainly have nothing to hide. I never have. I was a child model from birth, literally. Born to a fashion designer mother and a male model father, my squalling, red-faced arrival was published in the pages of *Vanity Fair*. I did more commercial photo shoots by age five than most working models get in their lifetime.

Then my parents split. Mom buried herself in her work. Dad traveled the world in search of a fountain of youth to keep him in the biz.

And I retired at the ripe old age of six.

I don't miss it.

I turn to my orange room. Such an odd hotel, but I like it. Monica brought me here to install six of my mixed-media assemblage art pieces in various suites. She likes my aesthetic.

I lean against the wall to assess the location of the three-dimensional spiral peel of an orange. It hangs over the bed, close enough to the wall that no one should bang their head on it.

Unless they're jumping on the mattress. I imagine a wayward five-year-old trying to hang from the strings.

I step onto the bed with my bare feet.

Nope. This isn't safe. It will have to go over the desk or in the corner. One boisterous kid or drunk adult could bounce on the mattress and the entire art piece would be toast.

Toast. I sit down, an image appearing in my mind. A suspended substrate textured like toasted bread, complete with a square of butter, slightly melting. And the knife, not gently angled as if to spread the butter, but piercing the toast instead.

Your toast is *toast.*

I stop everything to dig out my sketch pad and put

down the idea before it's lost. I have notebooks every-where — my backpack, my car, beside my bed at night. In a pinch, I'll make a quick drawing on my phone, although I prefer the scratchy sound of a high-quality pencil on textured paper.

Toast. I like it.

A *clunk* sounds from next door. She never told me her name. I set the sketch pad aside and move closer to our adjoining wall. She's opening and closing drawers, too quickly to be filling them.

I can picture every one of her features. The cascading hair. The well-cut hoodie, couture styled. The expertly slashed jeans showing flashes of skin on her thighs.

I return to my sketch pad and flip the page. I draw the bold lines of her shape and fill in the details. The sparkling Kate Spade sneakers and the generous curve of her ass in those jeans. The hoodie, tapered at the waist, the gentle stretch over her breasts.

Her face is etched in my brain. The soft mouth, high cheekbones, big eyes. Those lashes. I take my time on those. Lashes kill me.

When I'm done, I immediately have the urge to perfect it, fill it in, add color. But I have work to do here. There's this room plus two more that aren't complete. I'm not staying in this room currently. Monica told me I could have my pick, and last night I stayed in the coconut room where my husk installation perfectly houses an entire galaxy.

But I need to stop by the registration desk to move rooms. Because tonight, I want to sleep right here. Just on the other side of the wall from *her*.

CHAPTER 3

Lili

My mind is definitely on my neighbor as I carefully tape the skin beneath my chin sharply back to create a face shape that matches Indigo's profile picture.

If I'd known I would have to recreate this look in real life, I'd have softened Indigo's fake face. As it is, I'll have to use a sculpting technique I learned on YouTube, then cover the evidence with heavy makeup.

That's fine. Indigo is known for her vivid red and purple eyeshadow, heavily winged eyeliner, and massive lashes. Then the wig, long, lush, and cherry-red with a fat swath of deep purple that covers one eye, not too far off Jessica Rabbit's look.

I had the wig made when I was in New York last time, plus paid for a second version to be stored at the shop in case one got ruined or discovered among my things in the palace. I was on that trip with my parents' blessing, so I had real money to spend.

I carefully lift the wig from my backpack, unrolling it from the tissue paper and removing the net.

It looks good. I'll style it with the flat iron I packed from home, then pick up more styling tools with my beauty store gift cards. I need to shop for clothes. I only have two outfits other than the one I'm wearing.

But shopping is better with friends. I remind myself of all the expressions I've been practicing so that I won't sound like my Lili self, but Indigo.

What in thunder?

Are you a frazzlin, or what?

Bodikins!

Scat diddly!

Zounderkite!

My phone lights up on the bathroom counter. The Discord chat is heating up now that I've announced I'm in town.

Drag Scream: GIRLFRIEND! You had me at shopping! I have comps at H&M and three boutiques.

Me: Same.

Drag Scream: Are you at Monica's?

Me: A room like a lettuce head.

Drag Scream: I'm taking the subway straight to you!

Me: All right. Downstairs bar?

Drag Scream: Fab fab! I'm speaking at the Vampire Ball for Babes tonight. Come with?

Me: Undead suits me. I don't have the right clothes, though.

Drag Scream: I will snap my fingers and make you a vampire queen!

This is good. I have plans for tonight. Drag Scream will help me shop. Everything is going perfectly.

My phone lights up again.

Grim Weaver: Who said shopping?

Drag Scream: We're not putting her in a crochet jumpsuit.

Grim Weaver: That's your dream look and you know it.

Drag Scream: Shut your knotty mouth, my love. You coming to the bar?

Grim Weaver: And see the famous Indigo in person? Of course.

I angle the phone so I can see it as I smooth my real hair flat to prepare for the wig. This is so great. Drag Scream is a sensation, a horror-movie reviewer who is regularly invited to screenings in her outrageous outfits.

Grim Weaver is a tall, skinny skater-type who has knitted his way to superstardom on Pinterest and Instagram with his macabre wearables.

I have people to see. I won't be alone. And even though I miss my sister, and I left the castle in the middle of the insanity of a royal birth, this is worth it.

Drag Scream: 1 p.m.

Grim Weaver: At Monica's?

Carly Butterfly: I want to come to Monica's!

There's a pause in the rapid-fire messages on the Discord channel. I lean over the phone screen. No one else is inviting Carly. She can be a bit much.

But I will.

Me: We're meeting in the bar.

Carly Butterfly: There are at least fourteen toxins in every bottle of liquor.

Drag Scream: BYOB then.

Carly Butterfly: ?

Grim Weaver: Bring your own PB then.

Carly Butterfly: ?

Grim Weaver: Pro-biotics, wise one. Monica won't care. But don't diss her drinks on your feed. That will get you banned with a capital K.

Me: K?

Grim Weaver: OK!

I shake my head. Grim is two peaches shy of a bushel. I'm not sure if it's an act, or how he is. I guess I'll learn, because this is turning into a party.

The messages keep buzzing, but I have to focus on my face. I can't go anywhere without full Indigo, and that takes time.

I put on the hair net and glue the front. Even if people assume this is a wig, it has to look good.

I flip the red hair and dive into it, cutting baby hairs and tweezing the hairline, running a YouTube video as a reminder of the steps. Then I cut the lace, glue it down, and blend it all in with makeup.

I'm so different already. Princess Lilianne is almost gone. It's time to slather on Indigo's signature face and obliterate the old me.

Except now, I'll have to avoid the man next door. Because of my foolishness, he knows exactly what I look like IRL.

By the time I'm done, Grim Weaver has already messaged to say he's at the bar half an hour early.

I check myself in the mirror one more time. I'm wearing the ripped jeans and sparkle tennies. But the warm afternoon means I've switched the couture gray hoodie for a one-of-a-kind Rage Against the Machine T-shirt.

It's hand painted on top of the vintage lettering by an artist in Ibiza. She gifted it to me after I got her sixty thousand new followers with several key mentions about her beautiful work.

My backpack is a little on the nose, Louis Vuitton, but it was one of the few practical comps I've had. Hopefully, another option will come along, something more Indigo.

I take a selfie in the bathroom with my fingers in a sideways peace sign. I type, "Epic selfie incoming as we converge on Monica's incredible hotel bar."

I run the image through my custom filter and post it to Instagram, then quickly repeat the caption with a blowing kiss video on TikTok. It's wild running the filters on a version of me that already looks like the filter. But it works. I think I'll pass.

I'm about to find out.

I close my door carefully, trying to be quiet enough that the barefoot boy next door won't pop his head out and see that I've completely altered my appearance.

I tiptoe halfway down the hall before taking a normal stride toward the stairwell.

But, of course, as luck would have it, I round the bend in the stairs and slam straight into him.

"Whoa!" Jesse says, grasping my waist. "We must be Microsoft, because we just crashed."

He doesn't appear to have a clue who I am. He's not looking at me anything like he did in his room. In fact, I think I see disdain in his gaze as he takes in my hair and makeup.

"Go forth and selfie." He holds two fingers in front of his face, and my cheeks blaze that he's mimicking the exact gesture I made in my last upload. Am I that much of a cliché?

I shrug past him and continue down the stairs.

There's no way he would match the girl he met with Indigo. I don't recognize myself.

I pause by a mirror on the landing before heading into the lobby. Eye makeup on point. Lashes fully attached. Hair swooping. I straighten my shirt so that the lettering is perfectly centered over my torso.

A voice echoes down. "You can stop preening. You could already make New York traffic back up for miles." Jesse leans over the banister, peering at me.

So he hits on everybody. Natural-looking girls who stumble into his hotel room, and flame-haired vixens who pass him on the stairs. I definitely don't feel special anymore. Too bad. Because he is hot, hot, hot, and could have been a contender for USA Bucket List Item #1: Virginity.

I might as well complete the whole Gen Z, pretentious, self-indulgent, influencer stereotype. I turn around to lift both hands and double flip him the bird.

He laughs. "Loud and clear." But then he's up the stairs and gone.

Damn that smile. It's infectious. He somehow nailed both the male model and boy next door look at the same time. I didn't think that was possible.

But I don't have time to think about it, because as soon as I enter the lobby, a screech goes up. "Indigo!"

It's none other than Monica Best herself.

My hands sweat. She has no idea how instrumental she's been in my escape. Without the seven days in her hotel to get my bearings, I wouldn't have known where to go once I got off the plane. Maybe I wouldn't have come at all.

Monica is fiendishly tall, her height accentuated by four-inch platform ankle boots the color of tangerines.

She wears gold fishnets over her deeply brown skin, the tiniest gold wrap skirt, and a pea-green sleeveless turtleneck sweater.

Perfectly formed black braids spill over her shoulders. She has gold eyeliner, ear cuffs, and I want to be her when I grow up.

She waves the front desk girl over. "Sheba, let's do an entire series with Indigo. Look at that shirt. It's that Ibiza artist you featured, isn't it? I love it. The jeans. So on point. God, this hair. Epic. People could spot you in a colosseum. Brilliant."

I can scarcely breathe. I have no idea how to act. She's so over the top. I want to blurt out, "Marry me," but catch myself. I have to be chill. Indigo is chill. She also has to adjust her accent. I let out a breath. I've got this.

I toss my hair behind my shoulder. "Sorry it took so long to get here. I had to prioritize."

"I love it. Worth the wait." Monica leads me in front of a gigantic abstract painting on the back wall. "Standard set, thirty shots minimum." She waves at mango-haired Sheba, now wielding a pro-level camera.

Monica knows exactly what she wants. The photos are almost a dance, and she's the lead. Side to side, front to front, back to back, side to front, one foot forward, foot kicked up, bent back laughing, me rolling my eyes. The camera goes click click click click click. And then we're done.

Monica takes the camera from the receptionist and flips through the images. "God, these are epic." She turns to me. "You are perfect."

Indigo would reject the flattery, so I give a deadpan, "Sure. Whatever."

Monica claps her hands. "You're the best. In character to the end."

I head to the bar without saying goodbye. Indigo isn't into small talk. Putting on this persona is a stretch, but I can do it.

When I walk into the bar, Grim Weaver is seated at a long, narrow table ringed with stools.

There's nothing about his appearance that surprises me. All of us have been photographed and videoed from every angle. Grim Weaver is wiry, wearing a dark gray knitted vest over a tightly woven black sweater. He's got to be sweating in all that wool. His beanie is signature to his brand, a knitted black cap with an intricate gray spider sprawled over the top.

I slide onto a stool across from him. "Hey, Grim. Fancy seeing you in three dimensions."

"I thought this was the first time we've met!"

Oh, Grim.

A waitress drops off two pint glasses full of a bright purple something. He slides one toward me. "I ordered you something."

"What is it?"

The waitress sets two straws on the table. "Wheatgrass and beet juice with ginger." Then she takes off.

I unsheath one of the straws. "Do you have me confused with Carly?" She's the health nut among us.

He shrugs. "I wanted something purple."

That sounds like Grim. I lean down to take a sip through the stiff recyclable paper straw. It's tangy, textured, and sweet. "I like it."

He looks at something behind me. "There she is."

I turn, and Carly Butterfly heads our way. She's an eco-works, save the planet, zero footprint, green-tech influencer. She can work a discussion of humane food, climate change, and zero-plastic solutions into any conversation.

It's why many people avoid her. She judges everybody.

"Are your clothes made out of grass?" Grim Weaver asks.

I bite my lip to hold back a laugh. Grim can't help it. Carly's outfit does look very, well, *all-natural.*

She slides her hands over her textured pale green shirt and distressed brown cargo pants. She lays her hemp bag on the table. "You're a walking advertisement for doom."

"I've never played that game," he says.

Our eyes meet, and she raises her eyebrows. I get it. Grim is…Grim.

Her finger aims toward our purple glasses. "What in the world are those?"

"Alien blood," Grim says.

"It's wheatgrass," I say. "I think the beets make it purple."

"No," Grim insists. "I requested alien blood. They're among us, you know."

Carly plunks down beside him. "Ohhh-kay. Vegan organic non-GMO?"

"Probably," I say. "It's Monica's bar, after all."

Carly nods. "Right. Even her drinks have hashtags." She turns to Grim. "No aliens were harmed in the making of this concoction."

He shrugs. "Sure, they probably donate it."

Carly sighs and turns to me, her perky blond ponytail swinging. "How long are you going to stay in New York?"

"Not sure. At least a week."

"As long as Monica lets you?" she asks.

"Nailed it." I sip my drink. I liked it at first, but the thick sweetness might be wearing on me.

Carly nods. "You can couch surf at my place if you get stuck between gigs."

Grim laughs. "You have to like bugs."

Carly smacks his arm. "We all share the Earth."

He shakes his head. "We should give it to the cock-roaches."

Carly harrumphs. "I think *we're* the cockroaches."

Even though Indigo is supposed to be stoic and unaf-fected, I can't stop smiling. Both of them are just like their text messages. In fact, I get a pang of guilt that my Indigo persona is so far off the real me.

"Indigo is smiling," Grim fake whispers to Carly. "Should we be worried?"

"She's happy to see us. Even cool curmudgeons smile every once in a while."

"Don't count on it, frazzlins," I grumble, but I smile at them anyway.

The bone-jarring smash of recorded symbols makes everyone in the bar turn to the door.

It doesn't take long to figure out who's making an entrance.

Drag Scream has gone full vampire goddess. Sparkly black cape with deep purple edges. Dramatic headpiece with two horns. Her eye makeup shimmers. She's stunning. A real show-stopper.

She must have a speaker on her somewhere, because next is a steady drumbeat that she walks to. All eyes are on her and many cameras rise in the air as she saunters across the room to stand at the end of our table. "Bitches, I have *arrived.*"

I almost break into applause, but then remember Indigo would never do that. "All right, Miss Thing. You've made your entrance. Wave to your fans."

And Drag Scream does. She may not have the followers of Indigo, but she gets on television. She got shortlisted for *Ru Paul's Drag Race*. Her film reviews can be read on a ton of alternative and several mainstream entertainment websites.

Drag Scream taps her long black nails on the table. "Your drinks are unnatural."

Carly's face brightens. "Actually, it's all-natural wheatgrass–"

Drag Scream cuts her off. "I've heard enough. Unless it is fifty percent vodka, I'm not interested."

She nods at the bartender, who pulls a bottle off the shelf.

"Who's going shopping with me?" I ask.

Carly swivels to Drag Scream. "Are you going to H&M in that getup? People will think it's Halloween."

Drag Scream pins Carly with an evil glare. "Do not mention that holiday made for amateurs."

I bite back my smile. I love these people. Sitting here with them is like meeting the characters of a book you've always loved. Finally, they lift off the page and become real.

The bartender delivers a clear glass filled with vodka and one giant cube of ice, at least two inches across. Resting in a dimple on the top side of the ice is a single black olive cut in half with a mint leaf pressed beneath it.

"Perfection," Drag Scream says. Her gaze rakes the bartender so hard, it might leave a mark. "Just like you."

Carly, Grim, and I exchange glances, but we're not worried.

This is going to be the best afternoon.

CHAPTER 4

Jesse

By evening, all six art installations are complete. I've switched rooms to stay near the mystery girl and lie on the marmalade bed.

I'm fully aware the girl who fell into my room is the same one I saw on the stairs. An average person might not have recognized her, but I've drawn every detail from our first encounter.

I recognized the sparkly shoes, the ripped jeans. Those breasts were even better in that T-shirt.

And even though almost everything about her face was changed, the shape of her chin, the height of her forehead under the wig, and certainly the contouring of her makeup, something about her expression remained the same, particularly after she crashed into me.

I pick up my sketchpad. I've already drawn a diagonal line across the page that held the original sketch and added this new version of her. She's like a superhero. First the everyday girl next door, polished but still very natural.

Then the flame-haired wildling, probably the one who inspires two-point-two million followers.

I could look her up. It might not even be that hard to find the red-haired influencer with a European accent who uses alternative cuss words. That's distinctive.

But I want to learn about her from the source.

I hadn't planned to stay in the hotel past hanging the art, but I think I'll wait and see how it plays out with my neighbor. She intrigues me in a way I can't quite understand. I want more of it. See where it leads.

Voices in the hall make me sit up and listen. Mystery girl's door opens and closes with a tell-tale creak and metallic snap.

She's back. And this time, there's someone with her. The other person's voice is deep, but it's pretending not to be, as if they're putting on a persona.

I make out the words, "Try it on," before the voice dissolves into mumbles.

I shouldn't eavesdrop. I should let this go.

But I move close to the door between our rooms. With my side open, it's the thinnest barrier to listen through.

The deep voice is used to projecting, and from here I can make out almost everything.

"You are going to be a smash-hit at the ball."

Oh, so they are going to an event. That must be why the girl is in New York.

Then, "With your hair and this outfit, you're going to be a delectable vampiress."

Vampiress?

Huh. How many vampire balls can there be tonight in New York City?

Several, possibly. And they might be private.

But I can look.

I sit on the floor and do a quick search with my phone. Three come up instantly for today's date.

First, a vampire workshop where budding cosplayers gather to co-create.

My neighbor and her friend already have outfits. I can scratch that one out.

The annual tribunal of the Lower East Side Order of the Vampire.

Nothing about it being a ball. But regardless, such an event is probably closed to outsiders. The reference on a Reddit thread contains no details about the time or location.

I click on the third possibility. The Vampire Ball for Babes, a benefit for the Children's Hospital.

This might be it.

I read the event page. It's an annual event. Costume ball. Tickets, yada yada.

There will be an appearance by the venerable Drag Scream.

Drag Scream.

I consider the voice I heard. It fits.

I Google the name. Drag Scream is a statuesque figure in bold drag. Wildly decked out. Impressive.

I find a video of her introducing the director of a film from earlier this year. I press play and listen carefully. *Yes.* It's the same voice.

So if that's Drag Scream next door, possibly also staying here at Monica's behest, then that means the charity ball is the event they're attending tonight.

Mystery solved.

I should leave them alone.

I return to the bed, my head clasped in my hands, staring up at the ceiling, but I only make it five minutes before looking at my phone again.

Vampire ball.

In costume.

Masks and all.

This could work.

I click *Purchase Tickets*.

I need a costume.

Then I can go undercover to connect with the mystery girl in a way that means neither of us has to be the ordinary people we were when she fell into my room.

CHAPTER 5

Lili

For a while, I'm super nervous about Drag Scream adjusting my hair and makeup. This is, after all, a wig and not my real hair.

But of course, she knows all about these things. She's not sporting her real hair either. And her face is as doctored as mine. She also understands about my brand, leaving my fiery eye makeup, and when she works with my wig, she keeps my purple streak visible and draped over my eye.

She knows all the best costume shops, of course, and convinced one to loan me a costume. In return, we'll tag the shop in our posts.

This escape is already epic.

I wonder if I can check off my first bucket list item tonight. Go to this ball, hook up with someone. I'm doubly incognito between my Indigo look and the vampiress costume.

Yes. I'm going to do it. I'll make it happen. While Drag

Scream is busy touching up her makeup, I sneak a couple of promotional condoms into my boot.

I'll use them tonight. Even better if I don't know the guy and never see him again. Then that naïve princess problem will be taken care of. I haven't appreciated the innocence forced on me for twenty years via endless royal guards and lack of opportunity.

Where Drag Scream is all black and deep purple, I am scarlet and gold, like fire. Like my name. Indigo Flame.

When the two of us stand next to each other, we are something to behold.

I can get photographed and tagged as much as I want tonight. There's no way a single person from Avalonia, not even my sister, would recognize me in this getup.

"Maybe I shouldn't have eaten that last egg roll," I say, patting the cinched corset bodice of the costume. I can barely breathe.

"It will digest." Drag Scream sprays down a stray baby hair from her wig to her forehead. "We are going to slay tonight."

"Who were you going to take as your plus-one if I hadn't come into town?"

Drag Scream sets the can of hairspray on the counter. We binged on gift cards, and the counter is covered with supplies.

"I counted on fate, my dear Indigo. On the moon. On serendipity. I made space tonight for something amazing, and the world brought me you."

Drag Scream proclaims us ready. She has Lyft cards rather than Uber, so we use one of hers to get to the old off-Broadway theater where the vampire ball is being held.

Music from a rock band blasts through the space. The mezzanine is filled with seats in the upper rows, and a few spectators watch quietly from above as the primary activities occur below. The downstairs has been gutted, but there are still divots in the cement where the chair rows used to be attached.

The walls are covered from floor to ceiling with cascading fabric, mostly black, but lit purple.

When we first walk in, it's easy to keep my Indigo Flame persona active despite the nerves crawling in my belly. Drag Scream saunters across the ballroom floor, escorted by one of the organizers who greeted us at the door.

I try to match her confidence and keep my lids half-lowered, as if I'm unaffected by all the insanity around me.

Everyone is in costume. There might be a few mass-produced Halloween-style vampires here and there, but mostly, people are decked to the hilt.

Faces turn to watch us, some in masks, others ghostly white with lurid red lips and shadowed eyes. Everywhere are headpieces, dramatic hairlines, upturned collars, and long cascading robes. A few are gory, blood trailing from pointed teeth down their fronts, but most are richly decked in velvet, satin, and black lace.

Drag Scream scarcely nods as we pass through the crowd, but I pay attention to the ones she acknowledges. They must be important. We walk side by side, following a woman dressed in a black velour pantsuit, not a vampire exactly, but still divinely fitting in.

Just as we're about to leave the crowd to pass by security and head backstage, a figure in a perfectly fitted black tuxedo vampire costume catches my eye.

The suit fits him as if it is custom-made with broad shoulders and a tapered waist. If you removed the long velour cape with its starched collar framing his head, he could almost be at a formal event.

His black shoes gleam, and his white gloves are two bright spots in the shimmer of light.

He wears a mask that covers his eyes and forehead. Behind it, his gaze follows my every move.

Something about him intrigues me. My pulse jumps. Could he be the one?

My Princess Lili self wants to smile at him, but Indigo would never do that. So I merely raise an eyebrow in recognition of his attention, then look away as if I've seen better.

But inside, I'm screaming with hope. Please don't be a creepy weirdo! Please be a normal, totally sexy guy at a vampire ball.

The event is a fundraiser for the Children's Hospital, so many of the wildly dressed attendees will be smart, successful people. When I saw the price of the tickets, I knew this was no ordinary costume ball.

The woman leading us turns to make sure we're close behind her as we push past the boxy security guard watching over the crowd.

There's a space behind the curtains set up for the speakers and special guests. It includes five circular tables, chairs lined in red satin, and even two television screens with a live view of the ballroom.

The woman gestures to the tables. "There's a private

buffet and bartender. You can spend your evening here, or mingle as much as you like. It's strictly up to you."

A short, squat man in a black shirt and vest hurries up to us, holding a tablet. "Drag Scream, you are set to speak in fifteen minutes. Who is this?" He turns to me.

Drag Scream's voice could cut glass. "Do not embarrass yourself by acknowledging that you do not recognize Indigo Flame."

The man flashes the barest smile. "I'm so sorry. Of course. Indigo, pleased to meet you. It's an honor."

Scat diddly. I would never act like Drag Scream. But would Indigo? This in-person stuff is way harder than online.

"It's fine," I say, trying to channel my inner Indigo. "I am perhaps not your demographic."

The man gives a wan smile. "You're welcome to stay back here during Drag Scream's speech, or you may return to the floor to watch. I'll inform the guards that you may move about freely."

Drag Scream isn't letting it go. "Of course she is. And I'm quite certain that security has already recognized who she is and knows where she can be." She doesn't mess around.

"Thank you," I say, deciding that Indigo can be gracious even when she's stoic. Perhaps I need to tweak her personality.

The man hurries away.

"You're one intimidating beast," I tell Drag Scream.

"I have to be," she says. "People will take from you everything they can. I'm here on the blood, sweat, and tears of every drag queen who came before me."

Her gaze holds mine. "There are plenty of people who will tear down anyone who isn't like them. There are people who call me an abomination, a freak, a curse, a scourge. So I will be a beast. It's the only way to survive this world when you're someone like me. Now come on. Let's be fabulous."

We head for the bartender, and I consider what she said. Who would call Drag Scream an abomination?

I don't know. I've been protected from negativity all my life.

But I do know one thing — I will fight for her.

CHAPTER 6

Jesse

Damn, she looks good. I spotted my hotel neighbor the moment she entered with Drag Scream. The staff member leading them was clearly aiming for this corner of the stage, so I made my way here to see if I could catch the eye of this mystery woman.

And I did.

She looked at me, recognized my interest, and acknowledged it.

Does she know she met me at the hotel? I don't think so.

This is a wild and dangerous dance, and I'm totally here for it.

The Master of Ceremonies steps out to begin the program. I've met him. He's one of the directors of the Children's Hospital. He commissioned an art piece from me a few years ago for the entrance. I accepted and donated back the fee.

So I probably could have gotten an invitation to this ball. Hell, maybe I did. Mom's assistant Carina might not have found it worthy of forwarding to me. Carina manages most of my business dealings, and she knows I'm not a costume ball person, normally.

"The woman about to address us needs no introduction," the MC says. "She's a regular on entertainment shows, and a celebrity in her own right. Horror movie-goers rely on her expert opinion—"

I stop listening when my mystery woman appears from backstage, edging past the guard. Her face turns to the podium where it's still the MC talking, then immediately swivels to the crowd.

She's looking for someone.

Is she meeting a date?

I fall back into the shadow beyond the spotlights blazing toward the stage. She moves to a less tightly packed spot on the ballroom floor and keeps searching. Two white teeth catch the light as she bites a dark red lip.

Damn, these pants are tight. I guess both versions of her work for me. Or is this a third?

I take a chance and step forward so that the glow brightens my mask as her face turns in my direction.

She sees me. She stops searching.

It was me she was looking for.

My cock surges, but it will be unnoticeable in the costume. Capes are damn handy. I hold her gaze. I'm about to extend an arm to invite her to come to me when applause breaks over the crowd.

The MC has left, and the band plays a dramatic chord as Drag Scream saunters on stage.

Mystery Woman turns to the spotlight, smiling now that her friend is here.

Cheers rise from the audience. Drag Scream lifts her arms, purple and black webbing extending out, and encourages the crowd to grow louder.

They do. This isn't normal behavior for the socialite crowd, but the costumes do wonders for breaking normally reserved people out of their well-bred shells.

I consider moving closer to this woman, dressed like fire. I'm drawn to her like a moth seeking light. But I remain in place. I must let her come to me.

"Gentleman and queens!" Drag Scream says, prompting another cheer. "Straights and queers and in-betweens!" Another cheer. "We shall all come together for the children!"

The noise is deafening. I watch the woman gaze up at her friend. Gone is the practiced indifference. She's spellbound, like I imagine the first version of her I met in the hotel would be.

Drag Scream gives her spiel about the inequity of healthcare, the importance of loving each other no matter how life finds us, and to never forget to have a damn good time. She's great, and her friend clasps her hands together, enthralled.

The music blasts and the lights go down. Couples move to the dance floor or the bar. Some congregate at tall tables near the walls, positioned for holding drinks while people stand around them.

I wait.

Will she return backstage? Will she stop and talk to me on the way?

Forget letting her come to me. I will not let her get away.

When she moves toward the security guard, I step into her path. "A dance?" I ask.

She sucks in a breath, then corrects herself, standing tall, chin high. "My friend is waiting for me."

"Drag Scream?"

"Yes."

"Is she your date?"

"A friend."

"Do you have a date?"

"No."

"Then come with me." I take her arm and move her toward the dance floor.

She looks behind her. "Let me text her." We pause on the outskirts of the dance space, and she tugs her phone out of her knee-high boot.

She quickly taps out a message, then tucks the phone back in. "Since you insist."

"I do."

The music is a driving rock anthem. The dancers are random, flailing arms and gyrating. A few couples gamely spin each other.

I draw her to me, driving our hips together to the punishing beat. It's a relief to have her in my arms, no matter the music.

She smells of hair products and jasmine. Up close, her makeup sparkles as the dance lights catch it. Her red robe glitters. My hands rest on her cinched waist. Now that I'm near her, I want to melt into the swelling cleavage pressed upward by the corset. The warm trill of attraction I felt earlier today breaks into a deep, pulsing need.

And she's so close. I pull her even tighter, reveling in

the crush of her breasts against my ribs. Even in her platform boots, her face scarcely reaches my chest.

She seems tentative, but as the song goes on, we find a rhythm together. Her hair in its upswept swirl tickles my neck. Each move of her body against mine drives my desire into the red zone.

She feels it, slipping her arms beneath my cape to clutch my back. I know the moment she feels my erection against her belly, because she sucks in a breath.

Then she presses more tightly against it.

I'm glad for the fast, pounding beat of the song. It pushes us to drive our bodies against each other.

Our breathing speeds up. The song drops into a drum solo, and my heart competes with it in its rapid-fire beat. I want her. I'm going to have her. I won't let anything get in my way.

I don't know her name. Where she's from. Anything about her other than that she's staying at the same hotel as me.

But my dick says—we know all we need to know.

And part of that knowledge is the way she's holding onto me. How her face is turned up to mine. How my body is responding to her.

I lead us to the farthest corner of the dance floor. There, I lift my hands to her chin and hold her face. We forget to dance as my lips lower to hers.

She's hesitant at first. My mouth takes her more slowly than I planned, nibbling along the edges.

Then she sighs, and her lips part. I dive into her, tasting every sweet breath, our tongues slipping together.

I draw her close, letting my cape settle around us both.

My thumb slides down her throat and dips into that uplifted cleavage.

Her body responds, her breath catching as I reach inside the stiff edge of the binding.

The music changes to something slower and languid. More people come to the dance floor, and now we're surrounded.

She breaks the kiss. "I know where to go." She pulls away, taking my hand.

I didn't expect this. Conversation, sure. Drinks, likely. Maybe an invitation at the end of the night, but probably only a possibility of another meeting.

But a tryst at the ball?

Not in my wildest imagining.

She leads me back to the security guard. He nods at her, looking at me for a moment but letting it go.

We go down a short hall, then an open area that leads to the part of the stage behind the curtain. It's set up as a private space with tables and televisions. Drag Scream is there. She sees us and gives her friend a wink.

We pass all that and head off the stage wings to another small hall.

Dressing rooms.

"Drag Scream came here earlier to freshen up before her speech." She opens the door but doesn't flip on the overhead. A glow comes from the dressing table, the bulbs surrounding the mirror illuminated.

She closes the door behind us and turns the lock.

I waste zero time. If this is what she wants, I am ready and willing for service. I shuck my gloves to untie her cape and toss it to the floor, revealing smooth creamy shoulders that gleam in the low light.

I press my face to her collarbone, kissing this new territory. I decide to be on-brand for a vampire ball and bite her skin.

She laughs, and the sound of it sends my cock into overdrive. I reach for her skirts and pile them on my arms until I find her thighs. Then I lift her to straddle me, turning her to the wall and flattening her back against it.

She squeals and laughs again, lifting her arms to adjust her hair. The movement makes the corset sink, and she's so close to popping out the top.

I'll help it along. I unfasten the first two ornate hooks, and yes, the tension of the garment makes it fall open. Luscious pale breasts are revealed, tipped in pink.

She sucks in a breath as I lower my head and take one in my mouth. I keep working on the corset until all of it is free, and I toss it to the floor.

She's naked to the waist, her skirt piled between us as I hold her on my hips. I can't decide where to put my mouth, so I go everywhere. Lips, cheeks, jaw, collarbone, both nipples. I want to devour her.

She unfastens my cape, and it joins the other items on the floor. I want all this skirt out of my way, so I lower her legs to find the clasp.

There are multiple layers to this thing, and it takes some tugging and laughter to get it all gone.

But then she's in front of me, her lithe body naked other than tiny black panties and heavy boots.

My cock strains against the tight pants. She's like a

fantasy with her wild hair and makeup, pert breasts, and pale skin.

I lift her and turn to set her feet on the top of the makeup counter. Now she is bathed in light from behind.

"Turn in a circle," I tell her, my voice a rasp.

She stares at me a moment, hands on her hips. If I were sixteen, I'd have blown my load just looking at her.

But then she does it, slowly, elegantly, like she took dance lessons somewhere along the way.

The light brightens the tips of her breasts and curves along the slope of her back.

I shrug off my jacket and unbutton my shirt. She watches, sliding her thumbs in the elastic band of her panties.

This is a far cry from the girl I picked up from the floor of the hotel, who seemed skittish. Which one of these women is her? Or is it both?

I don't give a fuck at the moment. I want to be buried in that body, my face nestled in that rack.

I kick off my shoes, shucking my pants and socks as fast as humanly possible. Then I'm in boxers, and she's in panties and boots.

I wait, and she holds out the elastic of her panties and gestures with her free hand toward me.

I get it. I shove my thumbs in my waistband.

She mirrors my movement, and because I want the reveal to take its time, I slow the descent of my boxers.

She shifts her hips from side to side, but not like an exotic dancer. I don't get that vibe. But from some internal sense of what will drive me wild.

It's working.

I slide the boxers past my hips, and she does the same. Only when I'm about to spring out the top do I see the first hint of hair on her.

My mouth goes dry as I ease mine down farther, and my cock flies free. She slips hers down and my balls contract at the sight of the thatch of hair above a glistening slit.

I let the fabric hit the floor. She has to step out of hers with more care due to the boots, and I move forward to place my hand on her waist and keep her stable as she lifts her knee to pull her leg free.

She's wide open, right at eye level. I won't let this delicious treat pass me by. I sling her lifted leg over my shoulder and drive my face straight into that soft pink place I've been aching for since the dance floor.

She clutches my head, and my tongue slips inside her. I grasp her ass, holding her right where I want her. I push her forward so I can really get in there, finding that sweet swollen nub. The moment I suck it, her knee buckles, but I hold her up. I'm going to lick her so hard she collapses on my face.

Her breath comes fast. I feast on her, flicking my tongue rapidly against her clit, then diving in for a long, deep suck. She moans, her body curled over my head.

I don't know her or her kinks, but I slip a thumb into the crack of her ass. She draws in a sharp breath, but presses against it. I slip it through her wet folds, then return to press it just inside the tight pucker.

"Oh my God." Her body starts to contract against my mouth, so I dive in as deeply as I have all night, working both places as she shudders in my hands. This is definitely her thing.

"Ooooh, oooh, zounderkite!"

I would smile if my mouth weren't so occupied. She inadvertently played her hand with her antiquated curse word.

But she doesn't know she already met me. I may be buck-naked, but I'm wearing a mask, my pale hair slicked back in a way that makes it look dark.

She collapses against my shoulder, so I pull away and shift her to sit on the desk. She presses her red hair into my chest, panting. "Did you go to school for that?"

"I'm a fast learner."

She lifts her head. "Teach me what you like best."

"I'm happy to show you." I grasp her knees and spread them wide.

"Before we do that, I want to do something to you." She reaches for my cock and starts stroking it up and down.

"That's a good start."

She pulls me toward her by my length. "Do you like it between the boobs?"

I like it any way she does it, but I admire how she shifts, trapping me in her cleavage. "I think I saw this somewhere." She lowers her chin and when the tip of my cock slides close to her mouth, her pink tongue pops out and licks the tip.

Christ. That's enough playing. "I'm going to fuck you now," I tell her.

Her eyes go wide. "Yes. Let's do that. I have a condom in my boot."

She reaches inside and extracts a square packet. So she planned for this. I was just her choice.

It doesn't matter. She's naked in boots, her body lit by the vanity lights. I'm going in.

She tears the condom open with relish, but when she reaches out with it, those straight white teeth reappear to bite her lip. She hesitates.

"I've got it." I take it from her, and before she can even look up, I've got it on, and her knees are spread wide, and I'm exactly where I want to be.

Splitting her open.

I don't expect her to scream.

CHAPTER 7

Lili

I clap my hand over my mouth for the second time today.

"Sorry," I say, scrambling to come up with a reason for my surprised scream while also dealing with the white-hot shock of the pain I just experienced. "You're so *big*."

He nods and shifts my hips. It's immediately more comfortable, and I think I can manage. Holy scat diddly, this night has been full of surprises. Me, acting like a porn star. Thank God I watched some and knew what to expect. He stuck his finger in my butt!

And I...liked it? Oh my God!

I got comped a bullet vibrator once, so I know the orgasm part, but what he did was — whoa. It was whoa, whoa, whoa!

Right now is uncomfortable, though. The edge of the table is cutting into my thigh. I feel like I've been knifed in the va-jay-jay.

And I'm acting like a porn star, because I'm grinning and bearing it while pretending I like it.

But he stops.

"What?" I say.

He drapes my legs around his waist and lifts me. "Let's try it another way."

He walks toward a sofa in the corner. Then he sits and arranges my knees on either side of him.

Oh, this is already waaaaay better. He clutches my butt and moves me up and down.

When he doesn't get what he's looking for, he keeps shifting me, right, left, then, *what!* I feel it. A friction in the right spot. It's like a tickle, then an itch, then I'm into it, working with him. He catches a breast in his mouth, sucking on it. A jolt of pleasure moves straight from his lips to my clit.

Whoa. The pressure builds. I gasp against him, holding onto his head.

Then, at just the right moment, he does it again. Slips a bit of his finger into my butt.

I'm over the top. I buzz, I crack, I split open. It's different from when he used his mouth, deeper, stronger, harder. I let out a keening cry from this orgasm. I'm not in control of anything.

He moves me faster over him, somehow feeling even bigger than before.

Then he holds still, pulsing inside me. I breathe heavily, listening to him groan. This is it. Sex. A man. In me. Into me. I drove him crazy. He fucked me like I knew what I was doing. I fooled him.

I want it again. I want it every day.

He clasps his arms around my back. His mask crushes into my chest.

I don't even know his name!

I want to know.

I want to see him again. Do this again.

Will he?

He tilts his head back to rest on the back of the sofa. "This was an unexpected pleasure." His low, gravelly voice rumbles throughout my body.

"Indeed." I have to sound like Indigo now. If he doesn't know who I am yet, he'll figure it out if he looks at any coverage of this event on social media. I'll be tagged. My look is very distinctive tonight.

I lift my leg to dismount him like a boss, but as soon as I slide away, a long red streak smears between our thighs.

Right. Virginity. Gone.

He glances down.

Oh, God. What will he say? Will he out Indigo as a virgin? She can't be. She talks confidently about toys and lubes and sex positivity!

"Looks like Aunt Flow is coming to visit," he says.

Of course. "Sorry. She wasn't quite due."

"Looks like I invited her." He shrugs.

I rush for the dressing table and snatch up a box of tissues. "So sorry. Here."

"It's a period, not a crime," he says. "Though it does look like some violence may have occurred."

"I'm fine." *Shut up, Lili. Of course you're fine. Nothing to see here. No body parts were obliterated.*

He cleans himself up and folds the condom into one of the tissues. He passes the box over. "You might want these."

I wonder if I'll keep bleeding. Why don't I know these details? Stupid porn movies. And useless websites. I solemnly swear to do a TikTok on this so others will know. Actually, it might get me banned. I'll figure out a place where it can go safely.

I accept the box and tug out tissues. My panties are so tiny that I can't easily stuff anything in them. Would a tampon work? Of course it would. It's the same hole. I need to get one. I did not plan for this!

I try to breathe. This is a lot. I miss my sister terribly. I mean, as far as virgin-busting goes, I had it easier than her. She ended up surrounded by the entire royal guard. And our father.

Yeah, this was much better.

But maybe it's time I made my exit.

I snatch up my clothes and clutch them to my chest. "It's been an honor and a privilege," I say to the man, still lounging naked on the sofa in his mask. "I'm going to get dressed and find my friend. Have a nice life."

I duck inside the adjoining bathroom and lock myself inside.

Have a nice life? Where did that come from?

I'm grateful for water and paper towels. I clean myself up, relieved to see that there is no lingering bleeding. It seems done. Even so, I fold a paper towel and stuff it up my v-hole just in case and start redressing. The corset is hard to manage on my own, but I get it clasped.

My hair isn't as pristine as it was when I walked in, but that's fine. The ballroom is dim.

I assess myself when I'm done. My lipstick has worn off. I can fix that. I pull a tiny makeup case from my boot.

I repair what I can. I'm okay. This is okay.

I did what I set out to do.

USA Bucket List Item #1 — check.

And I learned something about myself in the process.

I like butt stuff.

I never would have guessed.

I kill the light before cracking the door open a tiny sliver. I want to make sure the masked man is gone.

The room is empty.

I let out a sigh. It's probably best if I let this guy be. Sure, he can figure out who I am. And if he wants to track me down, there will probably be some opportunity one day.

But I have no scheduled appearances in New York. I couldn't have. My escape from the palace wasn't planned.

By the time I have something concrete to promote on my feed, if I last that long in the US, he'll have moved on.

I swish my skirts to puff them back out as I walk through the dressing room. The lights over the makeup counter are still on.

I'm about to turn to the door when I spot something unexpected on the counter.

One of the tissues.

There's a lipstick beside it. It's not mine. Probably something left on the counter. It was used to write on the tissue.

It's a phone number.

I'm guessing it belongs to the masked man.

I don't want it.

Or do I?

I stare at it for a full minute. It's in my brain. But I don't memorize it.

Instead, I snap a picture with my phone, then crumple the tissue and toss it in the can below the desk.

I text the image to Drag Scream.

Me: Just hooked up with this guy. I don't want to end up one of those sad love songs where she ends up pregnant and can't find the guy, so I'm sending this number for you to keep should I ever need it. Otherwise, I'm deleting its existence.

I send her the photo, then erase it from my phone.

There.

Drag Scream: Don't tell me you barebacked.

Me: No, no. In case his swimmers are supernatural.

Drag Scream: Got it. I'll sit on it to the grave. Or until your vampire baby exits your belly.

And with that image in my head, I open the door and head to the backstage party, where Mr. Masked Man won't be allowed.

Now on to another item on my list. Epic twenty-first birthday.

CHAPTER 8

Jesse

I abandon the ball after scrawling my number on a tissue. I need to leave the decision in the woman's hands. I don't know if this is a normal encounter for her, or if she acted out of character, or if she regrets what happened.

I don't know anything.

I walk at a punishing pace for a couple of miles, trying to work off my resistance to letting her go. I stalked her there. As soon as she figures out that her mystery fucktoy is the same man sleeping in the room next door, she's going to jilt me.

Scat diddly.

I can't walk the entire island of Manhattan, so eventually I jump in a cab to return to the hotel. I realize it's too risky to show up in the costume. She could be in the bar or the lobby or on the stairs or in the hall. So I stop in a late-night tourist trap and change into an "I Heart NY" T-shirt and Statue of Liberty shorts before walking in.

The reception desk is empty, thank God, because I would never live it down if Monica saw me in this outfit. I sneak up the stairs and open the door to my room as quietly as possible. I don't let out a breath of relief until I'm safely in the mandarin room and the vampire costume is back in its canvas bag.

Only then do I let myself relive the night in my mind. Dancing with her. Following her to the dressing room. Her near-naked dance on the table.

Fuck.

Who is this woman?

I don't intend to search for her. But my phone obviously has triangulated my ticket purchase, my recent location, and possibly even who else was there. It serves up photos and a news report of the vampire ball the moment I flip it on.

There are pictures of Drag Scream on stage, then one of her walking in.

And, of course, right next to her is my mystery woman, all her socials tagged.

Indigo Flame.

A rush courses through me. I can see every side of her. The one in the hoodie in my room. The wild one on the stairs. Walking in with the vampire costume. Dancing on the makeup table.

Naked on my lap.

I'm screwed.

One thing I've learned about being an artist is that once an obsession takes hold, there is no way to ignore it. You have no choice but to dive in and get through it.

I do exactly that for the better part of the hour. Her Instagram feed, her TikTok videos.

There's precious little about who she is or where she

lives. Most of her photos are product endorsements. She's got everything. Clothing. Makeup. Phone service. Shoes. Bags. And the condoms she pulled from her boot? She promotes them.

I pause on a close-up photo of her face.

Wait.

Something's not right.

I've held that chin in my hands.

I've kissed those lips.

These older photos and videos aren't quite right.

I pull up photos from the vampire ball and zoom in.

I compare these to the images in her feed from weeks and months ago.

I start sketching, filling in details, morphing what I saw myself with those older videos and images.

They aren't the same. Her cheekbones are wrong. Her nose is different. Her eye shape has changed. The placement of her eyebrows is higher.

It's subtle, but definitely altered.

What's going on here?

I draw sketch after sketch, but then I fall into the memory again and now all the sketches are X-rated. Her dancing, breasts tipped with light. Her face, above mine, as she rode me on my lap.

I draw every part of her in scintillating detail, including each fold of her pussy, the exact texture of her pubic hair. I show my cock entering her. My thumb in her ass. I've never drawn anything like this. I do assemblage art in children's hospitals, for fuck's sake.

But I'm obsessed as hell.

I keep going, shifting into fantasy. My cock in her ass.

A blow job. I fuck her in the middle of Times Square, cameras pointed at us. In the fountain in Central Park, water cascading down her body.

I've lost my mind for her.

When the door opens in the next room, I nearly jump out of my skin. I slam the sketchbook closed as if she could see it through the walls.

I listen carefully. There's no other voice. No conversation.

I get up and press my hands to the door between us. She moves through the room. There's a rustle, then the clink of hangers. She's removing the cape, I bet.

It's quiet for a moment, then I hear a clunk on the floor, then a second. Her boots.

She sighs, and I bite my fist. I'm willing to bet that corset just came off. I can picture this, even the imprint the tight bodice left on her skin.

I want to knock, call out, beat the door down. But I only listen.

Water runs. There's a muffled, "Ouch."

What hurts her? I want to kiss the pain away.

Then a clearer, "Scat diddly."

I swallow, desperate to know what frustrates her, what's happening. Is she naked? I picture her leaning over the sink, breasts swaying over the porcelain.

I have *got* to pull myself together.

You'd think I never fucked anyone, never knew what it was like to be with a woman.

But there is no one like her.

I've seen enough to know.

The toilet flushes. Water runs. Then quiet. Has she

climbed into bed? I'd give my left testicle to slide in beside her.

I'm damn near ready to knock on the door between us and beg for her mercy when there's a faint buzz.

Her light footsteps run across the floor. "Octavia?"

Huh. That's an unusual name. I shouldn't listen.

But I do. Of course I do.

"I'm here. I'm fine."

I relax. Just a friend or family member checking on her.

They keep talking, but she's moved somewhere away from the wall, and the sounds are muffled.

I have to stop. I'm invading way more than her body. It's her privacy.

Pull yourself together, Jesse. You gave her your number. If she's interested, she'll call.

I lie back on my bed. Even though I have promised myself I will leave her alone, light has barely dawned when I'm up again, showering, choosing a shirt I think she might like, and heading to the nearest coffee shop to prepare for my next move.

I can't let someone like her get away.

CHAPTER 9

Lili

I wake up to a thousand points of pain.

A pinch in my back, likely from eight hours crouched in a suitcase closet.

An ache in both feet from walking all over the ball in unfamiliar costume boots that weren't quite a perfect fit.

A red-rubbed spot where the tight corset pressed the clasp of the layers of skirts into my skin.

And, lest I have forgotten, some well-worn parts down below, newly cherry-busted and thoroughly worked over.

I have to admit, that feeling is delicious.

As much as I've tried to put the masked man out of my thoughts since deleting the image with his number, he's plagued me. Common sense tells me I'm only overthinking him because he was my first. I don't get the fairy tale like my sister Octavia, whose first and only partner was also her childhood friend who became her fiancé.

I opted to bang a stranger in a dressing room and delete his number.

I roll over on the bed, taking stock of all the things that

protest movement. It's not too bad. Some ibuprofen, some stretching, and I'll be ready to face another day.

An oddly empty day. I thought I'd be wall-to-wall with meet-ups and things to do. But New York is expensive. I don't have gift cards for many activities, only a comp to a small museum and a couple of tickets to an off-off-Broadway premiere that's a month away.

I've never had to navigate the world on my own. This is the first morning of my life that my daily itinerary hasn't been delivered by the palace staff.

I can do anything.

As long as it's cheap.

Probably, I should take a walk. Look around. Get a feel for the city.

The idea of putting on the entire Indigo look feels exhausting. I'm only going to be walking around, not trying to drum up social media play. I'll put it on when I'm ready to meet up with the others, or finagle another sponsorship.

So I scrub my face of any lingering makeup or wig glue, brush out my real hair, and step back into my ripped jeans, this time pairing them with a soft blue T-shirt cut into fringe on the bottom. My belly button peeks out above the rhinestone belt I bought yesterday, but otherwise, it's a sweet, more or less wholesome look.

Unlike last night.

I lift the shirt to my nose. It smells of the palace. I breathe it in a moment. I'm not homesick, not really. But it's nice to have a familiar memory.

I slide on the sparkle tennis shoes and study the diagram by the door with the layout of the hotel and the fire exits. I want a way out of here that doesn't take me through the lobby.

And I need to buy a hat. It's not that anyone will recognize plain Jane me as Indigo, but last night Octavia said that royal guards had been deployed to the airport where our jet landed. They'd already figured out that one possibility was that I'd flown here.

However, the favored theory is that I used the tunnels to head out into the fields, then walked or took a donkey cart across the border to Belgium.

It's a plan I considered until Sunny went into labor. I heard the royal plane would be dispatched for multiple trips to fetch Sunny's family in the US, and that was my chance.

But if Father decides to make an international incident out of my disappearance, any camera anywhere could identify me. And no doubt, the security team is already scouring social media with facial recognition apps.

Still, New York is huge and, if Octavia is correct, only a secondary consideration. As long as I'm careful and don't get myself on television or a viral video (Leo, I'm looking at you and your cock speedo incident), I'm not in any imminent danger of being caught.

I memorize my route through the back of the hotel and start unlatching the locks to my door. I sling my bag over my shoulder and step out.

And immediately spot the man from the orange hotel room next door. He's in the hall, looking killer in fitted jeans and a melon-colored, short-sleeved button down that barely contains his biceps.

He walks slowly, his eyes focused on a takeout tray

holding three cups of coffee and several packaged danishes and bagels. He glances up as he approaches. "Are you a camera? Because when I look at you, I have to smile."

I roll my eyes. "What are you doing?"

He shifts to keep the overloaded tray balanced. "I might have gone overboard on the breakfast. Care to help me lighten this load?"

I hesitate. Why did he overbuy just to go to his room? And did he know I was about to leave?

He couldn't have. He came from the elevator.

One cup tilts, and I leap forward to set it right before it tumbles off the tray. "Why did you get so much?"

He shrugs. "I couldn't decide between a mocha latte, an Americano, and a macchiato. The guy behind me got testy, so I panicked and ordered them all."

"And all that food?" My stomach grumbles looking at it.

"I'm a growing man-boy." He angles his head toward the door. "Even if you won't help me eat all this, can you pull my phone out of my pocket and get the door? I don't know how I thought I was going to get inside the room with this load."

He turns around. His phone is sticking out of his back pocket.

I pull it out. It's a face-lock, so I hold it up to him. He grins at the screen. I pull up the hotel app and open his door.

"You're a lifesaver," he says, stepping inside. "You can set my phone on the dresser."

I follow him. The faint scent of orange in the room is pleasant and not overbearing. It pairs nicely with the coffee. And sugar. My stomach rumbles again.

Jesse places the pile of food and three coffees on the table in the corner. "Have a seat and pick one of these. I assume you like coffee?"

"I do." I hesitate by the door. I'm not quite buying his story, but maybe he's interested in me. Maybe this is his way of making it easy for me to stay or go.

Compared to the intense encounter with the masked man, this feels manageable. And I can't exactly judge him for flirting with both real me and Indigo me yesterday if I flirted with him and then had sex with a stranger on the same day.

Pot, meet kettle.

I cross the room. "Which coffee do you want?"

"I was hoping you would narrow my choices by taking something. I like them all."

I pick up the macchiato. "I'll go with this."

"Ah," Jesse says. "You want to wake up fast."

I breathe in the strong mocha smell. It's heaven.

I remember Starbucks from the last time I was here. We don't have them in Avalonia, but we ordered it a lot with Leo and Sunny at the hotel near Times Square.

I haven't tried approaching the coffee chain as an influencer. Probably they don't need my help. They're everywhere. But I might hang onto the cup for when I'm back in my Indigo look. I'd love to have some gift cards. That would solve one meal per day.

I take a sip and feel jolted by the strong espresso.

Jesse picks up the Americano. "Good?"

"So good."

He sits at the table, and I join him. Might as well eat.

He spreads out the baked goods in their paper sleeves.

"Classic bagel with cream cheese, cheese danish, blueberry muffin, chocolate croissant."

I'm starving. "I don't want to steal your favorite," I tell him.

He picks up the croissant. "Okay, I have mine."

I take the bagel. "When in New York."

"If you like bagels, there are some incredible places here, of course."

I nod. My head is spinning as soon as I take a bite. I didn't eat much yesterday.

If I want to be here long, I need more food comps. I couldn't do them while in Avalonia because I wasn't close enough to get the food for photographs. And there's no way to do a shot inside a restaurant that's an eight-hour plane ride away.

I have some straight-up Visa cards, but I've been hoarding them in case I need to travel. I hear buses in the US are cheap, but I'm not sure if they require ID.

"You're deep in thought," Jesse says.

"Oh, just trying to plan my day." I take another bite of the bagel with a happy sigh.

"Seeing the sights?"

"I'm going to walk the neighborhood. I've never been to Chelsea. It has a different feel from Times Square and Central Park."

"Is that where you stayed before?"

I don't want to give him the name of the hotel. I have a feeling it will say more about me than I want to, given its stature. "Midtown. Are you from here?"

"I've lived here off and on since I was a kid. My mother

is a fashion designer, so we split our time between New York, Paris, and Milan."

"Tough life."

"I was her favorite pin cushion to try on kid clothes."

"I knew you were a model!"

He shrugs. "Only until I was old enough to have a say."

"And your father?" I'm inhaling the bagel. I force myself to slow down before he notices.

"He was the real deal as a model. He still is. I don't see him often. He tends to fare better in Europe. America likes them young."

As he talks, something in my body heats up. It's weird. Why would this ordinary conversation be cranking my body? Is this what happens once you start having sex? You want it more and more?

It's something about Jesse. I mean, I found him attractive yesterday, in a friendly, good-looking way.

But the masked man was a dark, forbidden thrill. I can't believe what happened at that ball.

And yet, as Jesse talks to me, I get that same thrumming vibration low in my belly.

That's it, I must be a nymphomaniac. I'm one of those people who wants it all the time.

Jesse watches me with a half-smile. I realize I've frozen in place with the bagel halfway to my mouth.

"You okay?"

I nod and take another bite. Is it okay to be a nymphomaniac? I mean, we're all sex-positive these days, right? Consenting adults? As long as I'm protected. I mentally count how many condoms I have in my bag.

I should have brought more. Maybe I can contact the company and offer to do a promo for more.

Listen to me! Zounderkite!

"You seem out of sorts." Jesse's voice has taken on a different tone. "You're not allergic to cream cheese or anything, are you?"

"No, no. I'm sorry. I'm so distracted." I pop the last bite of the bagel in my mouth and wash it down with the macchiato. "And here I am, drinking your coffee, eating your food, and taking up your time." I stand up.

He stands, too. "You're not. I — I had hoped to catch you." He holds out his hands. "Confession time. I was hoping to tempt you with all this food. I thought I'd hear your door and invite you, but then there you were."

I'm not sure if I should be alarmed or flattered. "You don't even know my name."

"That's okay. You can be as secretive as you like. I'm an open book. Jesse Adams. Son of fashion designer Maggie Adams and model Jeff Brooks."

"You took your mother's name?"

I nod. "She insisted. Dad didn't care. They're both professional names to them. I'm not sure he was sold on my existence."

I sit back down. That's terrible. "How could he not be sold on having a son?"

He returns to his chair. "He didn't want anything to come between him and his ambition. Mom made the right call. When they divorced, it was nice for the two of us to feel like a family."

I expect he'll ask something about me, but he's true to his word and falls silent.

What should I call myself? Lili feels risky, even if it's a common name in America. Certainly not Indigo. I'm shocked at what a dirty girl she is, even as the thought of it sends a thrill through me.

Then I have it. My middle name. Ridiculously European.

"I'm Elizabeth."

He quirks an eyebrow. "Like the Queen of England?"

"Exactly like her. Most people call me Ellie." The lie slips out with ease. I'm getting used to a life of deception. It's a good one, though. Ellie sounds so much like Lili that I'll respond to it properly.

"Ellie. It's lovely and gentle. Like you."

Obviously, he hasn't seen me in a dressing room.

We grin at each other for a minute, and a different feeling washes over me. Contentment. It's so simple, having breakfast with a friendly, beautiful man. This is the life I could have led outside the palace all along.

"So, Jesse, what do you do now that you're a retired child model?"

"Art." He points to a sculpture of an orange peel hanging in the corner. "Mixed media assembly. I've sold a piece here and there. Monica bought some, and I'm here this week hanging them in rooms."

"I like it!" I walk over to the corner to examine it more closely. It's extremely realistic, as if a giant orange had actually existed and someone carefully cut away the peel in a perfect spiral. "So there are others?"

"Sure. Would you like to see them?" He jumps from his chair.

I turn to him. "Are you asking me for my company or

for my social media feed?" Maybe that's his angle. I have a lot of followers.

"As a friend. In fact, I'll insist you take no photos. Probably Monica has her own idea on how she's going to reveal the art."

Huh. So he simply wants to walk around with me. My belly flips. I like this. I like it a lot. "All right, then. Let's look at your art."

His smile is huge and genuine. I like it, but then something odd happens again. It should be that I merely smile back. But when my eyes fix on his mouth, my body flashes hot, and a slick feeling slides between my legs.

I'm super turned on.

By a smile.

By a kind, gentlemanly hotel neighbor who has done nothing but buy extra breakfast in hopes of sharing it.

I'm a mess.

I'll apparently have to be on my best behavior.

Somehow, after last night, I've jumped on a runaway train to fucktown.

CHAPTER 10

Jesse

I'm a mess. A lying, conniving, mess.

But maybe we can start over. She's here as her regular self, and so am I. I can set aside that darker part of me that fucked her in a back room then obsessed over her for hours.

What's gotten into me?

But she's here. I'm getting another chance.

I wonder if Ellie is some variation of her real name, or something she made up. I have no idea about that, only that she's also Indigo.

And what her screams sound like when I thrust into her.

Down, boy.

But I'm getting all these competing signals from her. Shyness. Uncertainty. Friendliness. Distraction. Then sex. I got blasted by that same tension that ignited all our actions last night.

I have to keep cool, though. I want to do this the right way.

The masked man version of me has to go.

We wander the hotel, taking the back stairs, and visit the rooms with my art.

She exclaims about them all and asks to take pictures after promising to keep them to herself until Monica's reveal. "I'd never dare upstage her," she says.

I don't want to let her go, so I offer to take her to the gallery next to the hotel. "It's full of metal sculpture. Really beautiful stuff."

"Okay." She smiles up at me, and my whole body lights up. I have to be careful, or I am going to tumble for this girl in a hurry.

If it's not too late already.

I turn to the elevator, but she goes the opposite way, out the back door. I follow her, assuming she's avoiding the lobby. I'm not sure how deep her Indigo secrecy goes. Am I the only one who knows? Surely not.

The heat bears down on us once we're out of Monica's air-conditioned hotel. Since we walked out the back, we have to circle the building to return to the street and enter the art gallery.

Ellie stares up at the buildings, then closes her eyes to breathe in deeply. I watch her, loving how she drinks New York in. She has the heart of an artist. I long to take her hand, but it's not something Jesse can do. It might be too simple a touch for even my vampire-masked self. There was no tenderness last night, just heat.

I don't how to best navigate this complicated situation.

The door to the art gallery opens with a jingle. Ethan has painted the walls bold colors to back the charred silver sculptures displayed throughout the space. Ethan himself is in the back, talking on his cell phone. He motions us in with the wave of a hand. I've known him a few years, as we've often attended the same openings and fundraisers.

Ellie and I turn to the first piece, an enormous globe framed with latitude and longitude lines in steel, hollow on the inside. Instead of continents, the world is decorated with flattened metal shapes of people, one dancing, one sitting by a fire, others holding hands or raising their arms to the heavens.

Ellie walks around it, her hand pressed to her cheek. "It's so intricate."

"You can touch it." Ethan rises from his desk. "The artist, Cam Reynolds, wanted to create something that could be felt as well as seen. There's one in the back that you can strike with a mallet and even hear his intention."

He turns to me. "Jesse! Did you get your work up next door?"

"Just finished."

"I'm still waiting for you to do a show here."

I shrug. "That's a lot of pieces. I'm a dabbler."

"Right. A dabbler with an installation at the Met." He turns to Ellie. "And two other museums. And the Children's Hospital. Did you go to their fundraiser last night?"

Ellie's gaze flies to me. I had hoped it wouldn't come to this, an out-and-out lie.

But I find a way around it. "I think Carina forgot to forward me the invite, if I got one." That's technically true.

"I missed it, too. I'm not much for costume balls." He glances at Ellie. "So who is this?"

"Ethan, meet Ellie." I have nothing to add. Officially, all

I know is that she's staying at Monica's hotel, and she likes macchiatos.

Not that I would tell him that she dances divinely naked, and that there's a spot I can reach with my dick, to the left of center, that makes her crazy.

"Ellie, are you a local?"

"No. Just visiting." She slides her fingers along the clean lines of the globe, and I almost shiver, remembering them gripping me last night.

"That accent!" Ethan holds up a palm. "Don't tell me. It's not British. Definitely not one of the islands. Belgian?"

Ellie's throat bobs as she swallows. She doesn't want to say. We didn't talk much last night, but during the little we did, she took care to minimize this accent, just like I lowered my voice.

We're a hot mess, that's for sure.

"She's an enigma, isn't she?" I say. "Please tell her about the metalwork."

Ellie's gaze crosses mine with gratitude that I cut off the questioning.

"Of course!" Ethan leads us to the back. "Don't miss the aural one. We also have one we have to keep away from the windows because the owners of the toy store across the street keep complaining to the building manager. I swear I'm going to buy my own space one day and not be at the mercy of a landlord."

Uh oh. I have a feeling I know which sculpture Ethan is leading us to. It will be interesting to see how Ellie reacts.

We pass a column and there it is, backed in red. I watch Ellie's face as she takes it in. She sucks in a breath, and the way her fingers clench tells me everything I need to know about how she's feeling inside.

"It's called *The Orgasm*," Ethan says. Then he seems to know to leave us to it as he disappears into the back room.

The statue is a circle, meant to conjure the science textbook illustrations of the life cycle of a butterfly, or any other drawing that explains the progression of a theme.

But along the metal ring are multiple images of a woman. There is nothing explicit about it, no body parts or acts-in-progress. Merely shapes. An arched back. A thrown-back head. An open mouth. An expression of serene bliss.

"It's lovely," Ellie says. "He cared a lot about each way a woman could feel." She turns to me. "You know him?"

"Sure. We studied together at NYU. Did you go to school?"

She shakes her head, and her hands clench again. Did she grow up in poor circumstances? I don't quite think so. She's so flawless, and she walks as if she knows her worth.

But it could still be. She may have made herself from nothing. Maybe she's done that well as an influencer.

"Is this artist famous yet?" she asks.

"He's up and coming. This is only his second show."

"Hmm." She stares up at the statue. "There is a one-two punch to building fame."

"Is this how you got so many followers?"

"It is."

"And what are the two punches?"

"Mystery and scarcity." She walks around the display. "First, you create some sort of question in people's minds.

Who you are. What you stand for. How you've accomplished something. Maybe even an explanation about what a thing is. Then, you take it away. Make it rare. Hard to find. Impossible to learn more."

"Interesting. And this works for you?"

"It has so far."

I want to learn more, but that's probably going to expose information about her account she might not want me to know. So I don't push.

She makes her way back to the front of the statue. "I like his portrayals of orgasm. But he left out a scream."

I clamp my reaction down. I can't show anything that might give her the slightest hint that I know exactly what she's talking about. "You're right. Perhaps he never experienced it."

Her gaze meets mine, and I see the woman from last night more clearly. My body stirs, but I have to will those thoughts away. Whatever she might have been then, she isn't that now. We're here for art.

I should confess. I should say it right now. The words are on my lips. "I'm the masked man from last night. I know you are Indigo."

But she reaches out to touch the statue, and my body vibrates. I can't let her go. What's happening between us is too new. Too fragile. Too easy to walk away from.

And she might, if she knows everything.

But I will tell her. If this moves forward at all, even just a kiss, I will absolutely tell her. I have to. The moment we connect, and definitely if we should ever get naked, she's going to know.

Because if she noticed even a fraction of what I memorized about her, our bodies will recognize each other in an instant.

Including her scream.

CHAPTER 11

Lili

It's great being a normal visitor and doing regular things. I don't know how much time I'll have before I'm caught, and I want to soak it all in.

After the art gallery, Jesse takes me to lunch at the crepe shop across the street. We watch the cook squirt batter on the round surface of the griddle, then expertly flip the partially cooked crepe.

Jesse orders ham and cheese, while I go with chocolate and banana.

"That's dessert, not lunch," he says.

I shake my head. "It's dessert lunch."

"Dessert lunch is not a thing."

I laugh. "It is if I say it is."

He relents. "You're right. I'm a convert." He waves to the cook. "Chocolate and banana for me, too."

The man nods, drizzling both of the crepes with chocolate, then dropping banana slices on top.

"Do you even like chocolate and banana?" I watch him peer over the glass barrier at the crepes.

"I don't think I've eaten a banana since I was twelve."

"What in thunder? Are you one of those meat and potatoes American men I hear about?"

He grins at me. "I think there are plenty of meat and potatoes men all over the globe. Are you going to make me eat salad?"

"Why, yes, I am. You can't avoid fruits and vegetables!"

He shrugs. "All right. Sounds like we'll have to have dinner at a vegetarian place."

Slick. He's getting me to have dinner with him, too. "Vegan. I don't trust you. You'll order nothing but cheese."

"But I love the idea of dessert lunch and cheese dinner."

I elbow him. "You're going to your grave by forty at this rate."

"Then you better save me."

The man hands us our crepes in their paper cones. Jesse grabs a couple of bottles of water and pays.

Another meal taken care of. But I admit to feeling worried. Calculating the value of my gift cards, I won't make it in New York a week. I can't go out with Jesse for food.

But I do like him. He's easygoing, non-pushy, and sweet. It's been a good day. Comfortable. I'm glad I'm not Indigo, even if it's risky to be out in public with my normal face.

We sit near the window, and he bites into his crepe. I watch him chew. "Verdict?"

"Bananas taste the same as they did when I was twelve."

"But you like it?" I take a bite of mine and almost swoon. It's delicious. We don't have crepe stands in Avalonia, and while I saw them on a visit to Paris, my sister and I weren't allowed to walk up and order one.

Mother insisted the royal chef could prepare them better, but having a server bring a plate of them to a formal table could never be half as good as eating them straight off the griddle with the sun beaming down.

He swallows another bite. "I think anything covered in chocolate is delicious."

I spot something in his eyes that makes me think of the masked man. Sex. Me, covered in chocolate. Him licking it.

Is that what Jesse's thinking? He's been a total gentleman.

I shake it off and keep eating. Once again, the earth moves. So good.

I'm tempted to take a crepe selfie and see if I can broker a deal, especially since they are so close to the hotel, but then I remember I'm not Indigo right now. Just plain Lili. Or, I guess, Ellie.

Tomorrow I definitely need to get back to Indigo. She's the only way I can make money.

My Discord chat kept chiming in the art gallery, so I silenced it. But my phone lights up repeatedly sitting on the table next to us. I turn it face down to hide the previews, concerned that something might out me as Indigo to Jesse.

"Your fans await," Jesse says. For a moment, I panic, thinking he's already figured it out, but then he adds, "All two-point-two million of them."

Right. He knows that part.

"Just some friends here in town," I say. "We met at Monica's bar yesterday."

"How was it? I've heard she has some strange concoctions down there."

"I drank something purple."

His crepe freezes halfway to his mouth. "Purple?"

"Some wheatgrass and beet juice thing."

"That sounds like Monica. We could go down there later if you like. I could get my vegetables in a glass."

My stomach flips. There's no way I can be seen in the bar at Monica's without my Indigo face. Anyone could photograph me, even accidentally, since it's full of influencers. Monica's hotel is one of the most dangerous places I can be seen without hair and makeup.

I sound casual as I decline. "I think I've had plenty of that. I like being outside. New York is so big." Also less likely to end up on a feed. Even in this crepe shop, two giggling teen girls are shooting mad selfies, thankfully faced the other way.

I wish I had my hoodie. Maybe seeing the town with Jesse was a bad idea.

But Jesse's inspired. "Then let's see New York. We can stay outside. Have you ever crossed the Brooklyn Bridge on foot?"

"You can do that?"

"Sure. And I know a great place for dessert on the other side."

"Lunch dessert for a dessert lunch?"

"Totally. You'll want it after that walk. It's a solid mile." He stands and gathers our trash for us. "Shall we go?"

"Yes!" This is good. Even if I can't use any selfies on my

feed, I can totally use the pictures. I can even make them backdrops for green screen TikToks. And with Jesse, I have a knowledgeable guide. I don't know how to get around town without guards and a limo. I've never paid for things. I don't even have American cash and there's no way for me to get it.

I also have a feeling my influencer friends from around here wouldn't be interested in these excursions. Picturing Drag Scream in her platform boots crossing the bridge midday makes me want to snort. No way.

We enter the subway station a few blocks down. Jesse buys a card to pay for rides and sticks it in both our turnstiles. The machines take credit cards, so I can use my Visa gift cards to get my own later. One problem down.

The first time a subway whooshes up to the platform, blowing back my hair, tears prick my eyes. I'm doing it! All the things an Avalonian princess isn't allowed to do!

The subway is crowded. I love every element of the ride, the smells and noises and people rocking back and forth with the movements of the car.

A man enters from another car, hat in hand, asking for money. Most people ignore him, but my heart squeezes when Jesse drops a dollar into his cap.

"Are you living here now?" I ask Jesse. It's clear most people are accustomed to people asking for money, and they ignore it.

"I'm not sure I live anywhere," he says.

The subway comes to a stop and most of the riders exit. We sit down near the door.

"What do you mean? You don't have a home?"

"I guess, technically, I live in one of my mother's places.

She has a home in Yonkers and a villa in Milan. In Paris, we tend to rent."

"So you live with your mother." I shouldn't talk. I also live with mine.

He laughs. "Sort of. We're rarely in the same country." He kicks back, hands clasped behind his head, legs outstretched. "I rotate between hotels and artist retreats where I do my work. I have a permanent studio space in Los Angeles where I store my unsold art. It has a sofa and a bathroom, so maybe it counts as a place."

"You have unsold pieces?"

"Tons. Not everything I do is great." He grins, and I'm caught staring at his lips. He's so damn handsome. Was the masked man good-looking? I have no idea. It was dim, and we were crashing into each other. I can't picture much of anything clearly. His hair was slick and dark. Was he tan? Maybe. He had abs. I remember that.

"I've lost you again," he says.

Oh, God. I was thinking about sex with a stranger while Jesse is showing me New York.

Good grief.

"Sorry. Everything is so new."

"But you were here six months ago."

Damn it. "Right. Yes. But I didn't get past the few places I was required to go."

"So, you were here on business?"

I don't want to lie. I have to stay sharp. "No, visiting people. There was no real sightseeing."

"Am I keeping you from them?" He sits up, dropping his hands on his lap, his face etched with concern. "I sort of ambushed you from the beginning."

"No, no. I'm fine. I'll probably have to message some of my friends, though."

"You can do that when we get off the subway. Not much signal down here."

I turn my phone over on my knee. He's right.

His hand rests on his leg, and as I flip my phone back over, the sides of our hands touch.

I'm shocked by the wild zip that goes through my body. I'm attracted to him, that's clear. But he's such a gentleman. I thought wild and demanding was my type, based on last night. I don't know. It's all so confusing.

I feel so naïve, despite all the work I've done to be informed. Street smarts don't come from studying. You have to get out in the world and take risks.

We enter another station. "This one's ours," Jesse says. He stands and turns to give me a hand to lift me out of the seat as the subway slows down with a squeal of brakes.

I take his hand, warm and strong. It feels good. Real. Like an ordinary encounter between two people getting to know each other.

What happened last night was an anomaly. It was me trying to check an item off my list. I shouldn't have done it.

But Jesse is real life. And an artist. A traveler. He's exactly the sort of person who fits me. Kind. Courteous. So beautiful.

As we head out through the tunnels, and he drops money into the case of a man playing a violin, I hold on to the hand he offered me.

Drag Scream said she made space for someone to come

into her life and take to the vampire ball, and fate handed her me.

Maybe I should do the same, and have faith in this man who turned up in the next room. He's opened a door to his life, one that is a perfect fit for the one I'm living right now.

If I'm attracted to him like I was the masked man, then I should be grateful I can feel it again. I don't have to be all impulsive and wild. I can take it slow with Jesse. Enjoy our time together.

The two of us can simply live in the moment, wherever it leads.

CHAPTER 12

Jesse

When we exit the subway station a few blocks away from the bridge, we stop for a moment on a bench so Ellie can respond to her friends.

A young girl in black braids with bright red bows on the ends feeds several pigeons wandering the space in front of a dim sum walk-up.

She has a handful of dough and pinches off bits to give them. The line of her red dress, her tiny shoes, and the way she bends to feed them sparks my interest. So I pull out a small sketchbook from my shirt pocket and draw the outer lines.

I've only captured the sweeping strokes when a petite elderly woman steps out. She speaks in Chinese to the girl, clearly unhappy that she's feeding the pigeons.

The girl blows kisses at the birds as she heads back inside. I flip the page and resketch the scene with her kisses floating to the pigeons.

Ellie has looked up at the commotion, then notices my book. "What made you want to draw her?"

I fill in details. "The way she bent over, the curve of her dress against the tall, straight lines of their shop. The colors, too, even though I can't put them in yet."

"I like it."

I finish enough that the memory is preserved and close the book. "You all caught up?"

"Sure. Just a bunch of chatter. There might be an opportunity to get tickets to a thing if we post about it. I'm considering it."

"Like a show?"

She shrugs. "Nothing that big."

She doesn't elaborate. I wonder if she doesn't want me to know about it because she's going as Indigo.

We stand up. I'd like to take her hand again, but I'm not sure if the moment has passed. "Is that what you do? Look for opportunities and follow them?"

"Sometimes. We talk amongst ourselves about the big ones, like Monica's hotel. Or if a shop has recently opened or a new clothing line is launched. We discuss if they're a good prospect to approach. Not every influencer is a match for every brand. We look out for each other."

"What is your brand?" We start walking and I decide, what the hell, and reach for her hand. She accepts it, and relief courses through me. This is working. Maybe if she tells me she is Indigo, it will feel natural to tell her I'm the man Indigo met at the ball.

"I'm not as defined as I should be. I'm hoping to clarify it during this trip." A woman with a tiny dog passes by, and Ellie smiles at it.

"What do you want to be?"

"I'm not sure. A generalist has the most opportunity,

but I don't think I have the right look for an ordinary fashion and lifestyle influencer."

"Why not? You're gorgeous and have an extremely broad appeal."

She flashes a quick smile. "Thank you. But I have a different…look when I'm posting. Something flashier and perhaps less mainstream."

This is it. The moment. I send a small wish into the universe that this will work out. "I'd love to see this look."

Another hint of a smile tells me she's about to lie to be nice. "Sure. Maybe sometime."

That's a no. I opt not to push. We're only hours into knowing each other as regular humans. The timing isn't right for a reveal, not on either side.

We reach the bridge, the towering stone and long cables looming above us. The wind is high, and Ellie releases my hand to capture her hair.

We pause at the Manhattan end of the bridge to turn and look out over the city. The afternoon sun shines on the buildings, making them gleam. I've sketched this scene a dozen times, so I don't feel the urge to pull out my notebook. But Ellie lifts her phone to snap shots.

I lean on the metal rail to watch. She's good, framing them nicely, capturing the lines and angles.

"You want me to take one of you with the city behind you?" I ask.

She shakes her head. "That's okay."

"Because you're not wearing your look?"

She shrugs. "There's filters for that."

Interesting. "You don't want it for yourself?"

Her gaze holds mine a moment. "Okay."

I angle her so that she's in the sweet spot of the image, the city shining behind her. "How about one of the two of us?"

Her eyes widen, then she catches herself. "Sure, we can do it with my phone."

I sense I shouldn't ask her to send it to me. I move beside her, extending the phone out with my arm. "I hope my shot meets the approval of a queen of selfies."

She reaches out and shifts my arm. "You could use a selfie stick."

I laugh. "I have a selfie stick right here!" I smack my forearm.

We look into the cell phone camera, and I snap the shot. I stare at the image for a moment, trying to freeze it in my mind to recreate later in my sketchbook. Maybe one day soon she'll trust me enough to let me have it.

She shoves her phone into her pocket. "I don't know anything about the bridge. Do you?"

We continue down the promenade, an elevated walkway above the car lanes. "There was a near-mutiny many years back when the city stopped allowing people to put love locks on the metal rails."

She holds onto my arm as we walk, and when she looks up at me, her hair flying around her face, I almost lose my breath at how lovely she is. "Love locks?"

I fight the urge to kiss her. "Couples would come up here with padlocks to commemorate their unbreakable bond. There was a long while when you could buy locks from vendors at either end."

"Why did they stop allowing it?"

We pass a "No locks" sign, hilariously decorated with a

padlock. "Something about structural integrity, yada yada. Dangerous to cars below. I don't know. People were upset."

We walk along for a while, and she says, "People want to leave their mark. It's comforting to know a piece of your love remains somewhere."

I squeeze her hand on my arm. "I agree with you."

We make it to the halfway point and stop for another round of photos. I pull out my phone, and it doesn't escape my notice that when I take a shot of the skyline from this vantage point, Ellie ensures she's beside or slightly behind me the whole time. Only when I put my phone away does she relax.

She really doesn't want images of her. Maybe she's avoiding someone. Or is private with her real identity. I can respect that. Whenever I get a scathing critique of my art, I wish I were less visible.

I regret stopping, because after that break, she doesn't hold on to me again. We walk like two friends traversing the bridge. I guess she's in her head and might be considering all the ways her celebrity self could be outed. I don't know how to convince her that all her secrets are safe with me.

The vision of her dancing on the table flashes through me again. I have to shove it aside. She's different here, wholesome and inquisitive.

But then, I'm not exactly behaving the same way either.

We reach the end of the bridge and walk into the streets of Brooklyn. "I think I promised you lunch dessert on the other side," I say.

"All right. I can be convinced. I think I already walked off that crepe."

"The place I have in mind is a few blocks ahead. It's been around fifty years. It franchised out a few decades ago, but this is the original."

Her hair is wild from all the wind. She looks like a goddess. "What do they have that you can't live without?"

"Cheesecake. There's a lot of good cheesecake in New York, but this one is the best."

We walk along the street a while until we get to a neighborhood. I keep my steps slow and measured. I want to extend this day as long as possible.

"Oh, this looks like the movies of New York!" she exclaims. "Brownstones, right? There are stairs going up to the doors!"

She runs up a set of steps, striking a pose on one of them. She looks incredibly beautiful in the sunlight, and that feeling of devouring her comes over me, the way it happened last night at the ball. It's almost as if there is this tiger inside of me, and the more time I spend with her, the hungrier he gets.

I'd give anything to snap a picture of her here, but I don't dare, not after her behavior on the bridge. I freeze this image in my mind, hoping I can store them all in perfect detail until I can get to my sketchbook. Maybe I can lay them out quickly at the deli while we're sitting down.

She runs back down the steps. "If I could sing, I would totally be belting the lyrics to *West Side Story*."

"I'm happy to be the Tony to your Maria."

Her eyes are alight as she turns in circles, taking it all

in. "I'm not sure I'm romance musical material. But I'm here!"

"Of course, we're in Brooklyn, not Manhattan."

"Oh?" She continues to turn, arms outstretched. "I haven't seen anything in Manhattan that looks as much like the movie as this!"

"I could show you more."

She stops to look at me, and that expression I remember from last night comes over her, right before we went to the dance floor. It's a hesitation before diving in. It's impossible for me to separate the two versions of her. At the core, both the wild vixen and this glorious, inquisitive woman are the same.

"All right, my frazzlin. What's in it for you?"

This stops me. What can I tell her that won't seem too outrageous? That I want all of her? Not just the wildling from last night. Or the skittish girl who fell onto my hotel room floor. Or even the one today, light-hearted and worried in equal measure.

I've only known her for two days.

But I come up with a reason. "I want to sculpt you."

"Me?" She presses her hand to her chest. "Wait, are you going to make me look like you've peeled off all my skin?"

Her horrified expression makes me burst out laughing. "No, no. I only did that for Monica's hotel. It was commissioned. I'm not that into skinned fruit."

She latches onto a street lamp and swings around it like she's ten years old. "Right. No bananas since you were twelve."

"See, you already know so much about me."

This makes her stop her twirl around the pole. "What

do I know? Jesse Adams. Artist. No real home. World traveler. Son of famous people. Age—"

"Twenty-nine."

"Oh, then eight years my senior."

"You're twenty-one?" That's younger than I would have guessed. Hopefully, it's not too much for her. I can't lose her on a technicality.

She hesitates. "About to be."

"Birthday soon?"

"Yeah. A couple of weeks." She lets go of the pole and starts walking again. "My father is fifteen years older than my mother."

"Are you close to them?"

"No. They are very strict and regimented. They didn't want me to come here."

This explains a lot. "Twenty is plenty old enough to do your own thing."

She nods. "And I'm doing it!" She wraps her hand around another pole and makes a quick spin around it. She can't stop smiling. I love this. Love everything about her.

We walk a few more blocks, and I consider what might be a safe question to ask. "Any brothers or sisters?"

"Yes, one of each. How about you?"

"I'm the one and only. Mom never got over Dad leaving her. Didn't take up with anyone else."

"I hear only children are spoiled." She quirks her eyebrow.

"We are. We get what we want." I pretend to snatch her, and she shrieks and dashes out of my way, laughing.

"I'm not yours to have!"

"Oh, yes, you are. I'm an only child! I get what I want!" I

chase her up the sidewalk, and we streak past several old men sitting on a stoop.

We come to a street, and she seems about to dash out into it. "Ellie!" I shout and grasp her waist, pulling her back to the curb.

She's still laughing. "There weren't any cars coming, you goof." She turns around in my arms.

And now she's close. We're breathing heavily from the run.

Everything about her body is familiar. I remember dancing with her, holding her close, lifting her to straddle me, pushing her against the wall.

Her eyes are on mine. I struggle with whether to kiss her. Will she recognize my mouth, how it feels? Can I kiss her differently to avoid recognition? Or do I want her to make the connection?

But then the moment is gone. An entire class of small children surrounds us, holding onto a rope. A nun leads them.

"Holy moly, this is out of a movie," Ellie says, jerking out her phone. She takes a million photos. "I'm living some sort of dream."

I would have to agree.

The children turn at the corner and keep going. The light changes, and Ellie and I cross the street.

"The deli is ahead," I tell her.

"Deli?" She slows down.

"Yeah. The cheesecake is at a deli."

Her voice has a shake in it. "What's the name of the deli?"

We pass a dry cleaner. "It's right here."

I take her hand and pull her beneath a striped awning. The moment she sees the words painted on the window, she backs away.

"No, no, no, no."

Then she runs.

CHAPTER 13

Lili

This can't be happening.

New York is huge!

Why of all the places, of all the restaurants, of all the delis, did we have to go to that one?

PACKWOOD FAMILY DELI.

It's the first Pickle Deli, run by Grammy Alma, the Pickle grandmother.

I've met her many times. She's Sunny's grandmother! My brother's wife! The one who just gave birth to the royal next-in-line!

I race back to the intersection, praying nobody inside saw me.

Thankfully, there's a walk symbol, and I keep running. I don't know if Jesse is behind me. I don't know if he thinks I'm crazy. But if anyone is in there that I've met, I'm done for.

I'm so stupid. I should have known not to go out in the city looking like myself. Now I'm drawing attention, racing down the sidewalk. People might film me. The video could be uploaded. I could get spotted by my father's staff, who are undoubtedly scouring footage, using AI facial recognition.

After four blocks of sprinting, I give out. I slow down, then walk, then stop to bend over and breathe.

I hear footfalls behind me. Jesse leans down, his face close to mine. He's obviously a runner. He's not even breathing hard.

"Ellie? What's wrong? The deli was closed. There was a birth in the family. I should have checked."

Oh, thank God. That's true. Grammy is surely in Avalonia, helping Sunny. That's why the plane was here, to pick up the rest of the Pickles. Grammy probably arrived with the first round that brought Sunny's parents.

Sunny worked in that very deli we saw. Leo wound up there, trying to avoid the royal guards. What was it about this part of New York that caused two royal siblings to end up here?

Does this mean I'm doomed to get caught?

Of course, I am.

I'm under no illusion that this reprieve will last forever. I wanted some time away. Time of my own to check items off my bucket list.

"Ellie?"

Right. Jesse.

"Please don't ask questions," I plead. It's all I've got. I could never explain it all. I've only known him a day. Two, if you count the five minutes after I fell on his floor. He'd never understand, and I can't risk the truth.

"Okay," he says. "No questions. How can I help?"

"Take me back to the hotel." My fear is overwhelming. I

glance to the right and the left, sure there will be someone I know, a royal guard, a camera ready to upload my image to the internet.

We walk along the sidewalk. I keep close to the wall. I don't make eye contact with anyone. Once the paranoia has taken hold, I can't shake it.

"Hey, let me get us something," Jesse says. He pauses in front of a tourist cart with "I Heart New York" T-shirts and small replicas of the Statue of Liberty.

I wait in a corner formed by a set of stairs leading up to someone's home. People walk by. Tall. Short. Young. Old. They are mostly in a hurry, focused on where they are headed next.

A shiny dark car rolls slowly down the street. I stuck in a breath. This is the sort of car my father hires when we're here. I flatten myself against the wall.

But it continues on.

Jesse returns with a Mets ball cap and an umbrella. "This might help." He sets the cap on my head.

I pull it low on my forehead.

He opens the umbrella. It's not what I expect, black on top with an image of blue sky and clouds on the underside. He angles it so that oncoming pedestrians can't see my face.

"Better?"

I hate that he's figured out that I'm in hiding. But I've taken such a big risk. If Leo could get caught in New York, how did I think I could escape detection for long?

But the hat helps. And the umbrella shields me.

I relax. We walk along the street back the way we came, toward the bridge.

Jesse's face is etched with concern. "Do you want to take the subway back, or can I hail a cab? A cab is more private."

I've calmed some. "The subway is fine." I tug on my cap. "I have this."

"We can pick up some sunglasses."

"I'm all right."

He closes the umbrella as we descend the stairs to the subway station on the Brooklyn side. I may have enjoyed our day, but I'm more aware than before that there are risks to being Lili out in the open.

I'm sad about it. I like spending time with Jesse. He reminds me of the best Avalonians, gentlemanly and kind and concerned. He's an artist. He really sees the world. We have this in common.

I would spend all my days with him if I could, but it's not safe to wander the city with the face he knows as me.

Maybe if I had met him as Indigo, this would have been all right. But now, our budding friendship, or romance, or whatever it was about to be, must end.

I simply can't risk it.

From this day forward, I am Indigo and Indigo only.

CHAPTER 14

Jesse

Damn it. I've lost her. I can tell.

She's shrunk in on herself, head down, not looking at anyone in the subway car. Thankfully, it's mostly empty.

Who is she, really?

I want to tell her I know she's Indigo. I could tell her I saw her on the stairs and recognized her shoes. Or that she showed up on Monica's feed.

But then I'd have to confess that I'm the man she met at the ball. That we know each other far more than she realizes.

She'd feel betrayed. I know it.

I have to admit that I've screwed this up. I did it the moment I went to the ball and didn't tell her. The minute we danced. And if not then, the second she locked that door in the dressing room.

And now, look what it's gotten me. I'm more convinced than ever that she's someone I can't live without. Every facet of her fits every part of me.

I don't know what to do.

So I sketch.

I draw the image of us on the bridge. I draw her twirling around the pole. Then my favorite, her on the stairs, looking saucy and excited.

She watches me draw as the car lurches through the tunnels. I'm well practiced in drawing against the motions of the subway. I enjoy sketching down here. There are always new people and scenes and expressions. One of my most famous assemblage pieces began with a sketch of an elderly woman on a train. She was broken down, hunched over, burdened with years of poverty and injustice.

I made a piece showing her falling to the floor of the subway car, slice by slice. I still get a lump in my throat when I come across a mention of that particular work.

"You're extremely talented," she says.

"It's my only obsession." Other than, possibly, her. Hopefully, it doesn't freak her out that I rapid-fired three sketches of her.

Not to mention page after page of extremely graphic ones in my hotel room.

She adjusts her cap as a man passes by. "I think it can take obsession to get that good."

"It definitely takes a lot of hours."

She leans against the back of the seat and stares up at the posters on the wall. "I'm not sure I'll get to that level about anything."

"Based on how you were framing your cell phone shots of the city, I'd say you have developed a good eye for photography."

"But I haven't been able to study it. I don't know if it's my thing. It's just something I do."

"But you like it."

She shrugs. "I don't know anything."

I close my sketchbook. "I didn't know anything for a long time either. I thought I should paint in oils, like traditional artists. I spent years perfecting my oil techniques before I realized I was trapped in a medium that wasn't serving me."

"What did you do then?"

"I went out and met more creatives. Sculptors. Graffiti artists. Mixed media. Whatever they did, I tried out to see how it fit."

"When did you settle on assemblage?"

"It was almost an accident. I was setting up my studio in L.A. when I opened a crate and one of my clay sculptures had broken apart. The pieces of it were stuck randomly in the glue of one of my mixed media pieces that had gotten too hot."

She laughs, and I'm relieved to hear it. It's the first laugh since she ran from the deli. "So it's like Reese's Peanut Butter Cups. Two great tastes that taste great together."

I love this. "Exactly. Both of the old pieces of art were ruined, but as I organized the space, I started looking at what would happen if I combined my mixed media textures with my old sculptures. I worked until I got the basics down. The mechanics of it, you know. How to make them fit and hold together. Substrates. Glue. Then I made new things."

"What was your first piece to get sold?"

She's clearly interested, her feet pulled up onto the seat, her arms wrapped around her shins. The skin of her knees peeks through the rips in her jeans.

"It was a boy breaking into pieces as another boy stood menacingly over him. I called it *A Bully in Five Parts*."

"Who bought it? How were you discovered?"

"I wish I could say I was self-made. But my mother displayed it on stage at one of her fashion shows for children's wear, and it became a sensation."

"Is that the one at the Met?"

"No. It was bought by a private collector for display in a building that houses a lot of therapists and mental health specialists."

"So you sometimes have a mission. Not just fruit."

I smile. "Not just fruit."

She closes her eyes. "I find it relaxing to ride this train."

"We don't have to get off at our stop." I don't want to, either. I'm afraid she'll disappear into her room, and I'll never see her again.

But maybe she's settling down. Something about the Packwood Family Deli scared the crap out of her. Or maybe she saw someone on the street. I wasn't clear exactly what spooked her.

We glide into the station where we started. "I think this is us, right?" she asks.

Damn. "It is."

She stands. "I think I have it from here. Thank you so much for breakfast. And lunch. Dessert lunch."

I stand next to her. She wants to part here. I have to let her. "If you need coffee tomorrow, knock three times on our adjoining door."

She says nothing to that, but as the doors open, she hurries out.

I sit back down. I don't want to follow her to the hotel or crowd her. I might resort to begging.

Strangers enter the car and surround me. At the last moment, I get off, too, walking slowly to ensure I don't catch up with her.

By a pillar between the platforms, a man plays a mournful tune on a saxophone, slow and sexy and full of woe, as if he's lost the object of his desire.

I stop to listen awhile, letting the notes wash over me, filling me with melancholy. I'm going to have to let this woman get away. I have no choice. She has another life. One she doesn't want to share with me.

After a few minutes, I drop money in his case and head out. I don't go toward the hotel. I don't go anywhere. I wander the streets, seeing her run up every set of stairs or twirling on every pole.

I've never fallen this hard, this fast. I've never had such a fucked-up introduction to someone.

I've never met anybody like her.

I have to find a way into her life.

There must be a way.

CHAPTER 15

Lili

The moment I get back to my room, I put on my Indigo look. Wig. Makeup. Eyelashes.

Drag Scream and I did some shopping before hitting the costume store yesterday, so I have some Indigo-appropriate attire.

I used my last Lili outfit with Jesse today.

But what I'm wearing now is *fire*. Red jeans, slashed within an inch of their lives, the gaps filled with glittery black fishnet. A black cropped shirt that glimmers with every movement.

Black boots, polished to a perfect shine. And finally, an Indigo-approved bag, a black leather pouch covered in rhinestones that fastens to a belt loop.

I try bra and no bra, unsure whether or not Indigo would show a nipple outline.

The one who met the masked man sure would.

My whole body whooshes with heat. Now that I've committed to setting Jesse aside, I can't stop thinking about last night.

I want to meet the masked man again. Do something regrettable. The need is dark and unrelenting.

But I created that failsafe of giving his number to Drag Scream for a reason. He will be my undoing if I pursue him.

Even so, I snatch up my phone and search for the deleted image. Damn. It's gone. I have my phone set to remove deleted images permanently because I'm constantly running out of phone storage due to the avalanche of selfies, photos, and videos I take. I have no way to download them to a larger computer here, and I'm not confident in the security of the cloud, not that I could afford to pay for that anyway.

It's gone. The only way to the masked man is through Drag Scream.

But I do spot something else while I'm looking.

The image of me and Jesse on the bridge.

We look so happy, the wind making our hair mingle. It was such a good day until I panicked.

Scat-fucking-diddly.

I know it's right to turn him loose. There's no way to have a relationship in my situation. At every turn, I'm one misstep away from getting hauled back to Avalonia.

I put on a bra. I rapid-fire text my friends. Drag Scream is at a movie screening but can meet up tomorrow night. Carly offers to make dinner at her place. Grim Weaver says he'll go anywhere for free food.

So, it's settled. We agree to descend on Carly's place for the evening tomorrow and look over our options for expanding our brands. I'm relieved to have something to do that won't cost much. I can take the subway to Queens.

It's afternoon here, but ten p.m. in Avalonia, so I text my sister.

Me: Text me if you can.

Octavia: I'm in my rooms.

Me: What's the latest?

Octavia: Baby Lucy is a doll.

Me: Send a picture.

One comes through. My little niece is wrapped up in a white blanket, asleep. My heart pangs that I missed meeting her. But she was my best chance to escape.

Me: Precious.

Octavia: A zillion people are reporting having seen you. It's crazy. Did you organize this? Because it will take years to follow every clue. Apparently, you're in Paris, Zurich, and Africa simultaneously.

Me: Really?

Octavia: It's so great. Have you recovered from your ball?

Me: All good today.

Octavia: No word on the mystery masked man?

Me: No.

Octavia: Will you try to find him?

Oh, I wish.

Me: I shouldn't.

Octavia: It's so daring. I'm in awe of you.

Me: I'm having dinner with the influencers tomorrow. I walked the Brooklyn Bridge and went to an art show today.

Octavia: I'm so jealous! Please have all the fun for both of us!

Me: I will. Thanks for the update.

I set the phone aside. This is good news. I'm not sure why everyone is sighting me everywhere, but I'm glad. I use Indigo's account to go view my Princess Lili Instagram.

I have a million tags. There are new hashtags. #Leave-LiliAlone #ISawLili and #PrincessOnTheRun

I never could have predicted this would happen. And Octavia's right. People are taking my images from Instagram and Photoshopping me in front of the Eiffel Tower, on a jungle cruise, riding roller coasters, and all sorts of things. Some have even changed my outfits, so it's not obvious the photo is from my feed.

Of course, now that I've engaged with Princess Lili's account, my news feed changes. I'm barely out of the Insta app when I spot a suggested article about my disappearance.

I click on it.

Princess Lilianne, youngest child of King Francisco and Queen Pulmaria of the European city-state of Avalonia, was reported missing yesterday morning.

Rosenthal Monroe, the cultural attaché for the royal family, said the young princess might have been influenced by a "negative element." He said, "Her Grace Lilianne has long been a part of certain social media platforms known for their misinformation and bullying."

He emphasized the princess has been sheltered and may not have the slightest idea about how to manage on her own without her royal guards and assistants.

. . .

Gah. I toss the phone on the bed. *No idea how to manage.* Right.

What a bunch of frazzlins.

Now I'm mad.

I'll show them. I'll make it in this town. In any town. I'll figure out a way to get by. Maybe I'll never go home.

My phone buzzes. It's Carly. *Feel free to come early tomorrow if you want. I dropped a pin to my place. Buzz when you get here.*

See. I have friends. Places to go. People to see.

Men to bang in dressing rooms and never learn their names.

Ha.

Sheltered princess. Can't manage on her own.

My anger carries me right out of the room, through the hotel, and out onto the street. I head toward the subway, then stop. Food. I'm Indigo. I can drum up a sponsorship.

I walk into the crepe shop. The same man is there, large and bald with a wide mustache. It's quiet midafternoon, and he's wiping down the counters.

"Who's the manager here?" I ask.

He looks up. "I own the place."

"Awesome. I ate here earlier, and it was unbelievably good. I thought I'd absolutely died and gone to heaven."

His face breaks into a smile. "Nice to hear it."

I open my phone and show him my Instagram feed. "I have over two million followers. I would love to make a deal so I can eat here once or twice while I'm in New York in exchange for publicity. I'll post every time I come."

His eyes scan the feed. "How many comments you get?"

Oh, he knows. Good. I like it when they understand how it works.

I click on a recent post. "This one got five hundred and eighty-three. Typically, I can convert around three percent, maybe less since you're only local. But I can get you seen. I can get it to spread beyond me."

He looks me in the eye. "You probably don't eat more than a mite."

I shrug. "I wolfed down a chocolate and banana crepe in about three minutes."

He laughs again and pulls a card from his pocket. "I like you. Here's a card for ten free crepes. Post as you like. You do you."

He scribbles "Ten free" on the back and his signature. "On weekends, you'll probably see Pablo. He'll know what this means."

I take the card. "Great! Thank you so much!"

He lifts a hand. "See you soon. Indigo? Was that it?"

"Yes, Indigo."

"I'm Marco."

"So nice to meet you, Marco." I wave and push out the door into the afternoon sun.

Ha. So there, Rosenthal. I got enough food to last me a few days. Breakfast. Lunch. Dinner.

Dessert lunch.

As quickly as the gentle thought of Jesse arrives, I have to push it away. I have no time for romance. I got my virginity business done with the masked man. I have a place to stay and a backup for when it ends. I bought new clothes and makeup.

Now I have food.

And tomorrow I'll meet up with my friends, pick a direction, and go on my next big journey.

I don't know where it's going to be, but I'm definitely going to manage *just fine*.

After a long day of hitting the streets and drumming up more sponsors, I sleep fitfully.

I pay way too close attention to any noises next door. What is Jesse doing? Is he thinking about me? Will he plot another way to get me to see him?

Maybe I was hasty. I freaked out over the deli, feeling exposed.

Why hadn't I met him as Indigo?

But morning goes by with no sight of him. I open my door a time or two and peer into the hall. Nothing.

I dress as Indigo and eat a crepe for breakfast. Then I wander a public park and convince a burger shop to sponsor a meal in exchange for two posts. I'm getting there, one victory at a time.

Then it's time to find my way to Carly's.

I get lost in Grand Central Station and have to make a thousand transfers. It doesn't help that the subway makes me think of Jesse. Pondering this makes me miss a stop, and it's not always easy to get back to where you were.

I'm glad I left early to get there. It takes an hour more than I thought it would. By the time I arrive, Grim Weaver is also on the stairs. He waits for me to catch up and we go in together.

Carly's excited to see us, although I notice her gaze

lingers on Grim. It could be his outfit. Today he's wearing a jumpsuit completely knitted in big black and gray blocks.

"You make that?" Carly asks him.

He spins on his heels. "Every stitch."

Carly's place is a long, narrow room with a kitchen on one end and a bathroom on the other. The door is in the middle, then a futon that turns into a bed, a sofa, and a tiny table with two chairs.

It works for Carly, who is as dainty as her apartment. Today's cargo pants are the color of wheat, and her shirt is wrinkly blue cotton.

Grim Weaver and I sit on the sofa, and Carly cooks on the hot plate, since only the oven works, but not the burners on her stove.

Naturally, I don't mention that the whole place is smaller than my clothing closet at the palace.

There is no closet here. Carly stores her minimalist wardrobe of all-natural fibers, vegan shoes, and hiking boots in plastic bins under her furniture.

I haven't sat on the sofa for more than a minute when something big and black scuttles next to my feet. I screech and jump up onto the sofa. "Get it! Get it! Get it!"

Carly glances over. "Just a cockroach."

"Don't talk to Indigo like that," Grim says.

Carly sighs. "I mean that's what made her jump."

"The other day you said *we* were the cockroaches!"

I sit back down, this time crossing my legs, my feet securely tucked in. Carly ignores Grim and returns to stirring the sauce on the hot plate.

Grim leans in and whispers, "If we're the cockroaches, what do we call the bugs?"

I pat his knee. I think he's being ironic, but maybe it isn't an act.

Drag Scream arrives about the time Carly is done boiling pasta in her coffee pot.

Instantly, the room feels smaller. With her platform boots and her piled-up hair, Drag Scream barely fits from floor to ceiling.

"You really living all up in here?" Drag Scream asks, pointing at the corners of the room.

Carly shrugs. "Unless I have six people sharing the rent, I'm not going anywhere else." She bends down to open a cabinet and pull out four wide bowls.

Drag Scream considers her furniture choices and selects the empty futon. She's dressed down today, wearing an emerald-green pantsuit and no jewelry other than earrings that dangle to her shoulders.

"So, question," Grim says. "Are you always Drag Scream or is this your superhero persona?"

I've wondered the same thing, but never dared to ask.

"Drag Scream is my alter ego." She smoothes her hair, tucking in any strays. "Most days I sell radio ads."

"As Drag Scream?" I ask.

"No, no, I'm Ferdinand at work. Khakis and polos like a good corporate shill. And male presenting. It works as a day look." She examines her nails. "I don't like to be put in boxes, always this or always that. Your generation understands fluidity more than mine."

Carly looks up from where she stirs the sauce. "But it's

she/her for your pronouns when you're Drag Scream? He/him as Ferdinand? I want to get it right."

"You can always address me as Queen. The Queen's car. Give it to the Queen."

Carly smiles. "Of course, Your Highness."

I admit to liking Drag Scream the best out of our New York contingent. There are a few other influencers from our chat in the city, but they haven't been as active or as interested in meeting as these three.

"Soup's on," Carly says, passing me and Grim a bowl. She takes one to Drag Scream, then sits on the narrow chair at her table.

I take a bite, and it's surprisingly good, rich and creamy. Who knew you could make a dish like this with a hot plate and a coffee pot?

"I thought you were vegan," Drag Scream says. "This divine creation must have cream."

Carly shakes her head. "Nope. Vegan queso is the base of the sauce. It's made with cashews and nutritional yeast."

"Insane." Drag Scream spins another bite on her fork.

Grim is eating so fast that he's going to get indigestion.

Carly takes her time. "So Indigo, what's your next move?"

"I'm hitting the pavement for sponsors. Got some tickets and some food comps. I found an incredible crepe shop."

"Good for you. Over by Monica's hotel?"

"Yeah, I had lunch there yesterday." My mind flashes to Jesse, and I catch Drag Scream pausing, her fork partway to her mouth. She's onto me, somehow.

Carly swirls her fork in her pasta. "Where are you going to stay after this week?"

I shrug. "Not sure. I still have several days."

"You got a home somewhere?" Grim asks.

I've prepared answers for questions like this. "I left home. Seeing what I can do on my own."

"I hear you," Carly says.

Grim nods and looks around the small apartment. "I wish I could afford some digs. Carly, how do you do it?"

Carly's face goes pink. She takes a huge bite of pasta to avoid the question.

"Daddy pays," Drag Scream says. "Isn't that right?"

Carly nods and stares at her bowl like it's a crime to have parents who help.

"I think that's great," I say. "What about you, Grim?"

He tugs on his knit cap. "I live in my parents' house. No shame in my game."

So none of them really live as influencers. It's a side gig. Not even Drag Scream, who gets paid decently for her appearances. She has a regular job.

Oh, boy. Why did I think more people were doing better than they are? A low panic forms in my belly. How long until I have to go home? Or do I get a job?

No, that's not possible. I'm not a citizen here. To work, I would have to produce identification. I'd be outed.

"You're deep in thought, Miz Flame," Drag Scream says.

"I'm living by the seat of my pants," I say. "And I'm stuck in New York."

"New York is a great place to be stuck," Drag Scream says.

"But it's expensive," Carly says.

"And nowhere to live," Grim adds.

They're not helping calm my panic. "I'm trying to figure out what to try."

Drag Scream sets her empty bowl next to her on the faded futon. "I have some options. There's a house party upstate that's supposed to last three days. I'm invited. I could take you. Or even all of you." She waves her dagger nails at Carly and Grim.

"A house party!" Grim exclaims. "I mean, like, aren't all parties in houses? I guess it could be a beach party. Or a forest party."

Drag Scream presses her fingers to her forehead. "It means people are invited to stay at the house."

"How do we get there?" I ask. "I have zero comps for travel."

"My parents have a car," Carly says quietly, almost as if she doesn't want to admit it.

"Rad!" Grim says. "You got a license? Because I don't have a license. I mean, I tried, but there was like, a *test!* Who knew you had to pass a test to drive a car?"

"Everyone," Carly says. "Everyone knows you have to pass a test to drive a car."

"You okay with driving?" Drag Scream asks. "I have a license."

"You'd probably be better," Carly says. "I don't do it much and people who honk scare me." A big black bug scurries across the table, and she easily scoops it up and takes it to the window to let it out on the fire escape. "Shhh, Monty."

We all whip our heads around.

"Did you…name that cockroach?" Drag Scream asks.

Carly closes the window, but I notice it isn't all the way shut. "Maybe."

Grim sits up straighter. "You're like, Cinderella, then."

She smiles at him. "Maybe a little."

Drag Scream stands to take her bowl to the sink. "Okaaay. Anyway, back to the house party. I'll confirm that I can add you all to my invite. It's in five days."

"That's one more day than I have at the hotel." I take Grim's bowl and follow Drag Scream to the sink.

"Offer's still good to sleep here!" Carly chirps. Monty squeezes through a gap in the window and heads for Carly's dish.

"Thanks." I press my hand to my stomach, trying not to lose my pasta. There's no way I can handle this place. I wouldn't sleep a wink, even if the cockroaches *do* have names.

"We have a plan," Drag Scream says. She turns and spots me staring at the bug. "Carly, thank you for your hospitality. Indigo, we can head home together. My place is one stop from Monica's."

After my trials getting here, I'm relieved at her offer. We say our goodbyes and clomp down three flights of stairs.

"Please never allow me to agree to dinner there again," Drag Scream says. "I've seen fewer insects in a Louisiana swamp."

I avoid touching the wall, which is smeared with an unidentifiable substance. "But the food was good."

"If you're willing to share it with your six-legged friends." Drag Scream shakes her head. "But good for her for finding a place of her own."

We head toward the subway entrance. It's a few blocks down. Night has descended, and only a few random souls walk along the sidewalk in front of building after building of housing like Carly's.

Once we're settled on a seat, Drag Scream asks, "So, how are you really doing here? It's only your third day."

"I've done a lot."

"Who'd you spend all that time with yesterday?"

I swallow. "The guy in the next hotel room."

"A random man?"

Heat rushes to my face. "He's installing art in Monica's hotel. He was fine."

"All right, boogie-boo. I guess if you can get buck-wild with a masked stranger, you can tromp around New York City with an artist."

"Thanks, Mom."

"You all right about how it went at the ball?"

I hesitate, not sure what to say, how much to reveal.

"Ahhhh," she says. "You're thinking of him."

"I might be obsessed."

"He was that good?"

"So good."

Drag Scream fans herself with a piece of paper from her purse. "You want his number now?"

I stare out the window as the tunnel walls whiz by. "I shouldn't. It's not like he's relationship material."

"But he excites you. Makes you feel alive."

He does that.

"I tell you what. I was invited to a black and white masquerade on Friday. I wasn't planning to go — it's too tame for my taste. But I'll make you my plus one and text your masked man to tip him off that you will be there. If he can finagle an invitation, then destiny has played its hand."

Her face flashes dark-light-dark-light as we enter our station. Do I want to see him again? Do those things again?

My body stirs.

I believe I do.

CHAPTER 16

Jesse

I should check out of this hotel. The art has been hung for days. Listening to Ellie move about her room next door, coming and going, has made me nearly insane.

Three or four times a day I almost bang on our adjoining door, insisting she talk to me.

But then I swing the other direction. I have to get her out of my head. I have to leave. Move on. Recognize that I've screwed up, and it's not fixable.

I got as far as packing my bag, but I couldn't walk away. It's impossible for me to leave before she's gone. As long as she's here, there's a chance I can figure out a way to make this work.

I call Ethan and meet him for lunch just to talk about her, to say her name out loud.

But he assumes everything is normal, and mainly he wants to bug me about doing a show in his gallery. He only met Ellie for three minutes, so there isn't much to go on. And I won't confess that I met her at the vampire ball. No one can know that was me until Ellie does.

If I get a chance to tell her.

That's the thing I'd say. I've pictured the moment in my head a hundred times. I put on the costume and knock on her hotel room door.

She sees me and takes a step back, wondering how I could have possibly found her.

Then I remove the mask.

In some versions of this fantasy, she's thrilled I am the same person who walked with her through New York. We embrace and find that knife's edge between the passion of the night at the ball and the easy camaraderie of our day in the city.

In others, though, she's angry. She slams the door in my face. I lean against it, asking for another chance while drawers open and close, and she packs. Then leaves. And I have no way to contact her again. Just endless scrolling through her feeds, watching her live life as Indigo.

It's an obsession. I know it. But it won't release me from its grip.

I almost reach my breaking point, the anguish over her forcing me to make a choice — go see her or leave.

But then my next art piece comes to me.

I told Ellie I wanted to sculpt her, and the agony of being so close without being able to talk to her fuels my work.

Once the decision to begin is made, I eat little and sleep hardly at all. I settle on my materials and get started. I need more sketches, and I make more, drawing again and again, perfecting the lines, adding in pencil coloring.

Ellie on the subway.

Ellie running from the deli.

Ellie smiling at the children holding the rope.

Ellie. Ellie. Ellie.

When I find one that I'm satisfied with, I carefully cut the image into a long, narrow oval and prepare it for sealant.

By Thursday, I have dozens of sealed sketches drying in curves, like flower petals.

I'm overcome with the need to do this work. And grateful. Otherwise, I'd fall into a hole, sitting on the floor, collapsing in on myself over this woman I met by chance and lost by whim. It's the dark place, the abyss that often seems near, but never quite gets me.

I've seen artist friends fall in. At first, they do great work, manic and wild. Then they need something to sustain the energy. They drink. They snort substances.

They ruin themselves. Some lose their edge. Some almost lose everything.

I will not go there.

I will not ruin myself, nor Ellie, nor invade her life without her invitation.

But I will do my work. Pour this torment into art.

I forget to check my phone, and on Friday morning when I finally think to plug it in for a charge, a message sticks out among the ones from my mother and friends.

UNKNOWN CALLER: Your vampiress doesn't want your number, but she wants to see you. This is the party. Find a way in. Do not disappoint.

Attached to the message is a snap of an invitation to a black and white masquerade.

Holy shit. Is this her?

I write the number back, but an automated message says it is no longer accepting replies.

It has to be her. Or her friend. I won't question it.

The stiff paper petals rustle, disturbed by air currents as I rush around the room, pacing wildly. I'm surrounded by Ellie in every sketch, permanently preserved.

And now I'll get to see her. The other her.

Maybe if Ellie isn't the way, Indigo is.

I don't recognize the names on this invitation, but I'll ask everyone I know. Someone will have a connection. And even if not, I will show up. Bluff my way in.

I will absolutely attend this ball.

And this time, I will not fuck up.

Fuck her? Yes. Most certainly that's what she wants.

But lose her again?

Not a damn chance.

CHAPTER 17

Lili

Entering this costume party feels the same as when Drag Scream and I made our way through the crowd at the vampire ball.

She leads, and people watch her walk through the room. I'm almost an inconsequential afterthought.

But there is one difference this time.

I'm only here to meet the masked man. Drag Scream told him to come.

The mansion is enormous. The foyer is comparable to the palace. Marble floors. Multiple pillars towering over us. Flower arrangements the size of trees.

I shift my hips so the shimmery length of my gown doesn't get caught in my legs as I walk. I'm easy to spot, all in red like before, when everyone here wears black or white to fit the theme. It's a bold choice. Even Drag Scream is all in black. I'm starkly in contrast, like a rose lying on the keys of a piano.

My gaze passes over the crowd. Men, women, gowns,

tuxedos, masks. It's elegant and understated. A small orchestra plays in the corner.

I inhale sharply when I see him. He wears a black tux with a white tie, similar to most of the other men here. But his lapel bears a red bloom. The mask is the same, fixed to his head while so many others carry theirs on a stick to lift and lower as they speak.

I recognize him more easily than I thought I would. His mouth, the only part of his face that is visible, is familiar. I can already feel it on my lips, my body, between my legs. This part of him is an essential part of me, without being mine at all.

It will be tonight.

Drag Scream turns, almost in slow motion, to see if I have spotted him.

I give her a nod, holding his gaze.

She leans in. "Do all the things, baby girl. Live in the moment."

Then she's gone, swishing her way toward a group, arms outstretched in greeting.

I stand in the center of the foyer, everyone murmuring in conversation all around me. I'm frozen here, unsure of when to make a move, or if I should wait for him to make his.

He watches me, lifting a drink to his lips. There are no gloves this time, and I can picture those hands on my skin, clutching me, slipping inside all the dark places of my body.

The need for him pools in key places. My throat pulses. My breath comes fast. My heart knocks against the shimmery fabric of my gown. I wear nothing beneath it. The surface was too smooth and all manner of underwear created creases and lines. The dress skims my body before flaring to the floor.

Already, my nipples have tightened. I don't take my eyes off him.

A waiter passes him with a tray and, almost as if there have been frames cut from a movie, everything speeds up. His glass, on the tray. His feet, striding toward me. Then his thumbs slip beneath the thin shoulder straps of my gown.

"Tell me something." His voice is low and gravelly, as if he's as full of dark need as I am.

I raise my gaze to those eyes. I don't wear a mask. Mine is painted on in bright colors, red feathers attached to my face with the same glue I used for my wig.

My chest is so tight that I can barely breathe out the word. "Yes?"

"If I were to slide these straps off your shoulders and leave you naked in the middle of this party…"

I suck in a breath. Would he do it? It would be easy. The dress plunges to my waist in the back. I didn't use any tape to keep it in place.

"Then what?" I ask.

"Could I fuck you in front of everyone? Would you let me ravish your body for their enjoyment? And would you scream for all of us?"

My brain goes white. Would I? God. Liquid heat slides through me. I expected something bold and dark from the masked man. But this?

What sort of gathering are we at? One where such a

thing could happen? Have I stumbled upon some strange sex party? Did Drag Scream leave out that key detail?

He pulls on the straps, teasing them over my shoulders.

The low neckline slips down. The edge catches on my tight nipples. One slight movement means it will fall. I don't breathe.

Would I?

I'm so hot at this. So overwhelmed with the darkest need I've ever felt. I didn't know such thoughts existed.

I realize with a thunderous acceptance that I would do it. I would let them watch. I would scream and let it echo off the ceiling, the walls.

I can't hold my breath any longer, letting out a small gasp, my chest heaving. The bodice slides down, my nipples revealed. The masked man still holds the straps, his eyes taking me in.

I don't move, letting it happen, feeling bolder, slicker, hotter.

"I see you would. Good." He hesitates, letting me breathe into this moment of nakedness, my breasts exposed. Then he lifts my straps, covering me again.

I quickly glance around. No one has paid any attention to us. He stands close. Most likely, no one could see me but him. I teeter between relief and disappointment. Maybe the fire is in the fear. The anticipation.

"Follow me." He turns on his heel. At first, I'm stunned statue-still. What just happened? Have I agreed to something?

But then I rush forward, following in his wake.

We exit the foyer and go down a hall. There are

drawing rooms filled with more partygoers, laughing, talking, drinking.

He keeps going, not even checking to see if I'm behind him.

We arrive at a back staircase. I lift my hem and follow him up.

We reach a second level, but he continues. Then a third.

The stairs open onto a round railing made of glass topped with steel. Above us is a circular cupola painted with angels. The noise from below filters up.

He approaches the rail and turns to me.

I stand next to him and look down.

The party is below, filling the main foyer. I can see the very spot where I stood moments ago.

"Take off your dress," he says.

I consider defying him, but I want this too much. I don't know what I've engaged in, but it's more like me than anything I've ever experienced.

I lift the straps like he did below, then let them slide down my arms. The silky dress slithers to the floor to puddle at my red heels. I wear only the shoes, elbow-length red gloves, and a tiny wristlet with my phone and lipstick and condoms.

I wait. He looks at me, then reaches out, running his thumb down my throat, between my breasts, crossing a nipple.

My breath comes fast and shallow as his hand slips down, tracing my stomach, then his fingers drag through the wisps of my hair and enter my body.

I gasp, my hand reaching out for the rail. There is no

hiding behind it. The base is clear. Anyone who looks up will see me there, naked, his hand inside me.

But then he curves his fingers, thrusting them deep, and I no longer care.

I grip his shoulders, rocking on his hand. I'm so wet, so in need of him, of this.

"Work it, my red dragon," he says. "Come on my hand."

I close my eyes. I'm so slick. So ready. It feels like forever since I saw him, since I felt this way.

The tension builds and tightens around him. It's so close. I want it so much.

"Yes, my flame," he says. "Come for me."

And I do, my body clamping down where he works me. I cry out against his jacket, hanging onto his arms, legs collapsing.

He snakes an arm around me. The full contact of my naked skin against his tux drives me into a second round of pulsing. I'm heady, lost in time, nothing but sensation and pleasure and the swirl of darkness that has taken over.

"Beautiful," he says. "Now turn around."

He whips me away from him and pushes me to bend over the rail. He shifts my legs apart, calves lifted by the heels. Both of my arms are extended wide over the steel barrier, and my head and breasts float over the crowd.

I watch the people below, feeling high and wild and incredibly alive and afraid and a million more things at once.

The masked man unbuckles his pants, then I feel his cock against my bare back. I turn my head enough to see him slide a condom onto its thick length. Then he cranks my head back to the scene below.

"If you cry out, they will look up. They will watch me fuck your naked body until you collapse. It's up to you."

Oh, God. He grabs my hips, then slam, he's in me, and I'm sucking in a breath. Below, a woman places her hand on a man's arm. He steps closer. Someone else sips their champagne.

Servers walk around with trays of drinks and food.

And the masked man begins a leisurely thrust in and out of my body.

I feel like I'm flying, like one of the angels on the cupola. My breasts sway over the crowd, a long lock of my red wig slipping over my shoulder.

He places a hand on my back, holding me firmly as he increases the pace. The tension gathers again. I could not be more wet, more ready, more hot for someone.

Everything else is lost. His thrusts become unrelenting. My vision goes hazy, the crowd below a blur of moving figures. Then his hand slides down, gliding between us to gather the fluid there.

And he's slipped a finger down the crack of my butt. When he's inside me there as well, I see stars. Everything goes black and silvery. The pleasure is so intense, so vivid, I can't hold anything back.

I hear myself whispering, "God, God, God. Yes." Then the pulsing is everywhere, orgasm sprouting from every place. I feel him pushing harder, unleashing.

And I can't stop myself. I cry out, a keening noise. The ghost of any past fear, any hangup, any shyness, all gone. I'm obliterated, nothing but fire and showering light. I start to cry, my body shaken.

It takes several moments to realize I'm no longer on the

rail, but leaning over a cushioned bench near the wall, lost in shadow.

He's still inside me, his hands massaging my back, my shoulders, shifting the hair over my shoulder.

He reaches around me to hold my breasts, squeezing lightly as if he wants to memorize the feel of me. Then he slides along my waist, reaching around, touching every part of me, gently, with curiosity and tenderness.

He kisses my shoulder, wrapping his arms around my ribs and drawing me against his back. I'm overwhelmed by this part of him, this side that wants to fix me after pushing every boundary.

We breathe together, reveling in the aftermath. I don't know when he moved us, when I cried out, who might have seen. It's done. I did it. I have no regrets.

He shifts and slides out of my body.

"Will I see you again?" he whispers against my hair, then tenses as if he shouldn't have asked.

"Yes," I say. "Apparently you're my addiction."

"Then you should know who I am."

My heart pounds. Will knowing him spoil this? Can I go to dinner with him? Would I walk across the Brooklyn Bridge with him, the wind whipping our hair, like I did with Jesse?

No.

I can't do that.

Not with him.

It's too intense for real life.

He's a fantasy I get to live every once in a while.

I scoot the bench away so I can escape him. "No," I say, scrambling for my dress.

I clutch it to me and run for the door. "I know how to find you. If I can't make it without you, I'll call again."

Then I tear down the stairs, jerking the dress over my head.

I have to get out of here.

Back to my hotel.

I have to think.

I have to figure out which side of me is who I want to be.

Jesse's Ellie?

Or the masked man's Indigo?

There doesn't seem to be any way to have both.

CHAPTER 18

Jesse

I don't know if I should return to the hotel, ever.

Ellie has made herself clear. She wants to fuck me as Indigo, as this other self. She wants to get wild and lose herself and behave in ways she can forget.

But she doesn't want to face me any other time.

I sit in the back of the limo I rented for the event, thinking this would be where we had our next tryst. That I would have time with her. Talk to her. And eventually, tell her who I am.

But then I looked up in that ballroom and saw the glass rail. And I lost all reason. I wanted to shock her. To shock myself. To play a dangerous game.

The obsession came over me. It's as if some alter ego called the shots, exposing her body in the middle of that party, then fucking her above five hundred prying eyes.

People saw us. Maybe three or four. But they sipped their drinks. This is not a cell phone crowd. They didn't alert anyone else.

But I got jealous and pulled her away. She is mine. I

won't share her, not even to be watched. And she was so wild, so free, so uninhibited.

I'm in love with her in some dark, forbidden way. It's obsession and intensity, and I suddenly understand stalkers and serial killers — anyone who loses control over their thirsty soul.

I shouldn't see her anymore. I should shove this blackness to some deep place where it can never come out again.

But it's a match for hers. We burn when we're together. If she feels half as much as I do, and she said as much when she called me her addiction, then we won't be able to stop. Maybe we will fuck into oblivion until both of us cease to exist.

The driver is patient, but I sense his concern that we are simply sitting on the street in front of the mansion. "Go ahead and go," I say. "Take a long way back to the hotel."

Then I think better of it. If she's on the other side of the wall of my room, I will break it down. "Actually, take me to Greenwich Village. I'll find another hotel before we get there."

I'm set on my path. I'll avoid Ellie until her time at Monica's is done. Then I'll return to fetch the sculpture I'm doing of her. If nothing else, I should finish it.

Then maybe I'll burn it. Dance naked around the flames and pray for my soul to be free of this madness that torments us both.

The limo turns the corner and a swath of red catches my attention.

It's her.

She's staring at her phone, then looking out at the street. Probably trying to catch an Uber.

"Pull up to her," I tell the driver before reason can stop me.

She notices the car, then stares down at her phone again.

I slide my mask back on and open the door.

She bends down to peer in. "This isn't a red Buick."

But then she sees me. "Oh."

I lower my voice, like I did at the party. "I can take you home."

She stands. "Oh."

I take her phone and cancel her ride. It's miles away. "We can do whatever you want," I tell her. "Not even talk."

She glances up at the driver for a moment. She seems to consider my offer.

Then she steps in. She moves to the opposite side of the limo and settles there.

The driver walks around to close the door.

"I see we have a chaperone," she says.

I nod. It might be best to talk as little as possible. There's no background noise here. She might hear a hint of Jesse even though I'm trying to sound different, and she's made clear she doesn't want to know me.

"Where to?" the driver asks.

Ellie gives him an address that is not quite the hotel, but a few blocks down. She doesn't want me to know where she's staying.

She settles against the seat, her arm crossing her belly. She looks everywhere but at me.

Maybe being silent is the wrong tactic. I should take

this moment to force her to listen. To explain. I can take care of her. I can do anything for her. She doesn't have to live in free hotels or eat only the food that will sponsor her.

But it's a risk. Currently, I have only one role for her. She's already told Jesse goodbye. This is the only way I can have her.

The silence goes on. I watch her. She runs her hands over the leather seats.

But the red dress hides nothing. Her nipples pucker. Her breathing isn't an ordinary pace.

I know what I'm good for. "Would you like me to fuck you again?"

She presses her hand to her throat. "Yes. But I'm afraid."

I didn't expect this. "Of what?"

"Never stopping." Her gaze meets mine before darting away.

"Then let's not."

I reach out for her and drag her to my side. My mouth is on her, tasting her, destroying the red lipstick that I left untouched in our encounter before.

I pull the dress down to her waist. A quiet whir tells me that the driver has raised the partition between the front seat and the back.

I fill my hands with her breasts. I could touch her for years without stopping. My tongue slips alongside hers. Her hands clutch my back.

We shift to lying on the long leather seat. I pull her dress farther down, then discard it on the floor. She's mine now, and I move down her body, greedy to lick and bite every inch of her skin.

I return to that thatch of hair and the glistening folds. I dive inside, spreading her knees wide.

My mouth explores everything, her nub, which I suck until she cries out. Then I slip down well past those parts to the pucker she enjoys so much. I thrust my tongue there, eliciting a long, lingering moan.

I unbuckle my pants. I return to the nub, suckling as her heavy breath starts to fog the window next to us. My gaze skims her body, her back arched, those pert breasts heaving. She hangs onto the lip of the seat with all her strength, knuckles white.

I slide on another condom, then glide inside her wet pussy like it was made for me.

I move in strong, bold thrusts that make her breath come in sharp, hitching gulps.

I slip my finger through her wetness and press against her ass again, waiting to see how her body will respond. But I know. She loves this.

"Oh my God," she says, perfectly motionless. "God, God, God."

I reach up and grasp a nipple and pinch it, causing her to buck against me. Her eyes fly open. "Oh, shit! It's so good! So much!"

I take it easy, gliding in and out of both places with care. I focus on her face, her body, the way she moves. I slide a thumb against her clit and circle it.

It takes almost nothing to put her over the edge. She rocks against me, crying out. I relax into her, letting loose, working with the contractions of her body to drive the pulsing of mine.

It's outrageous, unrelenting, unstoppable. When I spill

into the condom, I feel weak, like I should be on my knees, bowing to her.

I collapse on her belly and pull out slowly before discarding the condom in the trash near the seat. She stares at the ceiling, then brushes her hand against her cheek. I realize she's crying.

I almost say her name but catch myself. This version of me doesn't know who she is. "You all right?"

She nods. "I feel so lost. I want you. But my life doesn't fit you."

It does, though. I know it does.

This is the moment. I have to take off the mask. I have to reveal myself as Jesse.

I reach for it, shifting the elastic band that holds it in place.

She sees me. "No. Please don't. Maybe sometime. Maybe soon. But not yet." She slides away from me. "But here. Give me your number." She looks for her wristlet, the tiny purse that survived our encounter, but it's on the other side of the car, the contents spilled on the floor.

The limo moves forward, and a lipstick rolls across the floor. I pick it up. I write my number across her body, bright red over her pale skin.

"You always write in lipstick," she says.

"I'm going to photograph this for me to keep. But not your face." My voice tells her she cannot say no.

She doesn't.

"Spread your legs."

She does.

I tug out my phone from my jacket and take the shot. Her well-worked body is close to the camera, deeply pink in the folds. Then her belly, my number written on her skin, the last digit below a heavy, pink-tipped breast.

I show her the image to prove it doesn't reveal her face. She nods. She likes this, her body glistening even more with wet heat. I start to harden again.

But the limo rolls to a stop. I peer through the dark glass. We're on the street of the hotel.

"You're here," I say.

She rolls away and pulls on her dress for the second time tonight.

I want to reach out for her, to kiss her softly, to assure her she is everything to me, the sun, the moon, the stars.

But that isn't the role I have in her life. Instead, I pass her the lipstick and wait as she collects her things for her purse.

Then I roll down the partition, signaling for the driver to escort her out. "Let him walk you to where you are going. I assure your privacy, but I want to know you are safe."

The driver nods in understanding. Ellie looks at me once more, then she's out of the car.

I can only pray she will use that number.

And that one of these times, she will accept me for all I can be to her.

CHAPTER 19

Lili

That night, I wake up amidst torrid dreams of the masked man. I'm confused and lost and full of longing.

I'm also out of time.

After a week of pounding the New York pavement for sponsors. I've gotten jewelry, clothes, tickets, and a few more food options.

But no hotels. No travel. Those are hard nuts to crack. I got turned down by all the chains. I even tried the place where I'd stayed as Princess Lili and got laughed at when I inquired about influencer benefits.

Scat diddly. The royal family will *not* be staying there again!

I've begun getting my Indigo look on when there's a knock at the hotel door. Great. I slide the wig into place and throw on some sunglasses since I haven't done my eyes.

It's housekeeping. "Checkout time is eleven, miss," the woman says. "You can tap on the app when you've vacated the room. Don't leave and come back at this point, because the locks won't work."

I nod. "Will do." Monica definitely knows how to make people move on. As hard as it is to get hotel comps, I bet she often has people trying to squat here.

I'm about to close my door when Jesse's opens. Oh, crap. I jerk off the sunglasses and wig and toss them behind me.

"Hey," he says. "Having a pleasant week?" He looks dashing and well-bred in a pale yellow polo and white pants. You could seriously do a magazine spread with him.

"Looks like I'm about to head out. My time here is done." I shift to stand in the doorway so it won't close and lock me out. "I'm surprised you're still here." I tilt my head toward the retreating woman with her cart. "I got my final warning."

"I switched to paying customer," he says.

I wish I could. "Not sure of your next move?"

"I've been working here. It's been a suitable environment." He shrugs. "Even if my neighbor won't share a coffee."

My belly flips. I did leave him, practically running out of that subway car. But the last thing I need mixing up my feelings is more Jesse. My belly is mildly pink from the masked man's number in lipstick. I couldn't completely scrub it off. I have no business leading on any other man.

But a coffee couldn't hurt. Drag Scream came through with the house party, but that's not until tomorrow.

I'd rather not show up at Carly's until afternoon. The less time with the bugs, the better.

"I could use a macchiato."

Something flickers on his face. "Really? Then I'll fetch one. And a bagel? Or something else?"

"I might try your favorite."

His grin is enormous. "Two chocolate croissants, coming right up." He glances at his door. "I'll need a minute. How about I knock on our adjoining door when I'm back with everything?"

I smile. "Sure." This might get tricky, since I'll be Ellie in his room, but have to become Indigo before I go to Carly's.

But I can figure that out. There are public bathrooms. I'll make it work.

Jesse ducks inside his room, and I head into mine. I pick up the wig and wrap it carefully. Then I prioritize the things I'll need to become Indigo and put them in my new black bag.

Everything else has to go into the Louis Vuitton backpack I came with, plus some shopping bags. I need a suitcase. I have way more stuff.

I'm puzzling out how to fit everything in the bags when I hear Jesse's door open and close. He must be back.

I shove the rest of my things in one of the hotel's plastic bags for dry cleaning and take a last look around. I think I have everything.

My current clothes aren't quite what he's used to, since I planned to be Indigo when I opened the door. Hopefully, it's not too jarring to see me in this razzle-dazzle black number with pink rhinestones and a plunging neckline. I jerk it higher so the cleavage isn't so intense, and sit on the edge of the bed to wait.

It's only a couple of minutes before I hear the tap on the door between our rooms. I open my side.

Jesse's there, smiling. "I'll help you with your things." He picks up the shopping bags while I shoulder the others. "You got some sponsorship spoils?"

"I did," but I don't elaborate. Could he cross-reference these bags and find out I'm Indigo by searching?

But he's not paying any attention to them. He sets them on the dresser in his room, and I drop my other bags alongside. On his table are two coffees and two matching packets holding the croissants.

"It's nice to eat something other than crepes." I tap my hotel app to sign out of the room and head straight for the food.

He closes the doors between the rooms. "You went back there?"

Oh, right. Another sponsorship that would out me. I've posted several images of Marco's crepes on my Indigo feed.

"Uh, yeah. They were good."

"Dessert lunch again?"

"Dessert breakfast."

"You could eat dessert three times a day!"

I sigh happily. "What a life!"

We sit down, and my body relaxes in a way I haven't all week. This isn't drumming up sponsors or figuring out my next move. And it's not the tension I feel with the masked man.

It's easy. I've forgotten how I feel around Jesse. I regret not seeing him all week.

But of course, I couldn't do it. Not with naked-Lili face.

And naked sex with another man.

I'm leaving anyway. We were doomed from day one.

"So what's next for Ellie?" Jesse asks.

"I'm headed upstate tomorrow with some friends. A house party." I take a sip of coffee and everything is suddenly better. "Oh, this is so good."

"Sounds fun. Where will you be until you leave?"

I grimace. "Staying with my friend Carly."

He laughs. "You don't seem too happy about it."

"She's a naturalist eco-type and believes in sharing her space with all the creatures."

He pauses mid-chew, then swallows. "She has rats?"

"There's rats in New York?"

He laughs so hard he almost chokes. "Oh, yeah. We're sort of famous for it."

I close my eyes in prayer. "Please don't let there be rats."

Jesse laughs. "Have you been to her place?"

"Yes. The bugs came in and out like it was the Roach Motel. But not the pest-killing kind."

"Yikes." He glances around. "I mean, you could crash here tonight if you wanted."

I glance past him. "But there's only one bed!"

He laughs again. I could listen to that all day. "I can sleep on the floor," he says.

"I've seen that movie more than once! I know what happens."

He holds up his hands. "My intentions are honorable. We were perfectly friendly the day we saw New York. No reason to change that."

He's right. He didn't make a single move.

Hmmm.

"What's in it for you?" I ask.

"I could finish some sketches I made of you from that day. Color them in." He rolls his coffee cup between his hands. "As long as you can handle me staring at you for a couple of hours."

His gaze holds mine, and heat pools in me. Uh oh. I had forgotten how he'd inspired the same feelings as the masked man.

And by now, I've been around enough men in New York to know that I wasn't on a bullet train to fucktown after all. Grim Weaver didn't make me feel that way. Or any of the men I'd talked to about sponsorships. Not even an ice cream vendor who'd given me a free cone and tried to ask me to dinner.

And he'd been very sexy.

Just not my type.

Apparently, my tastes are specific, and both the masked man and Jesse fit the bill.

Jesse has resumed eating his croissant with an amused expression. That's right. I never responded. "I guess it's fine. As long as you aren't going to draw me naked."

He chokes on his bite. "No. I mean. I'd love to. But I was thinking of you with the children and the nun."

My face blossoms with heat. Of course. He wants to make an innocent drawing and here I am talking about nudity.

Obviously, my heated feelings aren't mutual.

"That sounds fine. Will you let me snap a shot of one or two of your works?" I don't know why I ask. I can't put them on my feed and tag him.

"Deal." He holds out his hand and I shake it.

"I'll text Carly to tell her I'll see her tomorrow instead."

He nods, looking out the window. Yeah, he's not melting for me or anything. His mind is elsewhere, probably on his work.

I let Carly know I managed one more night at Monica's, and I'll see her in the morning to pack up her parents' car for the drive.

And now, I get one more peaceful day with a very nice, very adorable man. No makeup, no wig, no worries.

I like this.

I like this a lot.

CHAPTER 20

Jesse

By a stroke of luck and some fast thinking, I have Ellie to myself all day and all night.

I shove aside all the things I'd like to do to her and focus on the innocent sketches. I had to frantically move the erotic ones, as well as the partially constructed sculpture of her, to another room. If the woman at reception wondered why I needed yet another reservation, she didn't ask.

But there's nothing here that will tip Ellie off. No costume. No mask. No sketches of her naked.

Even if my hands shake when I draw her.

Last night rises up, more intense than the first encounter. Ellie as Indigo, the red dress slipping down her body. Her legs spread apart, looking down on the party.

I've gone mad. That's the only explanation.

But this part of me has always existed. I have a series of erotic sculptures in a sex club tucked away in Midtown. The owner is a dominatrix who dated Ethan for a while. He hooked us up, so to speak.

But until Ellie, I had never been so darkly intense in my personal life. It's like mixing vinegar with clay. Separately, the clay won't dry without intense heat, and the vinegar has no use in the sculpture. But if you spray the vinegar on the clay, it creates a reaction that forges a bond so tight that it can mend a broken piece, or hold together two separate parts.

I think she feels it, too. Not only the sex-driven mating of our alternate selves. But this easier, more comfortable co-existence.

But I'm unwilling to test the merger. Not yet. I need her to like Jesse enough to not run away like she did on the subway. To be ready to accept both sides of me into her life.

Hopefully, today will help with that.

My goals will be simple. To convince Ellie to contact me after today. Then maybe we can work slowly on building a genuine relationship.

I start again with the sketch from that day at the street corner, when the nun and children arrived, like I told her I would. She works on her phone, and we have a companionable silence that stretches through the morning.

Eventually, my stomach rumbles loud enough to break the quiet.

"Someone's hungry," she says.

"Room service or find a place?" I ask.

"Oooh, I never got room service," she says. "I wasn't sure what Monica included in her comp."

"Then let's try all the weird stuff." I open the app to pull up the menu.

"She has weird stuff?"

"You were in her bar, right? She has zero normal-colored drinks. Even if you ask for a rum and coke, it comes out blue."

"When my sister was a kid, she got scared one time because she ate blue frosting and it stayed blue all the way to the end result." She claps her hand over her mouth. "That's gross. I shouldn't tell gross stories."

I love it. "No, no. Blue poop jokes are the best. Probably we will have a rainbow toilet after this lunch."

She laughs so hard that she holds her belly. "Oh, my God. Maybe if we eat enough colors, it will all go back to normal, like when you mash all the colored play dough together, and it goes gray."

Now I'm the one who can't contain my laughter.

We sit close together, peering over the options on the screen.

She points at the pasta dishes. "The Big Green Monster? There's no description!"

"Then we're getting it." I click it and keep scrolling. "And what would be the Gut-buster, under soups?"

"I guess we'll find out!"

Sitting so near her makes every nerve ending tingle. That dark need tries to take over, and I have to force it aside. Sleeping with her in the room will be hell. I'll want to spread her open, lick her from end to end.

"Jesse?"

I snap back to Ellie. She's pointing at another line. "You think we should try the Juice Wallets?"

"What category are they under?"

"Breakfast all day."

"Done."

I confirm our choices in the app, and we sit near the window, looking out. I wish we were in one of the suites with a balcony, but Monica put Indigo in a standard front-facing room.

There are some incredibly swanky setups here. Most of my art went in wild rooms with staircases, sunken baths, or jungle fixtures. I'm not sure why the orange sculpture was relegated to this regular room, but I am not one to question the ways of Monica.

Ellie stares wistfully out the window overlooking the street. "Did you always dream of being an artist?"

"No. Originally, I wanted to be a Chippendales dancer."

She tilts her head. "What's that?"

Oh, great. I didn't realize she wouldn't know. "Have you seen the movie *Magic Mike*?"

"Nope."

"It's about male strippers."

She sits up straight. "You wanted to be a stripper?"

"Not exactly. So Chip and Dale are two cartoon chipmunks."

"Okay."

"And Chippendales was a chain of clubs with male strippers."

"Ohhh. I think I see."

"I thought Chippendales dancers got to wear chipmunk costumes. So when I drew a poster during career week in second grade, I titled it in a way that got a phone call home to my mother."

I laugh. "So you don't want to be a stripper?"

Before I can think better of it, I blurt, "I'd do it for you."

Oh, shit. I went there.

But her eyes fix on me. She doesn't crack a smile. "Have you ever? Stripped for someone?"

I've stripped for her, while she danced nearly naked on a makeup table. But I can't say that.

"Not deliberately."

She sits back in the chair. "Pity."

I'll follow this line of questioning if she's game. "And you?"

"Oh! No. I mean. Okay. Gosh." She's completely flustered, and I wonder if she is also thinking of the makeup table.

Or maybe, dozens of other matching occasions. She could get this wild all the time.

I realize I don't want the answer. "What does Ellie dream of being?"

She slides her phone across the table. "I'm not sure. I never thought much about it until recently."

"Do you like being an influencer?" I wave my hand toward the phone. "However you influence?"

She shrugs. "It's fun. There's validation in having people talking about your every photograph. And lots of trolls."

Her words spark an idea, and I pick up my sketchbook again. I draw Ellie, her phone held at arm's length. At her feet are a clamoring mass of heart figures and fluffy trolls, all reaching up to her. I give them big cartoon eyes. Ellie watches as I quickly add texture and shadows.

"I love it," she says. "Can I snap it?"

I tug the page from the book and hand it to her. "You can have it. No need to even tag me. Just an anonymous work."

"It's probably not on brand for you anyway." She snaps a shot of it, then tucks the sketch into the side of one of the shopping bags.

"Probably not. It's almost greeting card style."

She examines the digital version of it. "Maybe so." Then she asks, "Do you do erotic art?"

My heart hammers. I wondered when I would see this side of her, if she would give any hint of it to Jesse.

"I do."

"Like what?"

"Sketching the human form is part of any art education."

"Do one." She slides the sketchbook in front of me. "I know I was all accusatory earlier, but I'd like for you to draw me like your French girls."

The *Titanic* reference makes me smile. "On a sofa with a heart necklace?"

"Can you do it with me dressed?"

"Sure. I'll have to guess at what's under there." As soon as I say it, I regret it. It's an out-and-out lie that will bite me when I confess. Damn.

But her beguiling smile makes my heart speed up. "So, do your best guess. It will be amusing to see if you get it right."

No more lies. I pick up the sketch pad and a drawing pencil. I'm going to draw her exactly right. Perhaps this will be how our other selves connect all the dots.

She moves to the bed and lies on her side, propping her head with her hand.

I turn my chair to her. She wears the slashed jeans I know well and the sparkle tennis shoes. The black shirt has the sleeves and collar cut out. It dips deeply into her cleavage. Her every move makes a thousand pink rhinestones twinkle.

I start with the shapes. The sharp bend of her elbow. The fall of her hair. The curve of her hips and the length of her legs.

I add her chin and face, and the line delineating her thighs.

Then it's time for details I can't see. Will she make the connection? Ask me how I know?

I fill in her breasts, her belly button, that dark thatch of hair I've lost myself in. It's all familiar, as I've done so many sketches of her in the last week. I leave no detail untouched. She will understand that I know her.

I want her to figure it out, to accept me as the man she meets between the times she sees Jesse.

I fill in her face, her eyes meeting the viewer rather than cast down. She's daring us to look more closely, to stare, to take in the wonder that is her body.

I stir in making it. I want to touch her. This is way harder than I thought it would be, staying aloof while she poses on my bed, even in her clothes.

I set down the pencil.

"Can I see?" she asks. "Let's see what is in the imagination of Jesse Adams."

I pass it over.

"Not too bad," she says. "Jesse Adams, I proclaim you talented."

Interesting. There's no mention of its accuracy.

"Did I get it right?"

She tilts her head at the image. "I think I have more belly pooch than that."

She most certainly does not.

But she can't see herself as I do. So my perfect rendition of her doesn't matter.

I have a role to play, so I stand and give a flourishing bow. "Thank you, my great lady."

There's a knock at the door. "Room service."

"Better get your clothes back on," I tell her, closing the sketchbook. "Wouldn't want to give the delivery man a show."

She laughs and shimmies her shoulders like a burlesque dancer. This blend of sex and lightheartedness makes my head spin. So this is Ellie unchained.

I want this. I want the sass and the sexy and the food and the ordinary mornings doing our work together. And I want the dark thrills and intense fucking and pushing boundaries. I want it all, simultaneously, all the sides of us.

How can I get there?

I open the door. A young man wheels in a silver cart. The domes on the plates are all fanciful ceramics. Ellie spots them and claps with delight. "Look at those!"

The man transfers the platters to the table. "Enjoy your meal."

We uncover the dishes. The Gut-buster turns out to be a creamy orange soup with oversized meatballs. The Big Green Monster is a heap of sage-colored pasta with tendrils of noodles spreading across the platter. Olive slices dot the surface.

"That's a Big Green Monster all right," Ellie says. "What are the Juice Wallets?"

We open the last dish. Whoa. Inside are three pink pancakes folded in half, with a compote of strawberries artfully placed along the seams to be quite intentionally vaginal.

"Are you going to eat the pussy?" Ellie asks, and if I'd been drinking something, this would have been a spit-take.

I choke and cough until Ellie pounds my back. "Did I offend your delicate sensibilities?"

I shake my head. "I'm fine."

"Good." She picks up one of the pancakes. "Watch me for technique."

She sticks her tongue into the fold, lapping up some of the compote. "Oh, that's good." She turns the same pancake to me.

I lose my head for a moment, and rather than lick it, I bite it, nipping her finger in the process.

"Oh, you are a wily one." The pancake almost drips, but she quickly lifts it to her mouth to salvage the bite.

"And you're fast with your tongue." I go for the last bite at the same time she does, and our mouths collide.

I back away. I can't kiss her. It'll give me away. I'm sure of it.

The pancake ends up smashing against her lips, so she snatches up a napkin. She keeps the joke going. "Messy business, eating pussy."

But we don't laugh. The tension has zipped into the red zone. It was bound to, with the stripper talk, the drawing, and now the vagina pancakes.

We're playing with fire.

I sit on the edge of the bed, giving her some distance.

But she stands before the table, twisting the napkin in her hands.

"Jesse, I—"

I hold up a hand. "I apologize. I promised honorable intentions."

She nods. "We both have been pushing it."

"We'll focus on ordinary eating," he says. "We'll call them by their formal name. Juice Wallets."

This gets a smile, and we sit back at the table, more sober than before.

I force myself to keep things light and easy. I can't overplay my hand. Not when I've been given one more chance at the ultimate prize.

After lunch, we opt to watch a movie. We're back to light banter and good-natured squabbles as we argue about what to watch.

"I'm a man. I need action and adventure." I hold the remote over her head and switch the channel.

"I'm the girl. I want Hallmark romance!" She heaves herself up to catch the remote.

We tussle over it, switching between *Die Hard* and *Sleepless in Seattle* over and over again until she lunges and lands on top of me.

I'm rock-hard instantly, and there's no downplaying it as she wiggles her way off my body.

"Oh," she says. "Oh." She drops the remote between us.

I'm not sure what to do. You don't apologize for something you can't control.

But she's looking at me, then my crotch. Her breathing is fast.

"Honorable, I swear," I say, but that sends her scrambling backward off the bed.

"I shouldn't be here. This is too much."

She stands beside the bed, looking back and forth.

"Ellie — we're fine. It's fine. I'm not out of control."

But her eyes are wide. "I might be. I need—I need a moment."

She dashes into the bathroom and slams the door, locking it.

Shit. Thanks a lot, stupid dick. But it had been coming all day. The proximity. The drawing. The Juice Wallets. And playing around on the bed. I know what she's capable of. I've been buried in that body.

This ruse has to end.

When she comes out, I'm telling her. This is it. If she is angry or upset, I'll leave this room for her and stay in the one with all the stuff I stashed.

With this resolve, I sit at the end of the bed, waiting for her to come out. Our fate is about to be decided, one way or the other.

But my phone buzzes.

It's an unknown number.

I don't know your name. We met again last night and you left your number on my body. I need you. Tell me where you are.

Oh, shit.

I run my hands through my hair.

This is the moment. I can knock on the door and say I got her text.

I'll come clean. I go to the door. "Ellie?"

"Please. No. Just let me be."

Shit. Shit. Shit.

Another text.

Are you there? I'm willing to do whatever you want, wherever you want to do it. Public. Private. I'll do anything. Tell me where to go. I'm desperate for you.

Fuck. If I tell her who I am now, she has no place to go. Nowhere to turn.

I pace the room. What do I tell her?

But then I know what to do.

CHAPTER 21

Lili

Dusk settles into night as I sit in the back of the same limo I rode in the night before.

My bags surround me. The driver told me I could leave them in the car. He would watch them.

I use my phone as a lighted mirror while I put on my wig and makeup. I have to look like Indigo when I see the masked man.

I sit cross-legged on the seat once I'm done, wondering where we're going. The text from the masked man said only that he would have a car waiting for me at the hotel and to plan to spend the whole night.

I didn't say anything to Jesse. He simply let me go, no questions asked.

I did the right thing. The situation was getting heated, and I couldn't in good conscience sleep with him when I'd just been with the masked man. I've been wild, but not quite that wild.

As we pass through the darkened streets of New York, I feel no fear about meeting him. Both times we encountered each other, we were at elite private functions.

Not that serial killers can't be rich or well-connected. But it seems unlikely. He pushes me, but he's never done anything to make me afraid.

We turn into an alley, and my whole line of thinking shifts. Uh oh. Where am I going?

For a moment, we pass locked doors and crumbling steps, then we reach an awning. It's black with red lettering that reads, "Club Y."

What does Y stand for? Yes? Yellow? Yum?

The limo stops. A broad-shouldered man in a black suit opens a door beneath the awning.

"I'll be back here to fetch you when it's time," the driver says. "I can take you wherever you need to go."

I nod, organizing my bags to sit all together. I slip my phone into my back pocket.

The limo door opens.

"Miss?" the doorman says, extending a hand.

I want to ask him what kind of place this is. A hidden restaurant? A club? Am I dressed appropriately? I should have put on the red dress.

But it's too late. I take the man's hand and step out of the limo.

"Please leave any cell phones or other devices with your driver," he says.

Oh. I pull my phone out and toss it back into the seat. "I don't have anything else on me."

He looks me over and nods. "Mistress Sapphire is waiting for you."

I follow him through the door. Inside is a small foyer

with high-backed chairs upholstered in black with gold edging.

A woman in a bold blue kimono enters, her black hair sleeked back into a tiny ball at the base of her neck. "I'm here to prepare you."

Prepare me?

I follow her through a curtain of gold beads and down a long hall lined with doors. Each one has a strange rectangle of glass on the wall next to it. As we pass one, I spot the blinking red LED of a scanner. That's a high-tech lock compared to the classic styling of the decor.

Where am I?

We turn a corner. There are more doors, and several have a beefy man standing outside, like he's guarding it. Is this some sort of hotel, then?

I swallow the lump in my throat. "So, where am I exactly?"

We approach a door near the end of this hall, and Mistress Sapphire presses her hand to the scanner. There's a beep, and the door clicks open.

"Club Y is a pleasure club," she says. "I'm to prepare you for your guarantor."

I assume she means the masked man.

I hope she does.

What if this time he wants me to have sex with someone else? Or many people?

My heart hammers.

The inside of the room isn't scary at all. There are lighted makeup tables, two sectioned-off areas with curtains, and a manicure station.

Mistress Sapphire rolls a rack of clothing forward.

"Your guarantor has asked for you to select from these items to assess your mood for the night."

She lifts the first hanger. It's a black silk evening gown with a square neckline and short, fluttery, sheer sleeves.

"I like it," I say.

She nods. The next item is another gown, the color of my skin. The neckline plunges both front and back, reminiscent of my red dress, only even more revealing.

"Maybe," I say.

The next item is white and gauzy, so sheer as to hide nothing. It seems pointless. "I don't think so."

The next item is a left turn from the others. It's a schoolgirl outfit with a short plaid skirt and white shirt, only the shirt has no buttons. Knee socks are folded over the hanger.

"Not my thing," I say.

The next three are lingerie. A pink baby doll, completely sheer. A black lacy one-piece. And a short floral slip dress.

So I guess we're not necessarily doing something classy, like dinner. Or maybe we only do that if I choose the first two dresses.

"I don't know. All of those are okay."

I don't quite know what to make of the next item. It's a dress, but it's very shiny, like plastic, and bright red. Mistress Sapphire holds it up, and I reach out to touch the cool surface. "What is it?"

"A latex dress. It clings."

"Is it hard to get off?"

"Possibly."

I squeeze it again. Interesting.

I think I will go back to the skin-colored dress when she holds up the last hanger. My breath catches. I've never seen anything like this.

It's completely Indigo.

A black collar is fitted with a ring and a long chain. Leather straps are designed to surround breasts, but not cover them. More straps form a harness, wrapping the thighs, but leaving the rest open.

"Yes," I say before chickening out. "That one."

"I thought so." Mistress Sapphire pushes the rack away and leads me to one of the curtained spaces. "You can undress there. I assume you will need help donning the submissive wear?"

Submissive wear. Okay. Wow.

"Yes, I will."

"Let me know when you are done. You can leave your things inside."

I pull my shirt over my head, my heart a steady, heavy thump. I'm definitely not in Avalonia anymore.

Or are there clubs like this there? I wouldn't know. Octavia's fiancé Finley might, but I would never ask him.

I slip off my shoes and jeans and panties, folding them all together on a bench attached to the wall. I'm naked.

"I'm ready," I call.

Mistress Sapphire pulls back the curtain. I'm not as shy about this as some might be. I've been prepped and dressed by other people plenty of times in my royal life.

"We shall remove hair," she says, and her tone tells me this is not a suggestion, but a statement of fact.

She slides a black silk robe over my shoulders and leads me to a flat vinyl-covered table. "Lie back. I do not wish to injure any sensitive parts directly prior to your encounter, so we will do this chemically."

I nod. I stare at the ceiling as she moves the robe aside and something cool smears over my skin and hair down below. It smells like vanilla. I think of the Juice Wallets and picture Jesse biting the end of the pancake.

Jesse. Damn it. We should never have met. I had no idea that when I came to America, I would become someone who banged one man and spent happy, content time with another.

I shake the thought away.

"Is he used to you in the wig?" the woman asks.

I raise a hand to the wispy edge. "Yes. Hair and makeup have to be like this."

She nods. "That is fine." She wipes away the cream. I don't look down. This is one job the royal stylists never do. I think I was supposed to stay natural and unsullied until my engagement, but that ship has sailed.

A warm cloth cleans me up. "You are ready," Mistress Sapphire says. "Stand up."

I swing my legs to the side and stand.

Mistress Sapphire removes the robe and fits the leather straps to my body. They connect by rings. She snaps them together, and I step into the bottom section. She tightens them, then encircles my neck with the collar. The ring on it connects to the bodice.

"Hold your chain," she says, bending down to fasten two more circlets of leather on my ankles.

She slips the silk robe over me again. "Let's secure your hair since you will be bound."

Bound? Oh, boy.

She twirls it quickly into a tight bun and fastens it down with an elastic band. Then she moves toward the door. "Follow me."

I'm not sure I want to walk through the halls again, even in the robe, but we don't go out that way. She shifts aside the fabric lining of the opposite wall and opens a secret door.

Nifty.

This hall is very dark, and the floor is cool and smooth. Only the occasional subtle red blink lets me know we are passing rooms.

We pause before one. Mistress Sapphire presses her hand to it, and I prepare myself to see the masked man. Will he be masked again? Will today be the day I see his face? Will he be handsome? Does that matter?

The door pops open. Instantly, the disorienting flash of white light strobes through the space. I almost stumble, unable to find my bearings.

Mistress Sapphire takes my robe. "You will be positioned for his arrival." And then she's gone.

Two black figures arrive. They are completely encased in a shiny covering. The flashing of the lights means I can't quite see them coming. But then their hands are on me.

Will they have sex with me? Is that what this is about?

I want to cry out "Wait!" and wildly regret my choice. I should have chosen the dresses! Or the schoolgirl outfit!

I'm lifted into the air. I let go of my chain and it falls straight to the floor. I'm hooked into something, suspended in the air. My arms are tied in an outstretched position. My legs are spread and cool air blows straight up between them.

Before I can ask what will happen, the two figures are gone.

I'm alone. The room is so quiet I can hear the faint buzz of the lights as they move through their blinking sequence. The chain grazes the floor as I swing ever so slightly front to back. I'm not quite flat, floating over the floor. My feet are slightly lower than my head.

It's not uncomfortable. I feel well supported, like I'm hang gliding.

I close my eyes to stop the disorienting light. It helps, even though I can still see the faint pulsing through my lids.

I let out a breath. I chose this. I contacted him. This is a man who exposed me at a party, who fucked me in an atrium above a crowd.

But it's hard to trust someone you've only met twice.

Still, I remember him in the limo. The way we sat across from each other. He seemed different, calmer, ready to talk.

I was the one who asked him to have sex with me.

In fact, I was the one who insisted he come to the masquerade.

Who is the real aggressor?

Right. Me.

Cold air suddenly crosses my whole body, making my nipples tighten. I sense someone has entered and open my eyes. I call out, "Hello?"

Another figure walks through the room. He wears a black suit and a fedora pulled low on his brow.

But even in the flashes of light, I know him.

He's here.

I'm already slick. I can't even imagine what he can do to me like this. I'm completely at his mercy.

He approaches, and then his hands are on me. They run along one of my legs, a finger sliding into the thigh strap as if to check that it's secure.

He circles behind me, touching more, my waist, my arms. Then he's in front, cupping both breasts.

His face is right in front of me, but I can't possibly make anything out in the light. It's easier to close my eyes, let him touch me, let him do whatever he wants. Submissive. I understand the word now.

He kisses me, his hand on my throat. I open my mouth to him, and he lingers there, tasting me, his tongue exploring. One hand returns to a breast, tweaking the nipple, pinching it hard.

I suck in a breath. It's a quick shot of pain, but then the release is like a drug, like I'm high. He does it again, and I can't help but let out a moan. I had no idea the aftermath of a pinch could be like that until him.

He pulls away, and for a moment, I don't know where he is. But then I'm shifting in the air. My midsection moves higher, pulled by the waist until I'm bent over. My arms are tucked behind me. My legs remain pulled apart. At first I'm disoriented, then I find my balance again. I'm like a hummingbird, hovering over the earth.

Then he's back. My view of the room is jagged due to the lights, but I can tell that he no longer wears the black suit or the hat. He's completely naked, his dark hair slicked back. I could see him, if only I could focus.

But it's useless, the image broken into fragments. I close my eyes again. He spreads something down my spine, cool, then it grows warm. Then it's on my belly, my breasts, my thighs.

Soon, I'm overcome with the heat he's spread on me, and he tweaks my nipples again. This time, the hot pleasure shoots straight to my clit. Can someone orgasm from this? It feels possible.

He moves again, and this time his hands are on my butt. Something cool is spread there, but it doesn't change to warm. He spreads it, then slips something inside me. More pleasure trickles through me. At first I think it's a finger, but then it expands, growing wider. Then something flat rests against my skin.

A butt plug. I have one of these in a kit I promoted as Indigo. I remember it arriving in one of my secret deliveries at the palace. I'd held it up and known for a fact that something like that would never be put in my body.

And yet, the dark thrill of it sends me up the scale of intensity. I'm glad I chose this outfit. Maybe I could have sipped a cocktail in a private room in the beaded dress. And maybe I could have seen his face. And maybe he would have fucked me in that room.

But this. This is no ordinary experience.

His fingers press the edge of the plug, then rock it back and forth.

I absolutely gasp. Oh, God. This is a lot. So much. Too much.

He pinches a nipple, and that along with the motion make it happen. My body clenches, and I orgasm, crying out with no fear of being heard. The sound is long and guttural and I let it fly free. This is nothing, absolutely nothing like I expected.

I can feel his smile as his face presses next to my ear. His voice is gravelly and low. "You like it, my dear girl."

"Yes."

"Do you want me to do it again?"

"Yes."

"You will have to wait."

"Okay."

"Would you like to do something to me?"

"Yes."

"What is that?"

"I want you in my mouth. I want to try that again."

"Anything you like."

He pulls on something, and I'm lowered, then his cock is right there, next to my mouth. I close my lips over it.

Some people don't like this. I've read enough forum posts about it to know.

But with his hot skin throbbing in my mouth, I feel high, like I've taken a drug.

And when he pinches my nipples again while I do it, I know I never ever want to do anything else.

Jesse

Twelve thousand dollars well spent.

Fuck.

I could go broke here in this club, Ellie suspended in leather, sucking my dick. I'd pay for it every night of my life until I died.

She was made for this. For me. For what we do to each other.

I understand her. I can predict what she wants. What will do her in.

I want the flashing lights to go away. To really see her.

But it's not time for that.

Right now, we are this, and this only.

Her mouth fits around me, and I grab her head and push her down. When she gags, I pull back out. She gasps. "That's fucking hot. Do it one more time."

So I do.

Then she lowers her head. I shift the ropes to an easier position for her, like a swing. I pull her knees high and to the side. Her arms are spread wide.

"I'm going to eat your—" I stop abruptly. I almost say Juice Wallet. That would have fucked everything up.

"Pussy?" she finishes. "Do."

I lower my head. She's slathered with her own fluid, evidence of how turned on she is. I bury my face there, feeling her shift in the harness, her head falling back.

I reach for a nipple and move the plug. She gasps, her body heaving against me. She's coming so differently here, so hard, so loud. There are no sighs, no moans. Guttural cries, elongated screeching. She's lost herself in me. I've lost myself in her.

When she quiets, I shift her again, pulling a strap that will hold her in place. Now she's lying as if in a hammock, knees wide, feet dangling as if over the sides.

I worship every part of her body, this time using the cooling gel instead of the warming one. I tip her nipples, watching them pucker. I cool her shoulders, the insides of her elbows, the dimples of her knees.

I'm making this up as I go along. I've never used this club. I only installed the art. I got a tutorial on the ropes while Ellie was being prepped. I told the driver to take a long route to give me time to arrive before her. I chose a room but waited to see what outfit she wanted before deciding on a package.

I was assured my identity would remain unknown with this lighting scheme. It's a common request.

I can choose to turn it off at any moment and reveal myself to her. Or I can talk in a normal voice. Or tell her something only Jesse should know.

I haven't decided if I will.

When she is relaxed again, I swing her forward and

back, slipping the line until she is at the perfect level before me.

I slide on a condom. Then I enter her as she rocks close. She gasps, but then she swings away again and we're separated.

Then I'm sheathed in her again.

And away she goes.

I give her a hard push, and this time, when she returns to me, I slam into her body with incredible force. She lets out a cry, and when we're parted, she reaches out as if to grab me and keep me close.

But I push again, and this time when I ram into her, it's closer to a scream.

I focus, making sure I don't miss, but she's wily and wraps her loose feet around my back. I move with her, then on top of her, and she's got me.

We rock together, suspended, until I find my footing. She wants me to stay, so I grasp her ass and drive her against my body. Now we're full-tilt fucking, our bodies smashing together, her feet locked behind me.

The flashing lights make everything surreal, like we're inside some vortex where nothing else exists but our two frenetic bodies.

I reach for a breast and pinch a nipple as hard as I dare. She cries out, and this sets her off. Her body convulses around me, her belly muscles clenching.

I unleash, pulsing inside the confines of the condom, and my whole body feels ignited. She tilts, rising up in an impressive sit-up to clasp my shoulders. As the throbbing between us elongates, she holds me close, pressing her mouth to mine. We've never kissed in a moment like this, and despite the wildness of all that has come this evening, it's the most tender thing I've ever experienced.

My heart turns over. I've felt this interest in her, this curiosity. Then this unyielding lust and obsession.

But this is different. It's gentle. It's a connection.

What the fuck do I do with this?

I hold on to her, releasing the cables, and disconnecting her harness. We kiss through unfastening the leather straps, and then we're naked on the floor, cushioned by the clothes that I dropped.

We kiss and kiss as the lights keep flashing around us, making it impossible to really look at each other.

Then she sighs and puts her head on my shoulder.

There's a whoosh of air, and we're covered in blankets. Something brushes my shoulder. It's a thick foam mattress, covered in silk.

I roll onto it, taking her with me. I settle the blankets around us.

She doesn't let go, her body fitting against mine, our skin touching everywhere.

I run my hands along her body, smiling when I encounter the plug.

I slip it out of her, and she sighs. "I had no idea," she says against my throat.

"We'll do it again."

"Yes."

Then the quiet descends. Her breathing becomes regular.

I snap my fingers and the lights stop blinking. The room goes pitch black.

I have her. I will not let this night end until it must.

CHAPTER 23

Lili

I awake to blackness.

At first, I'm afraid. Where am I?

But I realize I'm still in his arms. We are on a mattress, covered in blankets.

I can't see anything at all.

I touch him, his chest, his shoulders. He's real. It's him. I know him.

And butt plugs.

Oh, boy.

I won't be able to explain that one to my sister.

He stirs. "You're awake."

"Yes."

My hair has fallen from the band. I run my hand down his body. When it finds that part of him, it quickly stiffens.

He lies there in the black silence, letting me touch him. I remember him sliding between my breasts that first time and shift down his body, trapping him there again. It's funny and interesting, but not my speed any longer.

I'm not on birth control and have no way to get it, but I

want to feel him, just for a minute. "Is it safe if I feel the real you for a few strokes?"

I hear him swallow. "Sure."

I angle over him, guiding him inside me.

It's nice, feeling his skin. He groans, and I want to find a way to get protected. He likes it.

I rise up and down a few times, savoring the sensation. Then I slide off. "I'm sorry. It's risky. I'm not on anything."

He shifts and I hear the rustling of fabric, then a tear. "Here," he says.

It's a condom. I work it a minute, figuring out which way it rolls by feel. Then I slip it over the tip of him and slide it down.

Then I go back to where I was.

I like this, the blackness, the sturdy feel of him below me. My knees are cushioned on the mattress, and my hair falls over my shoulders.

Every other sensation is heightened by the lack of visual. My thighs, rubbing against his hips. My hands, supported on his ribs. He can't see me, so I feel free, lifting my hands in the air like the porn I've seen, as if the cameras are taking in every inch of my skin.

The thought makes me hot. I'm a mess. An exhibitionist? I never knew. And can never be one. God, my father would fall over dead. His royal princess in an adult film.

I hold my own breasts, pinching the nipples like this man did last night. I need something to call him. A name to cry into the blackness.

"Who should I call you?" I ask, still rocking up and down on him.

"Do we need names?"

"I want something to scream out."

He chuckles, and something about that laugh strikes a chord. Have I heard him laugh before, at one of our encounters? I must have.

"You can decide," he says.

I brace myself and work him faster. "Zeus, maybe, like the God."

He laughs again.

I think for a second. "No, Poseidon."

"Don't be picturing Jason Momoa."

"Bernard."

He stills me with hands on my hips. "Bernard?"

"Got you."

"Okay," he says. "Call me Z. Like Zeus or Zorro."

"Oh, Zorro. But yes, just the Z. Got it."

"What would you like me to call you?"

Your wife, I think, and then laugh. Like that would happen. Way too many barriers. "You don't know who I am? I was tagged at the ball."

"I don't do social media."

Oh. Hmmm. "Then let's go with something that starts with A. We can be A to Z."

"Aria."

"Yes."

I pick up my pace again. I like thinking of him as Z. As something. I reach up to touch his face, gliding my thumbs over his eyelids. If I can't see it, I can at least feel it. "Z."

"Aria."

I move faster, harder, shifting over him. This is heady, only the touch, seeing nothing. The tension gathers in me.

I work him so hard, pushing my limit, until I feel exhausted, on the brink of collapse.

Then it comes, spreading over me, breaking across my body like lightning bolts. I gasp, feeling light-headed. "Z," I say. "Z. Z. Z."

He holds on to my hips, rocking up into me. "Yes, Aria. Say my name."

"Z!" I can't go any longer and fall over him. My body keeps tightening around him. He thrusts up into me, again and again, holding me tight against his chest.

Then he lets out a long, feral groan. "Aria…" He pulses again. I'm getting used to recognizing when he comes. My Z. I know your orgasm.

I'm crying. Why am I crying?

I want so much more of him. I want to have normal things. Normal days.

"Z?"

He rolls me to my side and wraps his legs around me to draw me to him. "Yes, Aria?"

"We can't have a normal thing, can we? It will mess this up. Everyday life wouldn't fit."

He cups my head and pulls me close. "I don't know."

"If I knew who you were, would I be upset?"

He's quiet a moment, then finally says, "Possibly."

My mind races. Is he someone important? A politician? A celebrity?

Married?

He kisses my head. "I don't bring others here. I'm yours in this space. All yours."

This helps. "Thank you."

He holds me, and I'm utterly exhausted.

The next thing I know, the lights are coming on, slowly, like a sunrise.

I blink my eyes. I'm tucked in the blankets.

The room is pretty with purple satin walls. There is no apparatus hanging any longer, although there is an intricate crosshatch of steel beams across the ceiling.

I turn to my side, although I already know what I'm going to see.

I'm alone. My clothes are neatly piled on a stool near my head.

There's a note. "Call me when you need me, sweet Aria."

I hold it to my chest.

I don't know when I can call on Z again. Or if he can come.

The uncertainty will remain.

And the times we collide will have to be enough.

Someone must be watching, because as soon as I am dressed, a woman in a black kimono leads me out of the club where the limo waits. Not only are my things there, but a shiny black suitcase rests beside them.

"For you," the driver says. "From Z."

"Did you tell him I needed one?"

"I took that liberty, yes. Where should I take you?"

I give him Carly's address and unzip the bag. It's beautiful and strong. I quickly repack all my clothes and makeup in it. This will make life so much easier as I acquire more things.

I ask the driver to give me time to fix my makeup. He's seen me without it, but I can't let it concern me. There's nothing I can do about it, and as long as there are no pictures, there should be no way for him to out me.

By the time I get there, Carly's parents have dropped off the car, and Carly and Grim Weaver are loading bags in front of her building.

They stare at the limo as it pulls up. When the driver opens the door and I step out, Grim Weaver whistles. "Indigo's got some class."

"Gas-guzzling, ozone-killing nightmare machine," Carly mumbles.

The driver helps me out, then pulls my suitcase from inside. "Shall I load it in the trunk?" he asks.

"I've got it," I say. Carly's shooting daggers at him, as if he personally controls the eco-safety of the limo. "Thank you."

He gives me a nod.

When the limo is gone, Grim says, "No, seriously, Indigo, who comped you a limo?"

I should have prepared an answer. I don't know anything about Z, where he works or who he might be affiliated with. Before I can think of the repercussions, I say, "Club Y."

Grim tilts his beanie-wearing head. "What's that?"

Carly pauses by the back of the car, waiting for my answer.

"A club."

Now they are both suspicious of my evasiveness.

"What kind of club?" Carly asks. The wind whips her fine blond hair around her head.

I'm saved by Drag Scream, who pulls up in a ride share.

"Oh, look!" I say, heading straight for the car.

Drag Scream requires a couple of rocks back and forth to pull herself out of the low-slung sedan.

"I'll help with the bags!" I hurry to the back.

She has two huge suitcases, both of which weigh a ton. I might regret volunteering.

The driver comes out to help. The two of us heft the bags out of the trunk.

Drag Scream sighs. "Compact cars." She sashays to the driver's side of Carly's parents' SUV. "This works." She peers in.

I roll the cases to the back. I don't think I can lift either one of them on my own. My hand wraps around the handle, and I give it a heave.

It barely lifts off the ground.

"Here," Grim says. He hugs the main body of the suitcase, but he can't lift it either.

"I'll help." Carly takes one end of the bag, Grim the middle, and I pull on the handle. It takes some grunts and pushing, but we get it inside.

And then there's another.

"These bags would never make it on a plane," Carly says as we chuck the second suitcase next to the first. They are enormous compared to my modest one, Grim's half-shredded duffle bag, and Carly's tiny hiking pack.

"I think she keeps her ego in one," Carly says.

"I heard that!" Drag Scream calls as she adjusts the driver's seat. "And yes, yes, I do."

Carly runs upstairs to make sure her apartment is ready for us to leave.

"I bet she's saying goodbye to her cockroach friends," Drag Scream says.

Grim shuffles his foot on the street. "I think it's cool she gave them names."

I shake my head. "Come on, let's get in."

I crawl into the back seat with Grim, but Drag Scream says, "Indigo, get your cute little butt up front. I won't make it if I have to listen to lectures about the loss of wildlife habitat for two hundred and fifty miles."

I shrug at Grim and move to the front. He leans forward between the two seats as Drag Scream adjusts the headrest. "But seriously, Drag Scream, those bags are way over fifty pounds. How do you get them on a plane?"

That's weird.

"How can a bag be too heavy for a plane?" I ask.

Both of them look at me, and I know I've said something dumb.

"This isn't an *aeroplane*, Mr. Weaver. And my platforms alone are fifteen pounds."

"Yeah, you probably have to wear those rather than pack them," Grim says. "Good thing they don't weigh a person."

Drag Scream adjusts the rear-view mirror. "You're getting into dangerous territory, mister."

"Like with missiles and landmines?"

Drag Scream sighs and checks her vivid pink lipstick. It's an exact match for her nails and the glitter sparkles on her black dress.

I don't think much of her letting us load her bags. I'm used to having everything done for me. She might be, too. Besides, she's doing the heavy lifting on the road, driving the whole way.

When Carly finally makes it down and has settled next

to Grim, Drag Scream pulls out her phone. "Tag your self-ies!" she says. "We have people to impress at this party. Make sure you drum up all your engagement."

She presses a suction cup phone holder to the dash and drops her phone in. "Smile, everyone!"

She takes several snaps and sends them to all of us. "Copy my tags. I want to see five hundred engagements minimum by the time we get out of this car!" she says. "Get on point, people!"

She's worried about whoever it is we're going to see.

I post my selfie with a fireworks GIF, then add a story, then crosspost to TikTok. I've been super active since arriving in New York, what with all the sponsors I've tried to sign on. My following is already up to two-point-*five* million in just a week.

But this makes me think of Jesse. I messed that up. Ditched him on a subway car? Ran from his hotel room to go to a sex club? If he knew, he'd never speak to me again.

Not that he can anyway. Unless I track him down, he can't find me. We never exchanged phone numbers or even my full name.

And I don't want him to look. If he somehow ran across a photo of Princess Lili, I'd be done for.

We get stuck in traffic, and Drag Scream drums her hands on the wheel. "Look lively, friends! We are in for an epic three days!"

My chest warms over. I've never gotten to do a spontaneous road trip with friends. I think I'm starting to tackle Bucket List Item #2.

Make normal friends.

CHAPTER 24

Jesse

I'm seriously considering facial reconstruction.

Ellie has officially blown off Jesse. There's nothing I can do about that. Jesse has no legitimate way to contact Ellie outside the hotel, and she took off to meet another man.

Who also happens to be me.

But no. The side of her who wants me the most is Indigo — Aria, now, I guess. And those encounters require me to avoid my face, my voice, anything that links me back to the artist she encountered in the hotel room next door.

I'm screwed.

After our encounter at Club Y, I return to Monica's hotel, but check out of the orange room. There's no sense staying in a space where the memories swing so wildly from wonderful to bad.

I know she has a good time with me as Jesse. We connected on the Brooklyn Bridge. We had deep talks on the subway. We shared history over crepes. And the room service debacle was the very combination of light-hearted fun and playful sexuality that I feel certain would define us, if only we could be those people without these alter egos.

But it's clear that when she starts to feel any sexual attraction to me as Jesse it upsets her. So she leaves. She seeks out the darkness. The stranger. The man without a face.

I've overstayed my welcome here. I carefully crate the Ellie/Indigo assemblage piece and ship it to my studio in L.A. It's close enough to finished that I can complete it later. I will have to add an entirely new layer for Aria.

I can sketch her in the harness, her breasts bound, her knees forced apart.

And I can draw images of us on the mattress, curled together in blankets, finally talking like real people and not characters from an erotic tale.

I crave her so intensely that it makes my hands shake. I want her all the time. I want her to know me. To meld these two sides of herself and choose me. All of me.

Damn it.

Unfortunately, Jesse the artist is now required to fly to Boulder, Colorado, to attend the presentation of more of my art. I was supposed to go yesterday, but I delayed so that I could spend more time with Ellie.

I can't put it off any longer. I have to oversee the installation of the pieces and attend a rehearsal for the colossal gala planned, not only for my art, but also for the grand opening of the entire wing of the facility.

I will be among strangers yet again, although I've met the owner and she's great. The event will be big, and there will be media coverage for days.

I collect all my sketchbooks and call for the limo. The driver confirms that Ellie left Manhattan with her friends, so even without this event to attend, there is nothing for me here. If I'm going to meet her again, it will have to be as Z, and it will have to be the last time. I can't keep up this charade.

There are only so many ways a man can wear a mask.

Lili

It's over four hours in the car to the lake property where Drag Scream's connections are spending three days in what she calls "brainstorming and debauchery."

Jesse is on my mind as we drive along heavily wooded roads. I wonder what he thinks of me, bolting from his hotel room, clutching all my bags.

He didn't even call after me, as if he knew this was how it all would end.

But what could I do? A friendship between us was clearly never going to work. There was too much tension. Naked sketches and Juice Wallets.

What is it about both Jesse and the masked man that brings this out in me?

I drop my head against the back of the seat.

"What's getting you, Baby Girl?" Drag Scream asks.

I shrug. "Life."

"Life's a bitch and then you die," Grim says from the back.

"No," Carly insists. "Life is a wondrous journey."

"A bitch," Grim shoots back. "Like karma."

"You're inviting bad karma just by saying it." Carly glares at him.

Drag Scream shakes her head. "Little wife, the children are squabbling."

This makes me smile. "Keep it down back there!"

They don't.

"I bet your glass is always half full," Grim says.

"I bet your glass is full of chemicals that will kill you," Carly says.

Drag Scream turns to me. "Thinking about a certain masked man?"

This quiets everybody. Grim sits forward. "What masked man?"

Drag Scream focuses on the drive like she didn't just start something.

"Are you seeing somebody?" Carly asks.

"I met him a few times," I say.

Drag Scream's head whips around. "A few? I thought two! And how? You were only going to go to him through me!"

Grim and Carly grin at each other as if they really are two kids and Mama just got in trouble.

"I bet that explains the limo," Grim says. "And Club Y."

Drag Scream slams on the brakes, then catches herself and takes the car back up to speed. "You went to Club Y?"

"She wouldn't tell us what it is," Grim says.

"It's a sex club!" Drag Scream exclaims. "What is an innocent peach like you doing in Club Y?"

I sink down in my seat. "I'm not that innocent."

Drag Scream smacks the steering wheel as she makes

each point. "I knew you were getting all wild in the dressing room. And I knew you probably hooked up with him somewhere at that party. But Club Y!"

"Zounderkite," I mumble. I'm so busted.

Carly is practically hanging between our seats. "What did you do at the sex club, Indigo? Bondage? Group?"

"Hush your mouth," Drag Scream snaps. "You don't know what you're talking about."

"I've seen documentaries," Carly says. "Was there a dominatrix?" She gasps. "Are *you* a dominatrix?"

"What's a dominatrix?" Grim asks.

I want to jump from the car.

"You better explain," Drag Scream says. "They're going to make it much bigger in their minds."

I'm not sure they could make it much bigger than it was. But I tell them the rough story. "I met a guy at a vampire ball. It's no big deal. Drag Scream took me to a costume party, and I met him again. Then last night."

"At a sex club," Grim says. I think he likes hearing the words out loud.

"That club has a hard-core history," Drag Scream says. "One of the organized crime rings used to punish people by forcing them to work at Club Y."

"You've been there?" I ask.

Drag Scream shakes her head. "No, but I know people who have."

"Are they still trafficking workers?" Carly asks. "Because that's messed up."

My belly quivers. "I only met one person. Well, two. Both women."

Drag Scream taps the steering wheel with her nails.

"There were upscale theft rings run by two families. They own quite a few shady businesses. But Club Y was sold to the women who had been running the clean side of the operation. It was cleared of thieves years ago."

"Why is it called Club Y?" Carly asks.

I'm glad she asks. I was wondering.

"Because they take it farther than an X," Drag Scream says.

"Kinky," Carly says.

Grim looks perplexed. "But what about Z? Isn't that the farthest?"

It certainly is.

"You going to see him again?" Drag Scream says. "Obviously you have his number."

"I don't know. He seems to come when I need him."

"Like Batman," Grim says.

He's perfectly serious, but everyone laughs.

I want to talk about something else, anything else. I change the subject. "So, who are we going to meet at this party?"

"There's a whole bevy of queens," Drag Scream says. "Some have transitioned since I saw them last, so I'm very excited to see the result."

"Who else will be there?" Carly asks.

"The owner of the property is an eccentric old billionaire. Think Hugh Heffner, but gay. So there will be plenty of eye candy, probably not any of you all's persuasion." She glances back at Grim. "Which way do you swing?"

"Haven't swung any way yet," he says.

Now we all look at him, Drag Scream using the rearview mirror.

"Virgin in the house!" she says. "Well, look around. There will be more hookups this weekend than at the Bassmasters."

Grim sits back in his seat. "What's the Bassmasters?"

"A fishing competition," Carly says.

"We're going fishing?" Grim asks. "Doesn't that involve worms?"

"Poor worms," Carly says.

"There will be worms, all right," Drag Scream says. "Squirming their way up any ol' hole they can find."

"Uh, guys," Carly says. "I think Grim is going to faint."

I glance back at him. His face is paler than usual.

Drag Scream waves her arm at the chunky bag she placed near my feet. "Grab a Red Bull out of there. Carly, make him chug it."

I fish out a slender can, sweating on the outside, and pass it to Carly.

She pops the top. "Bottoms up," she says, passing it to Grim.

He takes a swig. This seems to perk him up, so he downs it.

There's pink in his cheeks again. He crumples the can.

"You know, you don't have to do anything you don't want to do," I tell him. "We've got your back."

Carly pats his shoulder. "We'll protect you."

Grim shrugs. "I don't get out much."

"This is going to be a great experience for us all!" Drag Scream turns on her blinker as we approach a diner. "Let's get something to eat, then we'll take it on home."

The lake house we're staying in is enormous, twenty rooms easy. But it's rustic and comfortable, the property butting up against the lake.

Drag Scream knows everyone. She introduces us with her normal boisterous welcome, but there's an entirely new level of squeal when a tall, slender woman in a yellow sundress approaches us in the bright room facing the lake.

"Zah-roe-bee-a!" Drag Scream calls, emphasizing every syllable. "My friend, my queen!"

Drag Scream engulfs her smaller friend in an exuberant hug. The two of them sway back and forth for a full minute.

Grim, Carly, and I glance at each other. This one must be important.

They finally separate, but Drag Scream keeps her arm around her friend. "Zerobia and I used to do a drag review together in Vegas. I was Liza, Cher, and Britney."

Zerobia grins. "I was Lady Gaga, Beyonce, and Whitney."

Drag Scream shakes her head. "We never could find anyone to perform a decent Diana Ross."

Zerobia joins her in the long face. "The classics are hard for a reason."

"Remember the final number?" Drag Scream asks.

"Of course!" Zerobia cocks a hip, one hand in the air.

Drag Scream immediately mimics the pose, and I get an idea of what their stage presence was like.

"Five, six, seven, eight," Zerobia says.

They dance for a while, all kicks and turns and jazz hands.

When they stop, Zerobia says, "Velociraptor left me to fend for myself in Sin City."

"Velociraptor?" I ask. Carly, Grim, and I all turn to Drag Scream for an explanation.

"Because she was so fierce," Zerobia adds quickly. "She could make the chorus girls quake in their boots. Then she wrote a few horror movie reviews and attended an opening or two, and that was it." Zerobia drapes both arms around Drag Scream's shoulders. "But you will always be Velociraptor in my heart."

"You know that lifestyle was killing me," Drag Scream says. "You should meet my new crew. This is Indigo Flame, one of the most prominent lifestyle influencers of her day."

I blush. "Hardly."

Drag Scream moves right on. "This is Carly Butterfly, who is keeping the world healthy and clean for the rest of us. And Grim Weaver. His knotty knit creations show off his dark side."

"What a stunning group," Zerobia says. "Are you all from New York?"

Such a simple question, but it makes me stiffen. I try to never straight-up lie, because one day I will be found out. But it's hard to nuance an answer due to my distinctive accent. Jesse almost pegged me from the first time I said *hello*.

"Hoboken, originally," Carly says.

"Classic," Zerobia says.

"West Village." Grim adjusts his knit cap.

"Near my Queen." Zerobia squeezes Drag Scream again.

Everyone looks at me.

"No place worth mentioning," I say.

Zerobia's interest seems sparked by my answer, but thankfully another group arrives in the sunroom, and a fresh round of exclamations and introductions takes place.

One of them is a slip of a girl in all black. She has six lip rings and too many ear cuffs to count. Her long green hair streams from a gray knit hat.

She and Grim make eye contact, and I can practically see the sparks fly. I lean in. "Go get her, Tiger."

Drag Scream notices her, too. "I'll make the introduction."

When they walk away, Carly sighs. "This is a lot of people for me. I need to go outside."

"I'll go with you." I want to meet people at a slower pace to avoid questions with hard answers. Perhaps I should've fleshed out Indigo's past more clearly.

I've been going with Belgium, but lately I've been concerned that it's too close to the truth. The news reports Octavia sent me last week all mentioned Belgium as the most likely hiding place of the missing princess.

We head through a screen door and down to the lake. The enormous wooden dock ends in a platform over the water. No one has made their way there yet, so we sit at the end. Carly takes her shoes off. We're too far above the water to dip our toes in, but it's nice to swing our legs.

An easy silence falls, then we spot two figures in black taking a path into the woods. It's Grim and the matching-hat woman.

"Looks like we lost one," Carly says.

"So much for opposites attract."

"I know." There's a forlorn note in her tone.

"Wait. Do you like Grim?"

She shrugs her tiny shoulders. "Maybe."

Shoot. And I encouraged him to meet the other girl. "You should let him know. I don't think he's very experienced. He's just met this girl. The likelihood that it will come to something is low."

She shrugs again. "Except if he's inexperienced, he'll fall too hard, too fast."

"So you're giving up?"

"I'm a believer in fate," Carly says. "If it was meant to be, it'll happen. If he hasn't picked up on my signals by now, then probably it's not our destiny."

This makes me think of Jesse and Z. Both seemed to be fated in their own way. Jesse turned up next door. And Z was right where I needed him to be for my bucket list.

I wish I could've salvaged something of the easy camaraderie Jesse and I had. I've never met anyone who was as attuned to me as he was, other than my sister.

My sister. I check my phone. Too late to talk to her. It's already almost midnight in Avalonia. The time difference is a beast.

And I have admittedly been a little distracted.

We both turn our heads toward an unexpected shout. There's another dock in the distance. Three young kids push each other around, dashing about. We watch them for a moment, amused, then one of them chucks a white container into the lake. It floats and bobs on the water.

Carly jumps to her feet. "That's a Styrofoam cooler! It doesn't get any worse for the environment. Think of the fish! The birds!"

Before I can say a word, she has taken off down the

dock. She hops and shoves her shoes on as she goes, racing along the shoreline to the other dock.

Saving the environment, one piece of Styrofoam at a time.

Now I'm alone. The sun is starting to go down. It's not low enough to create colors yet, but the way the rays of sunlight break apart through the foliage of the woods across the lake is stunningly beautiful. I lift my cell phone to take a shot, reflexively running it through my usual Instagram filters.

No. It doesn't need anything.

I remove the filter. I think about posting it, but then decide that maybe I would rather send it to someone.

My sister. She'll get my message when she wakes up.

I send her the shot with a note. *At a house party in upstate New York. Feeling happy with the sunset.*

Carly has made it to the other dock. The kids have disappeared. I wonder if she's going to jump into the water to rescue the Styrofoam. She only brought a tiny knapsack. Does she even have an outfit to change into if she soaks this one?

But no, she's found a long stick. She holds it out, tapping at the Styrofoam, trying to move it closer to her.

This might take a while.

I spot my messages with Z. There's the one where I asked him to meet me last night. Him telling me to get in the limo downstairs.

I send him the picture of the sunset.

Then I write him, too. *Sometimes the loneliest people at a party are surrounded by everyone except the one person they want.*

My thumb hovers over the send button. It's probably too much. This is a man I have seen only a few times and even then, only for clandestine sexual encounters.

But we did have that moment on the mattress last night. Curled up together. Two humans who had done the most intimate acts possible between two people.

Then it doesn't matter. My hand twitches, and I accidentally punch *send*.

My heart hammers as I wait to see if he'll respond right away. What would Z do on a Sunday evening?

I don't have long to wait.

Z: Same.

Same? Is he surrounded by people, too? Am I the important person he wants?

Me: I'm not sure when I'll be back in Manhattan to see you.

Z: I'm not there, either. At the airport, about to take a flight to Boulder.

Boulder? I quickly look it up. It's in a US state called Colorado, sixteen hundred miles from here. I'm not clear how far that is so I convert it to kilometers. Two thousand five hundred!

America is so big, and that's only halfway across!

If he's waiting at the airport, he doesn't have his own jet. So he's a normal moderately rich guy who can send limos and book last-minute sex clubs. But not outrageous. Not billionaire level.

That's good. Billionaires probably get noticed. I don't need that.

Me: Something fun?

Z: Yes, actually. The opening of a haunted wing of a castle.

Me: In the United States? There aren't castles here. This is a baby country compared to Europe.

Z: It's new. Built for entertainment. Weddings and the like.

Me: People want haunted weddings?

Z: You'd be surprised.

Me: That sounds like something for Drag Scream.

Z: I can get her invited. You, too. If you want.

Do I?

Me: When is it? Tonight?

Z: No. In a few days. I'm here to help with logistics.

Another clue. Does he work in event management? Maybe he is an investor?

Carly has managed to get the Styrofoam close to the dock, but the water's too low. She hangs over the edge, but from my vantage point, I can see that she's at least a foot short of reaching it. She lifts the stick to stab it.

Back to my phone. There's a big problem with going to Boulder.

Travel.

One, I don't know if I can afford to get there. I quickly look up the price of a flight from New York to Boulder.

Six hundred US dollars. I could do it. But I'd be nearly tapped out on the Visa gift cards.

Wait. There are buses. Those are cheap.

There's a bus and train combination for two hundred. It would take two days from here.

But there's another problem.

Identification.

I've never had to do airport security anywhere, much less in a foreign country, but I've seen news reports and heard people complain about American airports. There's TSA and body scans. And you have to have ID.

So, do I just say no? Or confess?

Z: Aria?

Shoot. I guess I'll confess.

Me: I want to come. But I can't fly.

Z: Fear of flying?

Me: I don't have ID.

This is hard to admit. If he's picked up on my accent, he knows I'm not from America. And how did I get here without a passport?

Z: A commercial plane won't work then. Let me make some calls.

Me: I'll be here until Tuesday. When is the event?

Z: Friday.

Me: My birthday!

Z: Then it's extra special. I'll get you here. Did you want your friend to come?

Do I? What if this all goes south when we're together more than a few hours?

Me: That would be nice.

Z: Done.

Me: I look forward to it.

Z: Don't bring any panties.

I suck in a breath, already heating up for him. He's my addiction. I think I might also be his. I remember his words from this morning. *In this space, I am yours.*

I can't be jealous of any other spaces. He can't be part of all of mine either. Not the castle. Not my royal family. He can't even know about them.

But here, in my Indigo world, I am his.

Me: What if I want you to ruin them?

Z: I will do exactly that if you wear them.

Me: Promises, promises.

Carly is on her way back, the dripping Styrofoam cooler under her arm. When she's determined, nothing gets in her way.

Same, girl. Same.

CHAPTER 26

Jesse

I spend the next day researching options to get Ellie to the castle in Boulder.

But as I look into trains and planes and private options, I keep wondering, why doesn't she have a license at age twenty? Or identification of any kind? Even if you don't drive for whatever reason, you need some form of ID to do basic things. This means she's never had a job, either.

She's never said where she's from, but her accent isn't American. Maybe her family immigrated and are close-knit, maintaining their foreign accent.

Still, something feels off.

My research turns out to be irrelevant, because the next day, Ellie texts me to say that she and Drag Scream will be traveling to Boulder with one of Drag Scream's friends named Zerobia.

Zerobia already has an invitation to the castle. I don't doubt that this is going to be a huge event. I didn't attend the opening of the castle itself, but between the novelty of the new event space and the prominence of the families involved, it will be covered on every major entertainment and travel site.

This was part of what led me to agree to create works for it.

Ellie will stay at the house party until Tuesday, and then it will take them two days to get here by car. This will give me plenty of time to prepare for her arrival.

But today, I must work.

I buzz into the Great Hall with the maintenance key Havannah provided me. I'll need to assess all the areas where my art will be installed.

It's already arrived, crated in a secure vault below the castle. Havannah and I sketched out some ideas when she commissioned my work detailing where we thought they might go, but until I eyeball the spaces, I won't know for sure.

The ballroom is on the ground floor. The art I have here will be temporary, given that it is intended for the haunted wing. But Havannah requested that one of the statement pieces be visible in the main event space for the party.

Tours of the new haunted wing will not be available to everyone due to the size of the event and the limited space in the halls. Plus, most of the rooms will be rented out.

I'll start here to think about which of the pieces will debut in the ballroom before being moved to its final destination.

The enormous hall doesn't carry the haunted theme since it's a multi-use space. The vast waxed floor is inlaid with varying colored planks of wood placed in an intricate pattern. It's currently empty. I'm sure staff will begin staging it for the event over the next few days. On a table near the door is a folder labeled Jesse Adams, so I pick it up.

It's the schematic for the party. Many of the events will be spotlighted on the built-in stage at the far end. Two doors in the corners lead to the kitchen on one side and the staging area on the other. With no serving tables sketched in, she must plan for everything to be brought in by staff.

Another drawing has a conceptualization of the decor. The bright champagne walls will be swathed in red silks. There will be something called a "haunted mirror" installed on one side.

In the front right corner will be a social media selfie station, wildly decorated with black candles, red and purple floral arrangements, and a collection of urns.

Fitting.

I like the space. People will be standing in line to take photographs, phones in hand. If I were thinking like an influencer, I would say this is a great spot to place my art for maximum publicity exposure.

The other option would be the stage itself.

Of course, I have no idea how drunk and disorderly this group will be. It may not be ideal to have the art so easy to manhandle.

On a whim, I photograph the schematic of the space. Indigo would have a good idea about which location would interest influencers the most. That's her area of expertise.

I've selected the photo to place in the text message when I stop myself.

Wait. This is Jesse's art. I text her only as Z.

I can't talk to Indigo. I've never met her as Indigo.

I have to talk to Aria. And Aria doesn't know that I know she's Indigo. Or Ellie.

Or whoever she might really be. Is her real name any of those? Unlikely.

This is a mess. I'll never keep it straight over the long term.

I have to confess.

But not today. I delete the draft and walk along the inlaid floor, my footsteps echoing. I pause by a built-in bench below faux stained glass windows on the side walls and take a seat.

I have to keep my head straight. It's not time for the big reveal. We should be in person for that.

I'm staring at my phone when the main door creaks open.

It's Havannah.

"Jesse! I heard you were down here."

I wave. Havannah has always been super casual when I meet with her. Today it's jeans. A lightweight sweater. Stylish tennis shoes. Her hair is twisted up on her head in a messy bun. She looks like one of her vacationers.

"Have you narrowed it down?" she asks. "I will leave locations up to you."

"Thinking about it. How protected will the art be from the attendees? They're not incredibly fragile, but they could be damaged."

"An important point. I think I would be inclined to have the art on the stage. We can do a big reveal, and that's where the most eyeballs will remain on it. Were you thinking the mummy?"

"It is the largest. And probably the easiest to understand from a distance. Others require a closer look."

She nods. "I think so too." Her gaze takes in the space. "I'm always full of awe when I'm in here."

"Quite a thing to build a castle in the middle of the Colorado mountains."

"I had to. I went to a castle wedding in France, and I was hooked. So, I did a stint in another one for my certification in tourism. It was haunted."

"But your main castle isn't."

"No, the facility I imagined would be beautiful and fanciful. The ghosts came later."

"It's incredible. I love that you got artists and craftsmen to build it room by room."

"It was the only way to compete with those centuries of history everywhere else." She stands up and turns in a circle, craning her neck at the vaulted ceiling lined with pressed tile. "I wanted a space that could play into childhood, hopefully in a positive way. Whenever I see this room empty, my mind always fills it with people dancing, wearing big puffy dresses that spin when they twirl."

I chuckle. "That's the Disney in you talking. Cinderella's ball."

"There are so many balls in Disney movies." She looks at me. "What do you see in this big, empty room?"

"People, for sure. Well dressed. Music. Murmurs. Beautiful objects hanging from the ceiling, creating a universe over the party."

"I like it. I can see it too." She clasps her hands together, eyes focused upward. "Your artist's eye is perfect."

Her phone buzzes. She glances at the message. "There goes the daydream and back to reality. Message me if you need something. Especially if the vault doesn't open with your card. It might not. There are security guards down there. I'll make sure they know to let you in."

I stand to shake her hand. "Thank you for the opportunity. This will be a fun installation."

"I hope you have a great time at the party. They put you on the haunted wing, right?"

I nod. "A vampire suite." The very thought of bringing Ellie to it makes me smile.

She pauses. "I don't know if someone's meeting you here, but have you been informed about the bonus features of that suite?"

"You mean the reinforced hooks in the ceiling for adding attachments?"

She grins. "I thought you might have spotted those. There's a toy room where items can be purchased." She flashes a wry smile. "If you didn't already bring your own, that is."

"Excellent information. And noted."

That's a woman who understands her market.

She takes off and I make another walk around the room to determine if the mummy art will work here.

Otherwise, all that remains is getting the object of my obsession here, and not blowing it when I am forced to make the big reveal.

CHAPTER 27

Lili

The house party was far tamer than I imagined in my head. We drank wine around a campfire each night. A guitar player and bongo drummer kept us in music.

Grim Weaver met his soul mate, then she ditched him for the guitar player.

On the last night, while he sat on a log staring into the flames, Carly Butterfly mustered enough courage to sit next to him and nudge his arm.

He looked up at her like he always has, as if this friend of his had something to say. Then he must have caught the look in her eye, because he startled shuffling his feet and acting all nervous.

It was adorable.

Carly returned to our room that night, of course. Neither one of them moves very fast. But she said he'd brushed his hand against hers, and she was almost positive it wasn't an accident.

So neither of them was too upset to learn I would be leaving with Drag Scream and Zerobia for Boulder, and the two of them would drive home alone. Carly felt up for the task since she knew the way.

"Have great conversations," I tell Carly as she shoves her knapsack into the back of her parents' SUV. "And don't do anything I wouldn't do."

Carly lifts an eyebrow. "You went to a sex club. I don't think there's anything you won't do."

Is that true? I don't know, but I laugh as she expects me to. I round the SUV and put my hands on Grim's shoulders. "Take care of Carly. Don't get lost."

He digs his toe into the dirt, eyes downcast. "Will you come back to Manhattan?"

"I have no idea." And I don't. "I'm not sure where I'm headed after the Haunted Ball."

"That sounds so cool." He looks into the car as Carly slides behind the wheel. "But so does this."

I clap him on the back. "You two have fun."

Zerobia pulls up in a type of car I've never seen before. It's way longer than most cars I've seen, the rear extending well past the back seat. It has no top, only a front windshield jutting up in front. You can see right into the white leather interior.

Drag Scream rubs her hands together. "I haven't been in the Judy Garland for years."

"The Judy Garland?" I ask.

"It's the name of this sweet, sweet ride," she says.

Zerobia honks the horn as if she needs to get our attention even though we're only a few meters away.

"Attention whore," Drag Scream says. "And she's earned it."

"I've never ridden in a car like this." I grab the handle of my suitcase to roll it over.

"Hardly anybody has," Drag Screams says. "This is a Cadillac DeVille. It's a rare classic, a gift from one of the best MMA fighters of all time."

"Oh."

Zerobia opens the long front door to hop out and pop the trunk. When I move forward, she holds up a hand. "Just a moment. I must prepare Judy for packing."

She pulls a heavy blanket from the trunk and spreads it across the lip of the trunk and over the red paint and bright chrome bumper.

"There will be no scratching my baby with clumsy suitcases." She takes my bag herself and carefully lifts it into the enormous trunk.

Drag Scream brings her monster bags forward, and Zerobia shakes her head. "Duffles from now on, woman," she says.

"Your strong, meaty arms can handle it."

"You forget, Miss Thing, that you are the strong one."

"Oh, for Pete's sake," Drag Scream says. "I'll do it." She hefts the first bag into the air. It almost bumps the blanket, but Zerobia catches it and the two of them set it in the trunk. The two suitcases easily fit, even with my stuff and Zerobia's.

Then we're off, Drag Scream pinning a scarf over her wig, and me quickly braiding mine as the wind whips over our faces.

The morning is cool, and I lift my chin to feel the sun on my cheeks. I'm reminded of riding a horse in Avalonia this time of year. Taking off across the fields into the hills was one of the few times I felt like I was totally free.

And now, my whole life is free.

Even though we're heading to a haunted castle to meet Z, oddly enough, when I look at the empty spot next to me in the back seat, it's not Z I wish was there.

It's Jesse.

We spend a night in a hotel in Iowa City. Zerobia pays since it's part of the travel budget she got to do the gig at the castle.

Everyone is tired. The late nights on the lake and the long drive get to all of us. Even so, both Drag Scream and I are up early to fix our wigs and faces. Both of us have a role to play.

Zerobia tells us we'll be stopping in Des Moines to pick up Lady Pendragon, the event casting agent who chose the acts for the Haunted Ball.

"I was picked three months ago," Zerobia says as we load up her Cadillac. "I've been looking forward to this weekend for ages."

I had assumed someone named Lady Pendragon would be another drag act, but she turns out to be a middle-aged lady with natural orange-red hair, graying over her ears.

We pick her up in front of a house on the outskirts of the city. She waits on the curb with her suitcase, long green skirts whipping in the wind.

"Hurry, hurry!" she says as Zerobia spreads out the blanket to protect the back of Judy Garland to fit Lady

Pendragon's bag. "It's nine hours to Boulder and the first rehearsal is at four!"

"We'll make it," Zerobia assures her.

Lady Pendragon slides into the leather seat next to me. "And who is this ravishing young thing?"

Zerobia turns in her seat. "This is Indigo Flame. She's a lifestyle influencer."

I'm about to say hello when Lady Pendragon reaches out to hold my chin, turning my head from side to side. "You could play a lot of roles. Do you have an agent?"

"No."

She releases me. "One of my royal court members bailed on me this morning, but the role calls for a big presence. You're too delicate."

"I'm sitting right here!" Drag Scream says.

Zerobia laughs. "Ain't many with a presence bigger than Drag Scream."

"Hmm," Lady Pendragon peers at Drag Scream as Zerobia pulls away from the curb. "Fine. You'll do."

"Such praise," Drag Scream says. But she adds, "Thank you. I like being on stage." She nudges Zerobia. "Just like old times."

Lady Pendragon's phone buzzes, and she sighs and punches the phone. "Hello?" She taps long orange nails on her thigh. "No, we don't need any gymnasts. Yes, I will keep looking for something for you." She slams her finger down. "So many people wanting work."

She sits back and lays her head on the seat. "What about you, Indigo? You looking for work?"

Am I? "I don't think so. I usually find sponsors to pay

my way. But I'm open to things." Unless she needs my real name, that is.

"Good. You do anything? Sing? Dance? Fire juggling?"

I shake my head. "Just take pretty pictures and convince people to buy stuff."

"That's a real talent." She closes her eyes. "Ahh. Peace and quiet and the open road."

I think she falls asleep. Zerobia cranks the radio, and she and Drag Scream sing show tunes for a while. They're good. Eventually, Lady Pendragon opens an eye and says, "I should put them in an act."

"We already did that, remember!" Drag Scream says. "Six years in Vegas!"

"Oh, right. And why did you stop?"

Zerobia looks at us in the mirror. "Insurance. 401k. Job security. You know, the finer things in life."

Lady Pendragon grunts.

Her phone buzzes. "I like this one," she says to me before answering. "Jayda! Darling! I'm so looking forward to seeing you at rehearsal!"

Her smile fades as she listens. "But you're the princess! You get kidnapped! It's the highlight of the act!"

She listens more, her face pulling into a frown. "I mean, sure. You can't help it if your appendix ruptures. Of course, I'll keep you on my roster. This is one bobble. You take care, honey."

She punches the phone and tosses it on the seat. "Unbelievable."

"What happened?" I ask.

"We have a whole royal court for this Haunted Ball. There's a short skit, nothing major. No lines or anything.

A narrator speaks. But my princess just called from the emergency room. She can't be there."

Drag Scream turns in her seat. "Good thing you have someone with royal bone structure right beside you."

Lady Pendragon's face turns slowly to mine. "Yes, I believe I do. Can you act at all?"

"I don't know."

"You have the look. Yes. You'll do. We have no time for paperwork. We'll do a handshake, and I'll pay you when the dust settles."

"Offer her cash," Drag Scream says. "She's not outing herself to save your ass."

Lady Pendragon presses her lips together. "I have to account for the expenses."

"It's called petty cash," Drag Scream says. "And you don't pay that well."

"Fine," Lady Pendragon says. "Five hundred cash, payable Saturday morning after the show. You will attend rehearsals tonight and all day tomorrow, perform tomorrow night, and that's it."

"Deal," I say. Five hundred US cash! I can make that last me for a while. Between that and my gift cards, I can worry less about how I'll manage once this event is over.

Lady Pendragon sits back. "My job is so ridiculous." Then she closes her eyes again.

I'm elated. It's hilarious. If she knew she'd hired a real princess to play the princess, she'd fall over dead.

But it's the sort of ruse that makes this adventure all the more fun.

CHAPTER 28

Jesse

The day is long waiting for Ellie to arrive.

All the art installations are in place, just in time for the partygoers to check into the rooms. The largest piece is hidden under silk behind the curtain on the main stage. It will be revealed partway through the presentations during the ball.

The ballroom is chaos with caterers, decorators, and facility workers preparing the space for tomorrow night.

About an hour before Ellie's scheduled arrival, she texts to say she's been hired to play the princess in the skit at the ball. She'll be going directly into costuming, and then a rehearsal.

I tell her I'll have a key sent to her so that she may join me in my room whenever she is ready.

All the ways I might reveal myself are considered. Some are simple, such as sitting at the end of the bed as myself, as Jesse. Others are more elaborate, like wearing the original vampire costume and stripping down, including the mask.

Or hanging the sketches of her in all the ways I've known her.

But as the day wears on, and she texts to say the cast is having dinner in the ballroom to avoid a break in the preparations, I grow impatient to see her.

So, after dinner, I pull a hat low on my brow and head down to the ballroom to watch the rehearsal. The space is dark with only spotlights aimed at the stage. I'm invisible, lurking in the far corner, leaning against the wall.

I spot Ellie immediately. The royal court is decked in elaborate costumes, pale gray colonial garb with high white wigs. Fine cobwebs complete the outfits, lending a spooky air. The actors aren't in makeup, but I imagine their faces will be ghostly for the actual event.

Ellie — Aria — I must get that right if I am to be Z tonight, looks more like her usual self than her Indigo persona without the red wig and eye makeup. This makes me wonder if Jesse could make an appearance and recognize her.

This could work. What if Z stands her up and Jesse is there for her?

I wish I had seen her before I sent down the key. I can't go to that suite as Jesse. I'll have to get another room for this plan.

But the castle is booked solid. I already knew that, and Ellie confirmed it when she told me that Drag Scream has to bunk with Zerobia and two other members of the cast because there was no place to put her otherwise.

No. This won't work. Jesse has no place to receive her.

Damn. I have no idea how this will play out.

A woman shouts, "Continue!" from the floor. The

narrator stands off to the side in his red coat, the only color in the production, holding an oversized book. He explains the actions of the cast on stage. "But the Lafayette family could only watch in horror as their precious jewel, Princess Sabine, was carried away by a ghoul. They would lose her a second time."

A man arrives on stage in an impressive costume made of ragged black cloth that must be wired to give the appearance of floating around his body. He snatches up Ellie and carries her offstage. Her silent scream is a red "O" as she disappears into the dark.

"That was good!" says the same woman. She and another woman in a green dress confer for a moment while the actors relax. The ghoul and Ellie return to the stage.

No one looks in my direction. I feel safe here in the darkness. The tables edging the ballroom are all in place. The photo corner is partially assembled, full of urns and darkened electric candles. The fresh flowers won't be placed until tomorrow, so the arch is bare.

The production resumes. The ghoul carries Ellie off stage again. The king and queen fall in mourning. But the prince is determined to rescue his sister. He believes she has been taken to the haunted wing of a nearby castle.

Lightning suddenly cracks on the far right of the stage, and the silhouette of the castle we're in is briefly illuminated. A figure with floating strips of cloth carries a woman. It's only a silhouette, but it looks great.

"Stop!" the woman calls. "We have light bleed on the stage!"

I hadn't noticed.

I'm incredibly impressed by the production.

"House lights!" she says. "Someone adjust that flood!"

The overhead lamps flicker on.

Shit, I have to go. Ellie could come back out on stage and I'm easily seen in this light.

I slip through one of the back doors. This rehearsal could go on for hours. I'll simply have to bide my time, think through all the scenarios for tonight, and prepare myself for the possibility of rejection.

If Ellie falls apart upon learning that I am both Z and Jesse, I'll have to find some way to live with that.

CHAPTER 29

Lili

I've never done anything as wonderful as this production for the Haunted Ball.

If any of them knew their actress was a real princess pretending to be an influencer pretending to be a princess, they would absolutely die.

But I am able to take on my regal postures as I play the role of the snobby damsel-in-distress who gets kidnapped by a ghoul and hauled to the haunted wing of the castle, a clever play within a play that brings us back to the ballroom.

After the amazing effect of our silhouettes entering the castle, the ghoul and I re-enter the ballroom from the back. I get to scream and shock the partygoers as a spotlight leads us back to the stage.

It's great fun, even if my voice is getting scratchy. Drag Scream has me gargle warm salt water and drink loquat syrup to keep my throat healthy.

The ghoul is played by a man named Axel. He's not a

professional actor, but a family member of the owner of the castle and probably the only one beefy enough to carry me off stage.

Only a few roles are played by professionals. Geoffrey, the narrator, is one. Zerobia and Fatine are as well, because they have singing roles. The king, queen, and prince all have acting credits.

The prince in particular has made a big deal about his small role in some TV show. He's tried to hit on me numerous times since we met this afternoon, but with him playing the role of my brother, it's wrong on so many levels that I've simply evaded him since dinner.

I text Z whenever I get a moment. While the lighting crew adjusts yet another set of spots, I sit on the stairs and update him one more time. It's coming up on midnight already.

Axel sits next to me. He's friendly and has already redirected the prince several times when he seemed hell-bent on luring me to his room. Axel has my back.

"Your accent is interesting." He shifts so that he's not sitting on any of his floating costume strips. "Do you mind if I ask where you're from?"

"Europe," I say. "Are you from Boulder?"

"No, I moved here to help with the castle. I'm from New York."

"I love New York," I say.

"It's a great town. Not for me, though. I love back-packing through the mountains."

"You're a hiker, then?"

He nods, adjusting the strips around his rather impressive thighs. He's been forced to wear tights for this, and he looks like a bodybuilder ballerina.

One of the crew members, a young pixie-haired woman, walks by, lugging two huge spotlights.

"Excuse me," Axel says, jumping up so fast that his ghoul costume actually floats for a moment.

He rushes up to the woman, his eyes alight. "Can I carry one of those for you?"

She gives him a look of pure disdain. "You think I look too wimpy to carry these myself?" And walks on.

Oh. Dang.

He scratches his head and heads back to the stairs.

When I see his face, I know he's got it bad. "You like her," I tease.

He shrugs. "She won't give me the time of day."

"You know why?"

"Nope."

"How long have you been trying?"

"Weeks. I think she has some history. I try to be helpful."

"Keep doing it. Maybe she'll come around."

He rubs his hair with his hand. "Maybe."

Lady Pendragon picks up a microphone. "Reset, every-one! From the top! Camille is going to watch from the back." That's the director.

We stand up. Axel heads backstage to wait for his entrance. I join my royal family. Here we go again. Hope-fully, I'll make it to Z before dawn.

I'm going to be one tired princess.

It's almost one in the morning when I finally follow the signs to the haunted wing of the hotel. I haven't had a single moment to explore.

I want to take my time to admire the stonework, the decor, and the amazing details.

But this chick be tired.

You can't enter the haunted wing after nine p.m. without a key that opens the main doors. I pass the plastic card over the scanner and smile when the heavy oak doors make a low creaking sound as they swing open.

"Enter only if you dare," a low voice says.

Nice.

I pull my suitcase behind me. Z offered to have it taken to the room, but I felt strange about letting it go. I wanted it with me until I knew the situation with him.

A small bar fills a space beyond the doors, serving drinks. A few people talk quietly at tables that resemble a wild west saloon. The bartender wears an old-fashioned vest and white shirt and polishes a silver stein. He nods at me, then turns to reveal that the far side of his face is a skeleton.

Whoa. I guess everyone here is in character all the time.

I give him a nod as I pass. The carpet in the hall is deep gray, but occasionally, I spy a small flash of purple light from below. The floor seems not quite even, giving me an unsettled feeling that something might collapse if I step the wrong way.

The whole thing is brilliantly spooky, so I'm already off kilter when I turn the corner to another hall and encounter a full-on ghost hovering in the hall.

I stifle a yelp and let go of my bag handle. There's a slight decline, and it keeps rolling, passing right through the apparition.

It's a projection.

Good grief.

I approach it, lifting my hand. It starts to fade, then I hear a faint hiss. A gentle push of pale smoke enters the space, and he's fully formed again, the smoke providing a place to reflect the image.

Genius.

My bag rests against a wall. I wonder how many other things I might encounter as I walk, but I'm prepared.

Twice I step on something that makes a cracking sound, as if the floor will break.

I pass a seemingly innocuous ficus plant, and it rustles in an unexpected gust of cold air, as if a spirit has passed through.

I love it.

The doors get farther apart until I finally reach the Suite of the Dead.

It's time.

I pause and take a deep breath. I'm tired, but I know Z will have prepared something for me. He's hinted as much.

The door pops open at the wave of my key. I clutch the handle of my bag and push it open.

The interior is dark, a pale red light pulsing slowly in the far corner.

The front space is a living area with a sofa and chairs, then a small kitchen with a black marble bar and stools. Farther back, near the light, is the bed.

The bathroom door is cocked open, providing a sliver of white light that illuminates a strange chair. It's upright with an incline at a steep angle, and a lip at the bottom.

Then I spot the cuffs.

It's a sex chair. I posted about a similar one months ago on my feed.

I don't see Z. No one speaks. I roll my suitcase by the sofa and look more carefully.

There is a bright white note on the coffee table. When I reach for it, it sets off a small lamp that illuminates the page.

Your outfit is in the bathroom. After dressing, kneel at the base of the red chair. On the bar is an energy drink and a shot of whisky. Also a brownie with edible marijuana. It's legal here. Take any or none of them. Be swift.

My adrenaline surges.

I walk over to the bar, feeling like Alice in Wonderland.

The energy drink is small. I down it.

I smell the whisky. It's divine. I drink it, too.

The brownie?

Why not? When in Rome, I guess. I'm here for new experiences. It's a tiny square, quickly eaten in two bites.

There is a bottle of water chilling in an ice bucket. I uncap it and down half of it in a single chug.

I'm ready. Clearly, Z has some way of knowing I'm here and will arrive when I'm in position.

The bathroom is blood-red and gorgeous. The sinks and counters look like ruby glass. An enormous sunken red tub gleams in the corner. There's a black-walled shower as well.

I twist the red wig into a knot and take a quick shower, wrapping myself in a red towel. I don't see the outfit right away, then spot it hanging from a shelf of bath salts and candles.

It's full-length, red, and completely sheer. It is lined with red gems, but I can't figure out the pattern until I put it on.

It swirls, encircling my breasts and cascading down my length. The weight of them holds it tight against my body. The mirrors reflect me in three views. I'm pale and striking with the red hair.

There's a black box resting on the counter. I pick it up. When I open it, there's a necklace like something I would find in our royal vault, red and gold and heavy with rubies.

Okay, then.

I fasten it around my neck.

As I'm about to leave the bathroom, I spot a pair of glittering red stilettos by the door. I slip them on. They fit. Z paid attention.

My hand presses against the necklace as I leave the bathroom, returning the door to its sliver of light. There's a small red pillow at the base of the chair.

I kneel there and a low tone sounds.

Another door opens, one I missed in the dark. A figure appears in a black shirt and pants, barefoot. His hair is slicked back, almost black in the odd light.

Z. He doesn't wear a mask.

I make out only the roughest contour of his features, the heavy brow, straight nose, and full lips. But it's not enough to really see him. The light is too low, too red, too infrequent.

He comes behind me and kisses my neck, biting me like he did that first time we met.

I feel odd, a combination of wildly awake and languidly relaxed. Alcohol and drugs. If the King and Queen could see me, heads would roll.

I want to laugh at the thought.

But then Z's hands are on me, touching me through the sheer fabric. He fills his hands with my breasts, pinching both nipples. Wetness slicks between my legs. Him, the room, the substances I ingested. I feel so wild, out of control.

He leans close to my ear. "You are mine here."

I nod. "Yes."

"Turn around."

I do as he says.

"Unzip my pants."

I do it, reaching inside to pull him out.

"Take me in your mouth."

And I do, reveling in the hard length of him, running my tongue along the hot, throbbing skin.

He groans, but pulls away, lifting me and turning me around. "Thank you for not wearing panties."

He pulls the red sheer robe away. It falls to the carpet with a heavy clunk of the gems. I'm pressed forward onto the chair, my knees on the ledge.

Z takes my arms and fastens them into the cuffs. Then my ankles are locked down.

There's a soft click, then the ledge spreads apart, and my knees go wide. I suck in a breath, my chest crushed against the soft velvet. I see nothing but the slow pulsing of red light on the carpet on the other side.

Something cool slides between my cheeks, and that tight pucker is filled. Another plug, I guess. Z's silky hands run along my back, sliding my wig hair to one side.

"I'm going to fuck both places today. Are you ready for that?"

Oh, God. Am I? A dark thrill bolts through me.

Something enters me, but I don't think it's him. It's narrower and smooth. He works it in and out, occasionally also moving the plug back and forth.

Then the chair tilts slowly forward. When I start to feel the blood rushing to my head, it stops. My butt is in the air.

Fingers work my clit. It's dizzying, all the sensation, having my head low. I can't quite get a grip on gravity, on what is up or down.

The chair moves again, lifting my head. The rush of it goes straight to where Z is working me. I squeeze my eyes closed. It's so intense, painfully close to orgasm, but it goes on and on and on, the pleasure an unending stream.

Just when I think I can't stand it, he presses the plug in more deeply and that's it, I'm over the top, crying out, shaking all over. I gulp in air, completely lost. I'm over-come, but then Z brings me back into the moment, filling me, working the plug.

I slide from one plane of pleasure to another. The chair shifts me, the blood rushing back to my head. His hand is on my thigh, his mouth against my spine. He works me hard and fast in both places.

I see stars again, crying out, wanting to beg for mercy. It's too much. I might fly apart.

Then he pulls out, giving me a moment. The chair straightens, and he releases my arms from the cuffs. I hold on to the chair for dear life as my ankles are freed and the two sides brought closer together.

His hands run over my body with the cooling lotion. I relax as he works my muscles, warming them with touch, then chilling them with the cool gel. My head feels heavy.

"Tell me if anything gets uncomfortable."

I nod against the crook of my elbow.

The plug comes out. I tense up for a moment, but his hands soothe me again. Then I feel him at the edge of me. I think it will be a stretch, but clearly the plug helped things along because he eases inside me, and each inch is another step up the ladder of sweet, dark tension.

I suck in a breath. It's so good. So unexpected. I want him to move in there, to work all those vibrant nerve endings that are lighting up, so much deeper than the plug.

And he does. I grip the velvet, feeling high. Is it the brownie or what he's doing? Both, I think. The room swims in front of me. The skin of his belly goes flush against me and he's buried inside me, in a place I never thought I'd explore.

But for Z, I would do anything.

My center of gravity goes off kilter, but this time I don't grip the chair to hang on. I let go and let myself fall.

I become one with the pleasure of Z inside me. He slips whatever he had before back inside me as well, filling both places, and this time there's a faint buzz.

I'm shocked back into my body, coming so hard at this new sensation that it seems I might collapse in on myself. I scream, I think, but I can't concentrate. I can only spin, whirling through the darkness and the red pulse. It goes on and on and I think it can never end.

I will it to never end.

I refuse to ever let it end.

CHAPTER 30

Jesse

I work her so hard, spilling into this new space. It's ecstasy to be with her, to experiment, to be wild.

But there's pain, too. This might be the end. I'm so close to my reveal.

When we're done, I cradle Ellie against me and carry her to the round bed covered in silk.

She's out cold after a long day and how I worked her. It's almost three in the morning. She needs to rest. Tomorrow will be taxing yet again.

I can't sleep at all. I'm deathly afraid of what the morning will bring. I've taken care not to close the black-out curtains. When light dawns, everything will be clear to her. Me. Jesse. Her as Indigo. Who we've been to each other all along.

I'm terrified.

My fingers trail along the line of her jaw and down her shoulder. I want to memorize every part of this moment, since it might be our last.

The feel of her smooth skin against mine for the full

length of our bodies is so perfect that I'm not sure how to let her go. I want to close the curtains, bar the door, get her fired from the production, and never let her leave here. To burn together until we're mere ashes.

The need to sketch this scene, to cling to the moment and force it into permanence is too intense to bear. But I do not succumb to it. I must stay right here, connected to her, skin to skin, for as long as the universe allows it.

I can't miss a second of this time with her.

I stroke her hair for hours, but it's still full dark when a buzzing sound starts nonstop from Ellie's bag.

I slide away from her. She's out. Her phone lights up over and over. I pick it up. Drag Scream types, "Where are you?"

Then someone named Pendragon also asks where she is. To get her ass to the ballroom for rehearsal.

I check the time. Five a.m. They're back at it?

There are other previews of earlier messages. Happy Birthday from someone marked O.

And it is her birthday. This glorious naked creature in my bed is newly twenty-one years old.

I hesitate. If I wake her, she will rush out of here. There will be no time for explanations. For recovery from the news of who we really are.

And it's her birthday. I can't potentially wreck her. Not now.

No. It must wait for tomorrow. We won't see each other again until night. She'll have the shock of Jesse being here when my art is announced, but I can't help that.

They are friends. It will be okay. And it will help the reveal make sense.

If I hesitate, I can have her one more night. We can do more things. I will plunder her and make love to her and remind her that no matter what, we work, and we can be together regardless of circumstance.

She'll understand. She'll have to. I won't let her go. I can't. I can't live without her.

I know what I have to do. I carefully put on my pants and shirt and shoes. I pull a ball cap low on my head and open the door to the secret room of the suite, the bonus feature where I waited for her to arrive.

I look at her one more time, then I pick up her phone.

Her model has a slider on the side that turns on the ringer. I kiss her hair, then flip it out of silent mode and crank the volume. I toss it on the bed next to her and bolt for the secret room's door.

It starts chiming immediately. Texts. Ringer. Reminders.

I pull the door closed and quietly latch it.

I hear the rustle of the bed. Her, "What in the world?"

I can only picture her perfect skin in the red sheets. The way the silk might be sliding down her body. It takes everything I have to stay where I am.

Her feet pad across the floor. Water runs in the bathroom. She rushes around. Her suitcase unzips.

She doesn't call for me, but a text comes.

Ellie: Where did you go?

I think for a moment.

Me: Ran to town for a special breakfast. Happy birthday, my beautiful flower.

Ellie: I have rehearsal!

Me: Then I will save the celebration for late tonight, after the ball.

Ellie: I'm so sorry. I have to go! Tonight!

A thump in the room sounds like her suitcase falling over.

Me: I will be waiting for more dark thrills for us both.

Ellie: Yes. Anything.

The outer door opens, then closes. And the room is quiet.

I step into the main suite. The sheets are awry. The bathroom light is still on. Dawn has started to creep over the mountains, bathing the room in a faint blue glow.

I sit on the bed, smelling her in the air.

She is my obsession, my utter addiction. She is everything.

Tonight, I will worship her.

CHAPTER 31

Lili

The day is long. No one but Z knows it's my birthday, and I don't tell anyone else. Even Z knowing is a huge mistake. I didn't change the date from my real one. So Princess Lili is also turning twenty-one today. Octavia sent me a ton of news reports, as it seems the whole country is mourning my absence on my special day.

I might hide well as Indigo, but unfortunately, my white wig and ghostly face in the production aren't like her at all. I'm afraid I look far too much like myself, particularly in the gown and tiara.

I forgot about the ruby necklace, and in my rush, showed up downstairs wearing it. Drag Scream noticed it immediately. She brought out a red crown from the costume box and twirled me in circles, saying I ought to be a real princess once our skit is over.

Mary in wardrobe looked annoyed and took it back.

I'm terrified of losing such an expensive gift, so I leave the necklace on, hidden beneath the high collar of my ghost princess outfit. It's nice to have it against my skin, a reminder of my night with Z. Every time I think of it, I shiver.

And there will be more tonight.

At lunch, a catering crew brings a spread from a local deli called the Tasty Mango. The food table is filled with sandwiches, potato salad, pasta, and several flavors of pickled cucumbers.

When we're all seated somewhere — chairs, steps, floor — Camille and Lady Pendragon stand on the stage to give us a pep talk.

"We have a special introduction for those of you who haven't met her," Camille says. "She's the reason we're here. This amazing castle was her brainchild, and she's here to give you a bit of history, Havannah Boudreaux-McDonald!"

Everything in my body goes still as Havannah walks on stage. I know her. She was at Leo's wedding, the one that didn't happen. Her sister married into the Pickle family.

The Pickle family of Sunny, my new sister-in-law.

I hunch over my crossed legs, grateful I'm sitting on the floor, but wishing I had my red hair rather than the white. At least we're not in costume at the moment, so I don't have a tiara or gown to give her any princess vibes as she looks at me.

"Welcome, everyone! We have such a special night tonight as we open the haunted wing of the castle!" Her eyes scan the cast and crew, but don't pause on anyone. I focus on my plate.

"A few years ago, I was a pregnant single mom with a dream of creating something magical with my hospitality degree. I attended a castle wedding in France and knew I wanted a castle of my own." She gestures to the side of the stage, and I sink down even more to see Max Pickle and his wife Camryn standing there.

No! They should be in Avalonia! The plane was fetching them when I ran away from it!

But that was two weeks ago. I guess they're back.

"I'm so thrilled to have almost the entire Pickle clan here for this amazing spectacle."

More family comes out. Oh, no. Oh, no! I had no idea there was a Pickle connection with this castle. I never would have come.

There's Jason Pickle with his wife Nova. And good grief, Anthony Pickle and Magnolia. I saw them six months ago when we were in New York. My sister Octavia and I taste-tested their new pickles.

"We are sad to be missing the great matriarch, Alma Packwood," Havannah says, "But you may have heard, her newest grandbaby is the royal princess Luciana of Avalonia!"

Her exuberance makes everyone cheer and clap. I join in so that I won't stick out, but inside I'm in a full panic. I can't be here. I can't be seen.

Drag Scream nudges me. "You okay, Indigo?"

I manage a nod and take a bite of sandwich to avoid having to say anything, even though I couldn't be any less hungry.

What do I do? Ditch the play? Run? How? I have nowhere to go and precious little money to get there. I'll get paid cash in the morning.

And then there's Z.

He knows it's my birthday. The Pickles surely know it

since I'm missing. I'm so glad I never mentioned it to Drag Scream.

This is the worst birthday of all!

Havannah talks more about the castle, but I can't listen to a word, utterly paranoid that we'll be asked to meet the Pickles and they'll spot me. When she's done and it seems like the family will mingle with the cast, I jump to my feet. "Bathroom break!" I tell Drag Scream.

I dump my food into a trash can and race through the doors to the hall.

What do I do?

We technically have a break until two, when we go to final wardrobe. We're done with rehearsals. The other speakers and musicians will be using the space from now until the event begins.

I need to kill an hour someplace safer.

Maybe I can go back to Z's room.

I would have seen him this morning, I guess, had I not run off. He seemed like he was ready to spend the morning with me since he got breakfast.

Am I ready for that?

Early on, he hid himself.

Later, I asked him not to reveal his identity.

Drat. I don't know if us having daytime activities would have changed the game.

I'm going to the room. It's time for me to see his face.

I head toward the hub of the castle so that I can branch back toward the new wing. The lobby is insane with guests checking in. Some are already in costume, blurring the lines between the attendees and the staff.

It's going to be a wild night.

Despite the run-in with the Pickles, I feel excited about my day. It's dangerous, for sure, but I could never have imagined a birthday quite like this. A haunted ball, being the princess in a ghost play, and spending wild, tumultuous nights with the masked man.

This is epic.

As long as I don't get caught.

What will happen after tonight? Will I run away with the masked man? A thrill zips through me.

I might.

I've passed the saloon and crossed the hall ghost, who is currently being selfied with a young couple, when my phone starts buzzing. What now?

It's Lady Pendragon. The royal family contingent of the cast needs to check in with the makeup crew because of a photo shoot. I'm required to get there immediately.

Great.

I immediately turn around and head back to the hall. At least doing this means I won't be expected to greet the Pickles.

Even so, I will have to tread incredibly carefully, or my first day of being twenty-one will be my last day in America.

CHAPTER 32

Jesse

It's torture avoiding the ballroom, but there's no darkness to cover me, and Jesse wearing a mask during the unveiling wouldn't seem right.

So I bide my time in private events throughout the castle and wait for the ball. It's excruciating, knowing Ellie is in the castle, and that this might be our last day together. But I resist.

I wear a pure white tuxedo for the evening. I'm not sure how Ellie will react to seeing Jesse here. This part I can't conceal. I'll be on stage. My art will be shown. It will feel like a coincidence, even though it is anything but.

The halls are filled with revelers in elaborate costumes heading to the main event. I pass by an entire coven of white witches, a zombie horde, and too many vampires to count.

When I enter the ballroom, I'm impressed. I don't know if Havannah and I are of the same mind, or if she considered my vision and was able to pull it off in only a few days, but incredibly realistic candles hover just below the ceiling as if they are floating like magic over the crowd.

Havannah herself comes up behind me. "It's very Hogwarts, isn't it? We'd already planned to place them through the wing, but I had them all brought here for tonight. Do you like it?"

"It's a real showstopper. The whole room is."

Havannah lifts an arm, a black sparkling sleeve dripping in an elaborate fall of fabric with her movement. "The walls are washed out in the low light, but otherwise, I think it turned out pretty close to the design."

A man in a black tux and cape comes up behind her and bites her neck. "I want to suck your blood."

She laughs. "Donovan, this is Jesse, the artist we'll be unveiling tonight."

I shake his hand. "It's a pleasure to be a part of this."

"It was Havannah's dream," Donovan says.

"You made it happen," Havannah adds.

"I never could have envisioned such a property." Donovan takes her hand and lifts it to his lips. "I was only the underwriter."

Havannah slides an arm around him. "We will see you backstage in about an hour?" she says to me.

"I'll be there."

The two of them walk slowly through the room. It's early yet, and only half full. Revelers stand in line to take photos at the selfie station or murmur together at the tables against the walls. Wait staff wanders through with trays of wine and champagne.

A group stands before the enormous full-length Haunted Mirror. I walk up to see what it does.

"You go," a red witch says to a woman all in white.

"You go!" she retorts.

Another woman, this one dressed in an elaborate purple and black robe, pushes them aside. "I'll do it." She stands before the mirror and presses her palm to the glass.

Smoke fills the mirror, and the woman disappears from the reflection. When it clears, she is back, dressed in a wedding gown. A man is behind her.

"Aiieeeee," she cries, whipping her head around to see if the man is there. He isn't. "What!"

The red witch nudges her. "The mirror doesn't lie. You're about to meet your future husband."

Interesting trick. They must use some sort of video AI to create the illusion.

I pick up a glass of champagne and sip it as the orchestra strikes up a new set. The stage is empty, the black curtain closed, wisps of fog seeping out from below it.

My art is behind two layers of curtain, since it will be unveiled after Ellie's skit. I should have time to watch her before I have to go back, since there is a musical act between us.

Then I get an idea.

I exit the side door and use my card to enter the back-stage area. I stand by the wall for a moment, making sure the cast isn't in this part of the space.

As I expected, they are in the dressing room for wardrobe and makeup. The comedian who will open the show is there, talking to the stage manager. Members of the prop crew stand around in their black pants and turtlenecks, waiting for the signal to start.

And then I see who I'm looking for. The band.

They're a rock tribute group here to appeal to several eras. The lead singer is a tall woman in a silver vest and black tights. I head over.

"I heard your rehearsal. You were fantastic," I tell her.

"Thanks." She looks me over. "What are you doing tonight?"

"My art is in the new wing."

"Is that right?" She seems bored with me, but I plunge on.

"One of the cast members of the skit, the princess, it's her twenty-first birthday tonight."

The woman narrows her eyes. That can't be good. "Are you going to ask me to sing to her?" Her voice drips with disdain.

"Oh, no. No. That's a big ask. Never mind."

It was only a gesture. Maybe the orchestra could play it later. If they have music. Maybe not.

The drummer speaks up from where he's sitting on a chair a few feet away. "I'll do it. I always wanted to do a birthday drum solo."

The singer rolls her eyes. "I knew it was a mistake to give you a mike."

The drummer laughs. "Somebody has to harmonize with your shit vocals."

Another eye roll. "Fine. We'll do the thing. What's her name?"

I have no idea how she's referring to herself to the cast. Indigo? Ellie? Some other name? I think I'm the only one who knows her as Aria. "Just call her the princess. It's what people will know her as from the play."

"All right," the singer says. "Fine."

I walk away, elated. I don't know if anyone else knows it's her day. I hope it's been a good one. I only got a couple of random texts from her.

A door opens on the other end of the room, and several of the cast members come out, laughing. She's not among them, but that's my cue to exit quickly.

This is going to be a great night.

I've never been on stage like this. I'm nervous, my belly constantly sending waves of butterflies through me.

I'm glad I don't have any lines. I think they would have fallen right out of my head at the crucial moment.

As I stand to the side with my fake royal family while the narrator tells our story, I see more of the audience than I thought I would. I wonder if Z is out there somewhere, and what he will think of our skit.

Then it's time to be captured by the ghoul. Axel ambles toward me, and I'm heaved over his shoulder.

We get to the side wings, and he sets me down. His face is animated beneath all the black streaks. "That was fun!"

"It was!"

"You ready to sneak to the back?"

I nod.

We take the staff tunnel alongside the ballroom. At the end, one of the stage crew members waits. "Let me make sure the path is clear," she says.

Axel and I stand inside the door. A woman with a massive tray enters, and we move out of her way.

"You all look great!" she says as she passes.

The crew member returns. "It's busier than we counted on. We're going to take you in by the spotlight operators, so no one will see you until your cue."

I feel Axel tense up. The pixie-haired object of his affection is a spotlight operator.

We follow the woman to a short set of stairs. There's a door at the top, and then we're in a small space where the two spotlight operators position their lights at the mourning family making their plan to get me back.

Poor Axel can't keep his eyes off the girl, who is concentrating on holding her light on the king. She sees us and glances over for a moment before reverting her gaze to the stage.

"Don't even think about interrupting me," she says.

I bite my lip. Poor Axel.

"Okay, let's go," says our crew member. We cross behind the other operator and down another short set of stairs. "This is going to open right next to the far ballroom door. Go straight out and make your entrance on my signal."

She presses her finger to an earbud, nodding her head. "And...GO."

Axel and I push the door open. Another crew member is holding open the back ballroom door. "You ready?" he asks me.

"Of course."

He lifts me and throws me over his shoulder.

It's show time.

When the skit is over, the cast congregates backstage as the band sets up between the curtains.

"That was perfect!" Camille says. "Turn in your wigs and costumes and enjoy the rest of your night. We'll be here in the morning with the payment for those of you not doing it electronically."

I'm about to head to the dressing room when a man holding a pair of drumsticks takes my arm. "You're the princess, right?"

My heart jolts, but then I realize he means in the play. "I was, yes."

"Come with me."

I wonder if he's taking me to Z, but then we walk over to his drum set.

What is this?

The lead singer looks super annoyed. "I see you found her. Are we doing that first?"

"After the intro song," the drummer says. He hands me a tambourine. "Stand here until we tell you to move."

I'm tempted to run, but then the curtains open again. Applause breaks out over the crowd.

The lead singer yells, "We're After the Effect and we're here to rock you back to 1993!"

They slam into a chord, and I try not to be terrified. I've never heard this song. It was recorded way before I was born.

The drummer looks at my tambourine, and I tap it to the beat. What am I doing here?

The song goes on forever. The singer roams the

stage in her silver vest, mostly screaming into the mike. The crowd likes it, though. They are more animated than they were during our skit, that's for sure.

Finally, the song ends. I sigh in relief.

The singer says, "Joey's got something special for you." She steps to the side.

The drummer leans into his mike. "I know you all enjoyed the play, right?"

The crowd cheers.

"And how about this princess?" He points to me.

Another roar of approval.

"Well, it's a special night for our very own royal girl. She's twenty-one years old today!"

I freeze. How does he know?

No one knows it's my birthday but Z.

And he doesn't know I'm twenty-one. I specifically didn't tell him my age.

Someone knows I'm here.

Someone's outing me.

Joey slams his drumsticks down and they break into a rock and roll rendition of "Happy Birthday."

I can't move, stiff with terror. Everyone is singing, the entire crowd.

Where are the Pickles? Are they making a connection? Is anyone here watching the news and peering at me like I might be the missing princess?

I want to melt into the floor.

Joey yells, "Once more, with feeling!"

No!

But they do it again, and this time, I see the side

curtains move. It's Anthony Pickle, staring at me. Then Max and Jason!

They are talking animatedly. Then Anthony's on his phone!

No, no, no!

I don't even smile or wave, but take off across the stage, aiming for the other side. But Havannah is there, also on her phone, staring at me like she can't believe it.

I'm caught.

The stage is too high to jump down. I fight my way along the back curtain, looking for the part.

I find it and dive through. I run straight into something solid. It's heavy and covered in silk. It must be the art they are going to unveil. I stumble against it, catching the silk on the metal hooks of my costume.

I step back and the silk comes down.

It's a mummy stepping out of a sarcophagus, broken into a perfect spiral as if he's unraveling, or maybe coming back together.

Regardless, I immediately recognize it as Jesse's work. There's no mistaking it.

I back away. What is happening here? Why is everyone I know all in the same place? Is this a setup?

I back into something. A person.

Arms go around me. Z? Can he get me out of here?

I whip around.

It's Jesse. What is he doing here? Is he part of all this?

"Ellie," he says. "Are you Google? Because I've been searching for you."

I shake my head. "What?"

His expression shifts. "You okay?"

He's not asking why I'm here. He should be surprised! Why isn't he surprised?

I glance frantically at the side wings. No one has come into this section, even though I left through it. Maybe I'm wrong about the Pickles.

Jesse couldn't have followed me here. He was scheduled to come here well before I was. "They have your art here?"

"Yes, like at Monica's." He smiles wryly at the unveiled statue. "You got the first look."

"I'm so sorry. I — I have to go."

He frowns. "Ellie, what's wrong?"

I don't know what to tell him. That I'm Lili, the missing princess?

"I can't say. But I need help."

He holds out an arm. "Okay. Tell me what to do."

The band has struck up another song.

"You can't. You have to go on next."

"Fuck it," he says. "You're more important."

"But your art—"

"You're more important."

"But I left you in New York."

He grabs my arms. "Is someone coming after you?"

"Yes. All the Pickles."

He looks at me as if maybe I've lost my mind. "From when you ate lunch?"

"The family."

"Oh." Understanding dawns. "Did you run from them?"

"They know my real name."

"I get it." He peers out. "Yes, they are all out there talking on phones. They look freaked out."

He snatches up the red silk that covered his art. "Put this on."

I wrap it around my head so that only my eyes are visible, letting the rest cover my dress and fall to the ground.

"We're going to walk very confidently past them and get you to my room. Then we'll sort out…" He hesitates. "We'll sort out everything."

I don't want him to miss his big moment, but I'm so grateful for his unconditional help. We move to the center of the next curtain and pass through. There's only a narrow walkway against the back wall.

"Ready?" he asks.

I nod.

We hurry to the side wings. The Pickles are all out there. Havannah is arguing with them, but I can't hear what they are saying over the noise of the band.

They look up and see me. Havannah stares at me, but we keep going. Jesse shouts, "I'll be right back," even though he might not.

We rush out to the hall.

"This way," Jesse says. We pass through another door and we're in the kitchens. Cooks and servers pause to watch the man in a white tux and a red-swathed girl dash between the metal rows.

Jesse opens a door that leads outside. "We'll go around."

The cool air is bliss. The door has slammed shut when I realize Jesse has gone a different way from me.

"Aria," he says. "This way."

I stop dead.

Aria?

He called me Aria.

Only one man calls me Aria.

He halts, spinning back to me. "Shit," he says. "Ellie. I'm sorry. I've been trying—"

I hear nothing else. I drop the red silk and take off in a dead sprint into the darkness beyond the castle grounds.

CHAPTER 34

Jesse

I've screwed up. In an instant, I've blown my cover as the masked man and spooked her even more than she already was.

She sprints into the darkness. I try to follow her, using my phone as a flashlight, but there is no telling where she went now that we're beyond the immediate vicinity of the castle. We went out a door that almost instantly leads into the woods.

The wind rushes down the mountainside and through the trees, causing them to drop pinecones. Every sound makes me whip around, but there is never anything but swaying branches and craggy rocks.

It's definitely colder tonight, and Ellie isn't dressed for the weather. I try to maneuver through the rocky terrain heading into the foothills, but the going is rough. How is she doing it?

There's a soft braying, then laughter? I shine my light to the side and spot a fence. I head toward it. There are donkeys there, leading into a barn. I quickly scale the simple wood beams and am immediately surrounded by the herd.

Hee haw haw haw haw. I've never heard a donkey sound like this, much less a whole herd. Are they laughing?

I head to the barn. Could Ellie have gone this way?

There's a glow of light as I enter the barn space. A man is spreading hay.

"Did you see a woman come through here? White wig, dressed for a play."

"Not a sign of her. Guests shouldn't be back here. The donkeys aren't ready for viewing yet. They just arrived."

I suck in a breath at his words. He has the same accent as Ellie.

"Where are you from?"

"A country you probably haven't heard of."

"Try me."

He leans on his pitchfork. "It's Avalonia. Near Belgium."

"Is that where these donkeys are from?"

"That's right. The lady who owns this castle is related to the royal family by marriage. She bought a small herd when she was visiting our new wee royal princess, and I came along to get them settled."

"Royal princess?"

"Yes, the Crown Prince and his wife gave birth to a healthy baby girl." He sobers. "Though the family is a mite in grief at the moment."

Something about his tone starts a low, incessant alarm ringing in my ears. "Why is that?"

"Their Princess Lilianne is missing. She'd be turning twenty-one today."

"Today?"

"Aye, today." The man resumes working his pitchfork. "Some say she's in Belgium. Others say she was taken by pirates."

Or a masked man, I think.

This is why she was running.

I outed her with her birthday song.

This is all my fault.

"Thank you, sir," I tell him and race toward the front of the barn. I have to find her, somehow. We'll have to look for her in the woods. I'll have to sound the alarm.

I hurry back to the kitchen door. It's locked, but my card opens it. I've barely made it backstage when someone grabs my arm. It's the stage manager. "You're late. We've been waiting on you. And someone unveiled the statue early. We'll just have to open the curtain."

"I can't," I say, trying to pull away, but this woman refuses to let me go. She leads me to the curtained space and madly gestures at the man working the curtains.

Before I can say anything, she's sprinted off the stage, and I'm revealed to the crowd at the ball.

The Master of Ceremonies gestures toward me. "And here he is, Jesse Adams, with his assemblage sculpture entitled, *Mummy, I'm home.*"

Applause breaks out. I give a quick bow, but that's it. Then I'm offstage again, searching for Havannah.

She's standing more deeply in the wings, surrounded by the Pickle family.

"What's wrong?" I ask, even though I know.

A beefy man who looks like he could bench press a

Cadillac says, "We've realized that the princess in the play is our missing sister-in-law. Have you seen her?"

So, it's true. I have to help her. "Yes. She ran through the kitchen."

Havannah turns to me. "She was with you, wasn't she? Wrapped in red silk?"

I nod. "I didn't know who she was, only that she needed help."

The man grabs my shoulders. "Where is she?"

"She took off into the woods behind the castle. I lost her in the dark."

Havannah lifts her phone to her ear. "Send as much security as you can spare to the barns. Bring flashlights. Roll the big lights out back as well."

She turns to me. "We're expecting a cold front. It's already rolling in. It's imperative we find her. She wasn't dressed for the Colorado mountains when it gets cold."

Everyone moves to the back hall. Out on stage, the party has moved on with another act. I couldn't care less.

I know I've lost Ellie for myself. But we have to make sure she isn't lost for good.

CHAPTER 35

Lili

Two miniature donkeys keep me company as I stumble up the side of the mountain. The pair of them, upon seeing me, jumped the fence that was way too low to contain the sprightly ones. Someone should have asked how high they can jump before building it.

I'm glad for them as I stumble in the dark. The moon keeps disappearing behind clouds, and we have to stop. But I trust the donkeys to take the most sure-footed path. They know better than I do how to traverse a difficult terrain.

It's cold but not freezing, and the work keeps me warm. I know I can't spend the entire night here. I don't know what I'm going to do. I'm trapped out here with nothing. No phone, no suitcase, no money, no way to escape.

Eventually, I stop. What *am* I doing?

Scat diddly. The jig is up.

The donkeys look back at me and bray their happy laugh. "It's not funny," I tell them.

They butt my thighs with their heads.

"Okay, maybe it's a little funny."

They are determined to make it to a dark spot up ahead, so I let them lead me there. It's a protected area in the rocks, not a cave exactly, but definitely out of the wind.

I sit there, and they snuggle up beside me. I pet their heads. "What are you doing here?" I ask them. Havannah must have brought some back with her. It's the only explanation.

Or maybe the Pickles got them. Regardless, I'm glad they are with me, a bit of Avalonia in America, here to transition me home.

If I'm ever ready.

The wind picks up, howling through the trees. We haven't gone that far, and the lights from the castle are visible below.

"So, what do I do?" I ask them. "Is it time for this princess to give up and go home?"

Tears prick my eyes. The donkeys seem to know not to laugh.

Do I miss home? Not as much as I thought I would. Everything's been new and exciting.

And there was Z.

Who is Jesse.

I reconsider all my memories with him in light of this revelation. How did I not see it? Now that I know they are the same person, it's perfectly clear. He must have realized at some point that I was the girl next door. Was it at the vampire ball? The masquerade?

My face burns about how I texted him from the bathroom and left him only to go to him anyway.

What a screwed-up situation. Maybe it's best that I escape it and go home.

It was a lie. All of it.

"And now I'm sitting on a mountainside with you two," I tell the donkeys.

One of them brays softly.

The wind howls again, this time penetrating our protected space. I shiver. "Okay, sweet donkeys, I have to get you home. None of us should be up here. I'll turn us all in."

I stand up and brush off the long skirts of the costume. The wardrobe manager is going to kill me.

Well, I guess until she learns I'm a princess.

I keep my hands on the backs of both donkeys to stay steady as we pick our way back down. I'm not sure what will happen to me. Most likely, whatever royal guards are in the US will escort me to the royal plane. But I should have a few hours before then.

Will there be time for another run for it?

Maybe I can slip back inside and get my phone. Put myself at the mercy of Drag Scream and Zerobia, and we can take off in her Cadillac like Thelma and Louise.

Could it work?

I'd have to leave Z. Avoid any Pickles. Avoid Havannah.

I should have left this castle the moment I knew it was hers.

My big mistake was leaking my real birthday. No one to blame but myself.

The back of the castle seems brighter than when I left. Jesse must have sounded the alarm. Traitor.

My anger burns hot. My suitcase is in his suite!

I think of all the times he tricked me and hid his identity behind masks and blinky lights and darkness. All so I wouldn't know he was Jesse! Why?

How differently that week at Monica's hotel could have gone.

My cheeks burn to think of it. Night after night.

But then we wouldn't have had the moment at the masquerade.

Or the sex club.

And it's not like I was honest about who I was. I gave him *two* fake names — Ellie and Aria.

And the biggest deception of all. My royal family. My duty. That I could never, ever stay. Or be his.

I gulp a half-sob. Worst birthday ever.

The donkeys bump into me as if to say, "We're here."

We make it to the last line of trees before we're back at the castle grounds. Security guards and facility workers are everywhere. A few of the workers have started climbing the rocks farther down.

I pause a moment before we enter the blazing lights. This is it. My last moment of freedom. I spot Havannah in her costume. I'm wrecking her big night. Then the Pickles, talking to each other next to her.

And finally, Jesse, holding a coat, probably meant for me. He looks so worried. He should. I'm so mad.

But also, I have to be glad.

I learned a lot about myself due to him. What I like. What I *really* like. Not to be afraid of new experiences. How I want to be treated, both among people and when alone with a lover in the dark.

He'll be a hard act to follow, but I won't settle. Father

can't make me marry anyone. Both Leo and Octavia managed to find their own perfect someones.

I will, too.

And with that resolution, I cluck at the donkeys and we take our last few steps until we're visible.

A guard spots us immediately, and a shout rises up.

Then I'm surrounded, the donkeys taken, and someone wraps me in a silvery blanket.

I spot Jesse, hanging back with the coat over his arm. I look away.

There's no point in us talking. He's part of the life I only got to lead a little while.

It's time for facing up to the consequences of what I've done.

Jesse

I have no way to talk to Ellie.

Aria.

Indigo.

Princess Lili.

She's quickly taken away with the Pickles. I can't get anywhere near her, and I'm not even sure she wants me to.

I end up in my room alone, staring at her suitcase. It feels wrong to open it, so I simply leave it where she parked it in her hurry to get to rehearsal. Maybe someone will come for it. I don't know.

Since I can't sleep, I sketch the two of us together on the Brooklyn Bridge, the Manhattan skyline behind us. I fill in the textures and colors and slip it into a side pocket of the bag in case it finds its way to her.

A knock the next morning sets my heart racing, but when I open the door, it's Drag Scream in a lavender pantsuit, looking deflated. She has Lili's phone and the outfit she must have worn to the rehearsal before she changed into her costume. She passes them to me.

"Indigo said this was her room." She stares at my bare face. "Are you her masked man?"

Since Lili hadn't known Jesse was Z, neither would Drag Scream.

"I am." I'm not sure what else is safe to say.

"Is she already gone?"

I shrug. "I was there when they found her, but I wasn't allowed to go."

"I miss her." She sniffs, tugging at her oversized collar. "Did you know she was the princess?"

"No."

"We were hanging out with royalty, and we didn't even know."

I set Lili's phone and clothes on her suitcase. "I'm not sure how to get her these things. No one came for them."

Drag Scream frowns. "It's all over social media. Her Indigo account has been outed as her. Of course, everyone's thrilled. She's got ten times the offers for sponsorship than before."

"Of course she does. She's perfect." I don't intend for this to sound as pitiful as it does.

Drag Scream reaches out to squeeze my arm. "She'll find her way to you. I've never seen anybody as hot for a man as she was for you."

I seriously doubt she'll want me after all this, but I keep it to myself. "You think they'll let her contact us?"

Drag Scream shrugs. "I've messaged her accounts. She hasn't logged into our private Discord. I hope that isn't the only way she has to get to us." She points at the phone. "If you can jailbreak it, you should. I don't know if they still lock princesses in towers," she sighs. "But if they do, I'm sure that's exactly what they'll do with her after this escape."

"Then I'll never get to her."

"Now, mister," she says, cocking her hip. "If a Disney prince can fight a dragon and cut through thorns to get to Sleeping Beauty, then surely you can find a way."

I nod. "You're right."

She gives a wave. "You can find me on Instagram if you need me. And do let me know if you get her. Tell her that her friends are waiting."

"I will."

She takes off down the hall. I stand in the doorway for a while, contemplating what I can do from a castle in Colorado.

But I'm not due anywhere. I was about to head to L.A. to work in my studio.

Which is where my Ellie/Aria art piece is waiting.

And it's now an art piece of a *princess*.

I think for a moment.

Maybe I do have a way of getting to her palace.

No swords required.

CHAPTER 37

Lili

The response to my return to Avalonia honestly makes me mad.

The streets are lined with people waving flags with my face on them.

Ugh.

A special dance has been prepared and is performed in front of the palace as we pass through, something like, "Lili fair and true, the country pined for you."

Ugh.

They should be celebrating Luciana, who, admittedly is the only good thing about returning. The moment the guard opens the car door behind the palace, I take off for the Crown Prince's wing to see her.

By the time I've pressed my first aunty kiss on her forehead and laid her back in her crib, my parents are outside the nursery door.

Great.

Leo leans in. "Say nothing. Give them nothing. No

details. No apologies. Keep your chin up and stare them down."

I appreciate the last-minute pep talk, because Father's murderous glare would make dictators quiver in their boots.

Mother reaches out. "Straight to the royal physician for you," she says, and I assume she means to verify if my hymen is still intact.

"I'm not a virgin, so you can skip that part," I say.

Father's eyes get large, then narrow. "Who stole your innocence?"

"I did. With a big red dildo!"

I hear a smack and spot my brother Leo clapping his forehead. Right. I'm supposed to say nothing and give them nothing. But I can't seem to stop myself. "I bet you didn't ask about Leo's virginity when he got home."

Mother stands taller, her chin lifted. "We should know if you are already carrying a child, and the father must be brought to justice."

"Justice? Nice. You can call 1-800-Buy-a-Dick and see who was responsible for the manufacture of Hot Tamale. That's what I named my sex toy."

"Enough," my father roars. "I can see you have been poisoned with loose morals during your travels."

My blood pressure peaks. "I teach sex positivity, Father. There is nothing loose or immoral about that. Get out of the Dark Ages."

I try to pass them, but guards are lined up right outside the door. I'm trapped.

Zounder-fucking-kite.

I want to be in my room. I want the burner phone I

gave Octavia. I want to talk to my friends. I haven't been alone since the moment I stepped out of the woods. It was a long night waiting for the royal plane, then a long flight here. It's early afternoon in Avalonia and I haven't slept in days.

I need some time to think. Maybe to cry. Definitely to plot and plan.

"Excuse me," I say, but they don't budge. Right, the King's Regiment doesn't move for anyone but him.

"Dad, call off your stooges." I ram between them, like a royal version of Red Rover, Red Rover, but they're like brick walls.

But I'm little. They stand at attention, and there's a gap between their boots. I drop down and duck between them, and take off in a run.

My father roars, "Stop her!"

But Mother quickly adds, "No, let her go to her room. She needs to collect herself."

"Fine," he roars again.

Good.

I race through the foyer and past the guards to the children's wing. I have never felt more out of place. Octavia is here less, as she's preparing a home for her and Finley to live in once they are married.

My footsteps echo down the empty hall. I changed out of the costume, but I wasn't able to go back for my suitcase or phone. Things happened too fast, and by the time I thought of it, I had no way to contact either Drag Scream or Z — Jesse — to get them. Probably they would have been taken away anyhow.

I'm stuck wearing an outfit that was packed on the

plane after my disappearance, a demure pink dress with matching ballet slipper flats. I'm sure Father wanted me to look like a proper princess should photos be taken of me when I returned.

I burst into Octavia's room and slam the door behind me.

She's sitting on her bed but leaps up when she sees me. "You're here! I heard you were on a plane back! Tell me all about your adventure! You made it two weeks!"

I don't expect this to happen, but I burst into tears.

Octavia leads me to her bed. She looks normal in jeans and a sweater. I kick off my shoes. "Can I have some decent clothes? I hid all my good stuff in the broom closet outside the tunnel before I left."

"Of course. You stay here." She pushes aside the tapestry to the tunnels and disappears.

I had such a good plan, but I only got two weeks.

Did I make the most of it?

I met friends. Made new ones. I checked off all my bucket list items. It had certainly been epic, even if not the way I thought it would be.

If only it hadn't all fallen apart.

If only Jesse hadn't tried to be sweet by having the band sing me "Happy Birthday."

If only I hadn't told anyone I was turning twenty-one that day. I gave one secret to Z and another to Jesse, having no idea that the two of them could put it together and expose who I was.

So many regrets.

Octavia returns with a suit bag stuffed with clothes. "I didn't even think to check in the tunnel exits. Naturally, the guards walked the tunnels, but this didn't catch their attention.

I know it didn't. I'm good. I chose a plain canvas bag that would blend in with the mops.

"Do you have the burner phone?"

"Of course." She heads to her closet.

I unzip the bag and take out a pair of jeans and a hoodie. It's my second favorite behind the gray one I took with me. Those clothes that I wore in America are lost to me.

I brush my hand over my eyes. *Stop crying, you ninny!*

When I pull off the pink dress, Octavia sucks in a breath at the ruby necklace. I never took it off. "Is that from him?"

I nod. "I didn't take it off."

Octavia balls up the dress and chucks it in the corner. "Dumb outfit. I told them to put normal clothes on the plane."

I nod, tugging on the jeans and sweatshirt and pressing my hand to the necklace hidden beneath it. I reach out for the phone. "Can I take a minute before we talk?"

"Of course," she says. "We have all the time in the world."

"Until Mother barges in," I say. "I had a tiff with them a minute ago."

"I'm sure." She draws her knees to her chin and waits me out.

I log into Discord first, wincing when my avatar immediately shows the green dot that I'm online.

There's a whole channel called Indigo/Princess, but I

don't even click on it before my private messages start lighting up.

There's Drag Scream, Grim Weaver, and Carly Butterfly. Zerobia has joined our private chat. And a dozen others outside of New York I'd hoped to meet on this escape, but never got to.

I want to scroll through everything that was said about me after I was found out, but the incessant notifications keep me from getting to the old messages. Eventually, I start reading the new ones.

Drag Scream: She's here!

Carly Butterfly: Are you okay?

Grim Weaver: What do we call you now?

Grim Weaver: Are we allowed to talk to you? Should we bow?

Carly Butterfly: You can't bow on Discord.

Grim Weaver: (Bow emoji)

Carly Butterfly: Grim. Good God.

Drag Scream: Forget them. Indigo, are you okay?

Grim Weaver: How big is your palace?

Grim Weaver: I saw the princess tower on the news. Are you locked up in there?

Grim Weaver: I can climb vines if you have them. I don't think you have enough hair.

Drag Scream: Grim, knock it off. Indigo, are you there?

Indigo Flame: I'm here.

Carly Butterfly: You're alive!

Grim Weaver: Did you almost die?

Drag Scream: Did they take your phone?

Indigo Flame: Yeah.

Grim Weaver: HOW DID YOU ALMOST DIE?

Indigo Flame: It was yeah to them taking my phone. I had another one at home.

Grim Weaver: You mean the palace?

Indigo Flame: Yes, the palace. And no, I'm not in the tower. It's for brides.

The questions come hard and fast and I can't keep up. I sit back against the pillows. Octavia lies next to me. I'm glad for her easy, supportive company.

"I missed you," I say. "I wish you could have come."

"I'm so ready for more details. The time difference made it hard to talk."

"It did."

I private message Drag Scream, not wanting to talk about Jesse in the main chat.

Indigo Flame: I haven't messaged the masked man. Did you see him?

Drag Scream: I did. That was a big secret you kept.

Indigo Flame: I know. I'm sorry. I just wanted away.

Drag Scream: I get it. I saw Jesse the morning after you left.

Indigo Flame: How was he?

Drag Scream: Devastated. A wreck.

I can picture Jesse that way. Z, not so much. It's hard for me to put them together as the same person.

Indigo Flame: I'll write him. Send me his number again.

Drag Scream: Will do. The main chat is blowing up.

Indigo Flame: I can't deal with that.

Drag Scream: I'd bug out.

She's right. This is exhausting. I drop the phone on the bed.

"That all the friends you made?" Octavia asks.

"Yes, the New York influencers. I got to know them

pretty well." I think of Carly and her coffee pot pasta and her cockroach Monty. And Grim's hats. Drag Scream's motherly guidance in decidedly non-motherly directions.

I stare at the high ceiling. "What do I do about Jesse?"

She frowns. "I thought you were more into Z in the end."

Right, she doesn't even know.

"They are the same person."

She sits up straight. "What do you mean?"

"I'm not sure how it all came about. If Jesse met me and happened to be at the vampire ball, or if he followed me there, or what. But they were the same person."

"And he never told you?"

"No. I can see it now, looking back. But our times together were so different." Although, maybe not in the end? Things got heated with Jesse. Then got softer with Z.

"When was he going to?"

"I have no idea. Jesse called me Aria like Z did, and that's how I knew. But then I got caught. We didn't talk."

Octavia picks up my phone and holds it out. "I think you better." She heads to the hall. "I'll let you know if we're about to be invaded so you can stash the phone."

She pulls the door shut behind her. She's right. I have to protect this last phone at all costs. Now that I'm outed on all accounts, there won't be secret phones arriving anymore. The royal staff will watch both my Princess Lili and the Indigo Flame feeds. They'll go through all my deliveries.

I flip the phone over. It can make international calls.

Or I could text.

It's morning in Boulder, and Z's already gone through a

whole day without me. Is he still at the castle? Did he go back to New York?

He could be anywhere, in any time zone.

But I remember his face when he realized I knew who he was. He lied to me. He didn't have a reason half as important as mine. I couldn't be with him at all if I was outed. What was his excuse?

My anger burns hot again.

I toss the phone back on the bed. I unclasp the necklace and shove it into one of Octavia's drawers.

I won't call him. I won't think about it anymore. I'm stuck here, and there's no way to fix what happened, or to move forward.

There's no point in torturing us both.

CHAPTER 38

Jesse

Donovan McDonald swirls his glass, making the square block of ice spin. "You sure you want to do this?"

He's asking me a little late. We're already over the Atlantic Ocean on the plane he and his brother Dell Brant own. I've never been where we're going. I hadn't known the small city-state of Avalonia even existed until I met its prized princess.

"You think I should let her go?"

He leans back in the plush leather chair, peering at the clouds outside the window. "I haven't done much with the Avalonian royal family other than attend a wedding that became a non-wedding that became a secret wedding in the fields with a different bride."

That sounds like a story. "Who did that?"

"Lili's brother Leo. They forced a bride on him, so he tried to elope with Sunny Pickle. I don't know the whole story, but the King is keen on controlling who ends up in the family."

"Didn't the older sister just get engaged?"

Donovan nods. "And that was another crazy tale. Apparently he's a royal guard who was her friend from childhood, but once any male turns seven, he can't be around the princesses until he's over thirty."

Damn. I've been around Princess Lili plenty. And over and under and inside various entry points.

That might be treason, or a federal offense, or who knows what in a country with a monarchy. Avalonia doesn't have any elected government or parliament or anything. The King literally rules.

Donovan tilts his head toward the crate I insisted go on board with us and not in the storage compartment. "So what's that?"

"A sculpture."

"A gift for the King to butter him up?"

"A gift for Lili. I told her I would do it, and I'm keeping my word."

Donovan sips his drink. He's all casual in jeans and a sweater, but I'm fully decked out in a three-piece suit. I don't know what to expect when we go calling on the palace unannounced. Probably we'll get booted immediately. But I will look presentable just in case.

"I've got to hand it to you, you've got balls."

But even as he says it, I consider how balls-deep I was with Lili. What a wild law to have, seeing no men between ages seven and thirty. How has she dated? Had a boyfriend?

Has she not?

Had she never done anything when I met her?

She bled that first night.

And let out that wild scream when I first slammed into her.

And shied away after we were done.

Fuck. That was her first time. I'm sure of it.

And her second? Naked over a ballroom.

I blow out a long gust of air. I would do everything differently if I could do it again. Take care of her. Be gentle. Maybe even hold off.

But that's not what she wanted. Maybe I would have been dull. Nothing special. She wouldn't have pined for me.

The more I think about it, the more I know it's true. We work at such an intense level exactly because of our explosive interactions.

Donovan slides the bottle of bourbon toward me. "It's a long flight. Take the edge off."

I think I will.

I'm glad for Donovan. He contacts Sunny straightaway. She comes down to the palace gates herself, looking other-worldly in fluttery white skirts and a long, flowing top. No less than four guards in blue uniforms follow her.

She nods at them, and they open the series of inter-locking pedestrian gates to let us pass through.

Donovan kisses her cheeks. "Motherhood looks good on you. Are you feeling well?"

She presses her hands to her belly anxiously. "I will when I can fit into my normal clothes again."

"You're perfect." He turns to me. "Sunny, this is Jesse

Adams. He and Lili were seeing each other while she was in the States."

Her eyes narrow. "She hasn't mentioned him."

"Did you not read the gossip?"

"Donovan, you know I don't read any of that. The international press thrives on ugly lies about royals."

"Ah, yes. I only brought it up because so many photographs of the Princess have been bandied about, many with Jesse here. I was merely proving his claim."

Sunny takes me in. "I don't know if she wants to see him. She's been holed up in her room since she returned." She meets my gaze with trepidation. "It's been a week since she got home. Have you spoken to her?"

"I'm not able to. She was using this phone when she was with me." I extract it from my pocket and hold it up. "She probably wants it back. We took quite a few photographs together on it, and I don't know that she has a backup."

"I better hide that," Sunny says, taking the phone and tucking it into some hidden pocket buried in her skirt. "I have no doubt that it's not an official palace device."

"So, what do we do with him?" Donovan asks.

"You're the one who brought him here," Sunny says. "Jesse, what should we do with you?"

"I'd love the opportunity to see Lili, of course," I say. "Perhaps with her phone, we can reconnect."

"She won't be able to leave." Sunny taps her lips. "Let me talk to her. Do you have a place to stay?"

"We can find one," I say.

"It's the autumn festival," Sunny says. "There won't be a

room to rent for miles. It's extra busy this year because Princess Lucy will be presented for the first time."

So I've chosen a horrible time to come. "I'm willing to wait in Belgium. I will wait any length of time, any at all, in the hope of seeing her."

This gets to Sunny. Her expression softens.

"I don't think I can get you in a room at the palace. The King is acting all crazy since Lili went missing. But I can tell you where to go to see her. It's private, and currently under renovation. Can you acquire an outfit that makes you look like a worker?"

"I can do anything."

"All right. I'll send Donovan the address. Be there tomorrow. It's to be her sister's house when she gets married next year. I'll make sure she goes there with Octavia tomorrow." She stabs my chest with her finger. "Don't screw up. There will be guards, and they will throw you in the brig."

"Don't go in the brig, bro," Donovan says. "Octavia's dude got tossed there. They like sending the men who sniff around the princesses into the dungeon. It's old-school as hell."

I nod. "Happy to do it. And happy to go to the brig."

Donovan shakes his head. "You say that, but you haven't seen it."

I don't care. I'll do anything, and I do mean anything, to get a chance to prove myself to Lili.

CHAPTER 39

Lili

When Octavia suggests I go with her to check on the renovations of the house she's fixing up for when she marries Finley, I jump at the chance to leave the palace.

We get assigned extra guards, which I figured, but it doesn't matter. I'm not exactly going to make a run for it. I know I'm stuck, probably forever. I had my fun.

My house arrest hasn't changed. I refuse to have dinner with my parents unless the baby comes. With only grown-ups present, my mother and father are happy to launch into long diatribes about how disappointed they are with me.

If baby Lucy is there, though, it's okay. All the attention is on her every movement. She gets passed around, and I'm just another lump on a chair, which is totally fine by me.

The evenings are hard. I've taken to sleeping with Octavia on the nights she doesn't sneak out with Finley, which admittedly, is most nights.

I got my period, which I'm sure was reported to my mother since I never did see the royal physician. Then it went, and in its absence, the need for Z returned with a fierceness that makes me vibrate. I won't cry over him. We both made big mistakes. But I long for how I felt when we were together.

I tell Drag Scream about it, because at least she has seen us and knows. Octavia listens, but she can't understand what I'm going through, since all she knows about him is what I've told her.

And that's not a lot, particularly about the hard-core details of our darkest encounters. I can't shock her. She might be hot for Finley, and maybe they did have their first night in the woods. But I have a feeling they're vanilla compared to what I'm like with Z.

Was like.

I've avoided looking Jesse up online because it's pointless. I can't get to him. But Drag Scream forwarded me an article about him in the *New York Times*. He's working on a new assemblage sculpture in his L.A. studio.

Someone leaked an image of his new work, and art collectors around the world started bidding on it. According to the story, it's already worth over two million dollars, and he hasn't even offered it up for sale.

Octavia bursts through my door, looking super young with her pink and blue striped hair tied up in the two tight balls she used to always wear. She's got old jeans on, and a sweatshirt. "I hope we get to paint some walls ourselves," she says, hopping on my bed. "Wear old things. Let's get down and dirty."

I select a set of gray sweats I never liked and twist my hair up inside a ball cap. "Let's do it," I tell her, and we head down the hall arm in arm.

When we get in the black car with windows tinted so dark it's hard to see outside, there are four guards with us.

"I think I might have set us back on the no-guard front," I tell her.

"Don't worry about it," Octavia says. "We'll have fun once we're in the house."

I haven't left the castle since I returned. Town Square is gearing up for the autumn festival with fall colors and harvest wreaths. The weather hasn't turned cool yet, at least not today, and I push up my sweatshirt sleeves.

It takes a few minutes to get to the edge of town where the Farthington Estate has sat empty since old Lord Farthington moved to a retirement home. Father scouted it when he realized Octavia wasn't going to give up on Finley, who works at a bar. I'm sure Octavia would be happy to live with him in any apartment, but a royal needs guards and places to house them. So Father bought this estate for them.

I realize how far away Octavia will be when she gets married. And she might move in ahead of the wedding. I don't know. I rest my forehead on the glass and decide not to ask her when she'll abandon me completely. I can't take any more sadness at the moment.

We're both surprised to see one of the royal cars already there, parked in the enormous circle drive leading under the porte-cochere at the front of the two-story structure.

I sit up. "Don't tell me Mother and Father are here."

Octavia shakes her head. "No, they were in the throne room when we left."

"Who's here, then?"

A guard jumps out to open the door for us, and we hurry through the front entrance. There are workers in paint-splotched overalls in the foyer, stripping the gold wallpaper that Octavia hates.

I follow her to the left, where there's an enormous drawing room that leads to an office with French doors thrown open.

And on an antique sofa near the front window is Sunny, baby Lucy on her lap.

"What are you doing here?" Octavia asks. She picks up Lucy and rocks her back and forth.

"We needed an outing," Sunny says. "Sometimes I can't handle someone popping in every time I move, asking what I need."

"I get it," Octavia says. "Maybe this house can be an escape for all of us. You're always welcome." She flattens Lucy's collar. "You're getting a double chin!"

"She's an eater." Sunny meets my gaze. "Octavia, I wanted to ask you about your wedding timeline. Lili, you could wander around if you like. The upstairs rooms are quiet and empty. I'm sure you are very sick of being surrounded by people."

She's got me pegged all right. "Will do."

Octavia nods. She sits next to Sunny on the sofa, and I wander over to the office. It has a giant cherry desk and a backdrop of empty shelves.

I like it here. I pass by Sunny and Octavia, who have their heads close together, and back to the foyer. I think about exploring the bottom floor, but something about Sunny's suggestion that I go upstairs to be alone appeals to me. There are workers all over the downstairs. It will be nice to sit by myself in a room, knowing no one will barge in. Some of my best moments were in the hotel room at Monica's. It was my own space. No one had a key.

I head up the curved staircase to the landing above. To the right is a hallway lined with doors. To the left is a matching set.

But the center is open with three big archways filled with light. There must be a cupola or skylight in the room beyond.

I step inside to see that it's a library, the side walls all built-in bookshelves, the kind with a rolling ladder that moves along a rail.

And in the center is a huge sculpture.

An assemblage.

I instantly recognize it not only as Jesse's, but I'm fairly positive it's the one from the grainy image in the *New York Times* article.

This is his two-million-dollar piece.

What in thunder?

Why didn't Octavia tell me she bought this? Or did Jesse send it?

The overall shape is that of an enormous flower blooming. There's a central stem, then petals slowly peel away from the core. It's pale pink on the outside, growing more and more red as you get to the middle.

Yes, like a vagina. Exactly like that.

I walk up to it and suck in a breath.

It's me.

Every petal is me.

On the outer layers, the petals are sketches of me as Ellie. On the subway. Falling on the hotel floor. Posing on stairs in Brooklyn. Gazing at a nun and a string of children.

The next layer of petals portrays me as Indigo. I'm walking into the vampire ball with Drag Scream. Posing outside of the crepe shop. Holding out a condom packet.

And in the hot red center of the flower are other images, more stylized, perhaps so much that only Jesse and I would know what they are. Me, floating over the masquerade ball. Suspended in ropes. Bent over a rounded chair. I'm Aria. It's the core of me.

I peer at the base, where a gold plaque is etched with two words.

Lili Blooms.

I step back. Yes, the shape is a lily.

All of these layers are me.

And Jesse knows them all. Understands them all.

Lost them all.

I can see his feelings in the mournful tilt of the flower, the way the petals look as if they are about to fall away.

But what is it doing here?

How did it get here?

I whirl around to confront Sunny and Octavia about it and crash straight into a stalwart chest.

I know this chest.

I know those arms.

The aftershave, like whittled wood.

Z.

Jesse.

How had I not realized the two of them smelled the same?

I look up.

He's watching me.

He's here.

"How?" I ask.

"Sunny."

"When?"

"Yesterday."

I take in his overalls. They are splattered with paint. "Did you steal these off the workers?"

He laughs, and my heart sings to hear that rumble. "We've been helping. I painted a yellow room."

"You painted a room?"

"I can wield a paintbrush."

I gesture toward the flower. "If your sculpture is worth two million, how much could a room be worth?"

He grins. "You looked me up?"

"Drag Scream sent me the *New York Times* article."

He tries to hold his expression, but it droops as he says, "But not my number."

"I had it. I just didn't use it."

"Oh." He takes a step back. "Should I go then?"

I step forward. "No. I didn't call you out of self-preservation. You're off limits to me now. I'm not free to go where I please. And my father is so mad."

"At me?"

"At anyone who corrupted me." I lean into him, wanting the smell of him to continue to wash over me.

"I'm guilty of that." He frowns. "I thought a lot about that first night. That wasn't your period, was it?"

He's figured it out. I shake my head. "It was something I wanted out of the way. You were perfect."

He pulls me to him, his arms pulling me into his chest. "I would have done things so differently."

"No. It was exactly right. I'll never forget it."

He kisses the top of my head. "I purposefully drove up the price of this sculpture."

"You did?"

"Just like you told me that first day. Create an air of mystery, then scarcity. I wanted you to have it. You can sell it and buy your freedom. You always had to fight for the money to go places. Use this and you can go anywhere, do anything. You won't need the palace. Or your father."

I spin around in his arms to look at it. "I don't think there is any price to buy my freedom. I'm a royal."

"Then keep it. If you're sure we won't work, let it remind you of when we did."

I lean against his chest. I know I was so angry, and maybe he was, too. We both made mistakes. We both held secrets.

"I don't know what to do," I say. "I'm allowed to choose who I love. Leo married an American. Octavia's about to marry a former guard."

"Then what's stopping you?" His question is gentle.

I turn around to face him. "We barely know each other. My parents will be opposed. We live on opposite ends of the world."

He brushes back my hair. "I can work anywhere. Unless your father bans me from Avalonia, I'm happy to be near you. I think your sister-in-law is on your side. She snuck me in here."

His face is so earnest. He wants this. He's willing to try. To see where it goes. Can I meet him halfway?

"Who are we to be to each other?" I ask. "Aria and Z? Ellie and Jesse?"

"We are all of those things and more." He runs his thumb over my cheek. "And I can't wait to explore each and every combination."

"Sweet, innocent Princess Lili with the rogue Z?"

"Mmmm. Wear all the jewels and nothing else."

I shiver. "Aria and gentlemanly Jesse?"

"She can tie him to a bed and use a leather crop on him."

The very image of it makes me shiver. I jump and wrap my legs around his waist. He catches me, his hands holding me in place.

"When can we start?" I ask.

He tilts his head toward the hallway. "I have a door with a lock. And some paint." He glances down at my chest. "I'm going to paint right on your skin."

I shiver again. "Then let's get in there."

He starts walking, still holding me against him. I reach for his head and bring him closer for a kiss. It's our first one bearing all of our unique selves, truthful to who we are, and a blending of all the personalities we've shown to each other so far.

I'm really, really glad to get to explore them all.

Naked.

CHAPTER 40

Jesse

Six months later.

So, yeah, I built a sex dungeon for Lili.

I go over each part of it while I wait for her to arrive. It's red and purple, in honor of her Indigo colors. Red silk bed. Purple rope suspension. Red sex chair, more elaborate than the one at the haunted castle. Purple toy wall, lined with every manner of crop, whip, and handcuff. Everything.

There's a camera recording it all. We discovered a mutual kink of fucking while running a recorded video of previous fucking. The King and Queen would flip if they knew the recordings existed. It's a closed system, though, with no Internet connection anywhere near the camera or the computer than runs the projection.

We're crazy. We love it.

I hear the front door buzz as she comes in. I carefully

close the door to the dungeon. As far as Lili knows, it's a home gym I've been renovating.

The house is within walking distance of the Town Square at the base of the castle gates. She often comes down with a single guard. We've provided a screened porch for him to hang out on by the front door.

And yeah, that was an important feature of the dungeon — soundproofing. We've had to keep the noise at a controlled level ever since I moved here, as we can't have the guard breaking down the door to save the Princess every time I drive her over the edge.

Because that's pretty damn often.

Lili's setting her bag on the sofa when I enter the living room. She greets me the way she always does, by jumping up and wrapping her legs around my waist. Unless we're having a dinner or some other activity first, she's ready to get down to business immediately. She gets pent-up at the castle, and her schedule doesn't always allow her to get here daily.

"It's been three days," she says. "I need it *now*."

I laugh. "Good afternoon to you too, my love."

"Stop with the small talk. I have better uses for your mouth." She drags my head to hers. I sit her on the back of the sofa so I can kiss her properly. She tastes of roasted sugar beets. The first spring batch must be ready. I haven't developed a taste for them yet, but I've been told I better. It's a staple in Avalonia.

She smacks the side of my head. "You're thinking. Stop it."

I laugh. She knows me too well.

"I have something to show you," I say.

"Your cock?"

I laugh again. I love every one of her dirty words. "I'll be shoving it in your mouth in a minute. But first, a trip through the house."

I shift her to my back, locking her ankles around my waist. She wraps her arms around my neck, and I carry her through the kitchen and down the stairs to the cellar, past the washing machine, and to the door to the dungeon.

I turn my head. "When you arrive, you are to strip down to your panties, kneel on the purple square, and place the blindfold on your eyes."

"Ooooh," she says. "I like this."

When I open the door, she sucks in a breath. "This isn't a weight room!"

She slides off me to look around. "Jesse! I love it!"

I flip a switch on the wall. Immediately, the room goes black and a white strobe breaks up our vision.

"Like the sex club!"

I turn the light to a slow red pulse.

"And the castle."

She runs over to me to wrap her arms around me. "We're going to have so much fun in here," she whispers.

"I know. Now get your fucking clothes off and assume the position before I decide you're a bad girl."

She squeals, kicking off her boots and jerking her sweater over her head. I enjoy the strip show and how her breasts bounce as she tosses her bra in the corner.

Soon she's only in black panties and kneeling on the pad.

"Blindfold," I bark.

She snatches it up and slides it over her eyes.

I head over to the wall to pick up a riding crop.

We're going to enjoy this room.

I can't wait to hear her scream.

Epilogue: Lili

My brother Leo gives me my final instructions as I prepare the table at the head of the ballroom. I'm already in my gown, tiara, and gloves even though the guests at the first birthday party for Princess Lucy won't arrive for another hour.

I have preparations of my own.

Leo straightens the ceremonial cloth made from spun gold. "Do you even have pockets to empty?"

I shove my gloved hands into the hidden pockets. Aisha, our stylist, designed this dress specifically for tonight. It's fiery red at the bodice and top of the skirt, then slowly morphs into a vivid purple at the bottom. I like being Indigo at times, even though I shut down her influencer account and retired the red wig. I've stopped posting as Princess Lili, too. My life of social media super-stardom has passed.

I do, however, have a super secret account called Aria's Dungeon where I post provocative images from Jesse's special room. Not so much what we do. That would get my account banned. But artsy pictures of panties and riding crops, or a handprint on a thigh. Stuff like that. It's titillating and fills my need for secret social interaction. Aria already has tons of sponsors sending us all sorts of dirty toys to try out.

We're never bored.

But none of that is for tonight. I'm Princess Lili, and my brother is tutoring me on the proper Avalonian procedure for an official proposal of marriage.

"Empty your pockets and explain the significance of each item. Make sure you're prepared to part with them for a while, as they'll be on display."

I nod.

He passes me the Avalonian royal betrothal ring. "You'll have to see what finger the ring will fit on. It's sized for a woman's middle finger, so it might have to be his pinky."

"Got it." I let out a long breath.

"You sure you want to do this publicly? I did it with Sunny in front of only her grandmother."

"You'd only known her for five minutes and were running from the royal guard!"

"True. Our sister did hers in the rose garden."

"I'm the least traditional sibling, so I'm throwing this bone to our parents."

Leo grins. "I think it's great. Dad might be warming up to him."

"You mean because he finally stopped having him thrown out of the gates?" The guards had a standing order to eject Jesse if he attempted to visit, rescinded by Father only last month. Eleven months of kicking him out. It was ridiculous. He's made Jesse work for it.

"Exactly. And he's coming to the birthday bash, isn't he?"

"It would be hilarious if they kicked him out before I could propose. And by hilarious, I mean, I would torch the palace."

Leo laughs. "I'll personally speak to the front guards and ensure his safe passage inside."

"Thank you."

I tuck the signet ring in my pocket. "I guess I'm ready."

"Good. I need to go check on Sunny and the guest of honor. She already spit up all over her birthday dress during the photo shoot."

"Oh no!"

"It's fine. We had three made." Leo steps off the platform. "See you at the party."

My throat tightens. I'm doing this. There will be press at the party, so my father can't stop me without creating an incident. And if I perform the ritual, Avalonian law states that it is binding.

Unless, of course, he says no.

Even though Leo has assured me that Jesse will be allowed into the palace, when Jesse texts me to say he's arriving, I go out the front doors to wait for him myself.

There is a line of cars dropping off guests, so I end up having to greet each family as I wait. It's not so bad, and accepting their bows and saying hello keeps my mind off the stressful moment ahead.

I'm not trying to overshadow Princess Lucy's big day, but Leo, Sunny, and Octavia all agreed it was the perfect time to stage an engagement coup. And it's also exactly a year since I stumbled through the unexpected hotel door and landed on Jesse's carpet, so it's fitting all the way around.

I just have to get it done.

Jesse arrives in a sleek gray classic Rolls Royce that fits in with the other cars passing through the driveway. He wears a black tux with a white tie, and looks so much like he did on the night of the masquerade that heat rushes between my legs.

Simmer down, girl. But he's had precious few visits to the palace. In fact, we've never even broken it in properly.

Later. Yes. I'm taking him to my childhood bed and doing all the dirty things.

He spots me and smiles. He knows the drill, standing before me with a formal bow and waiting for my nod to be released from the gesture. Then I take his hand and enter the palace with him.

Whew. He's here.

Technically, the royal family is supposed to make an official entrance as a group at half-past six, but I decide not to abandon Jesse. Thanks to my father, he's not familiar with royal events and might need some coaching.

Not that I care that much if he breaks protocol, but at this point, avoiding more reasons for my father to dislike him is a priority.

We walk along the side wall of the ballroom, picking up champagne from a waiter's tray as we go. The room is full. Guests know not to be tardy to an event like this.

An enormous birthday cake fills one corner and we walk closer to examine it. There are thirty-three tiers, thirty-two for Leo, and an extra one for Lucy, as they are now first and second in line for the throne.

"You're beautiful," Jesse says. "No one is going to look at the baby with her aunt nearby."

I elbow him. "Hush. This is Lucy's day."

He grins and sips his champagne, then glances up at the ceiling.

"No cupola or rail," I say. "Don't get ideas."

"Oh, you want me to get ideas."

I do, actually.

The orchestra quiets unexpectedly, then strikes up again with the Avalonian anthem. This is one moment Jesse must get right. We all turn to the flag-keepers, who are entering the ballroom.

Jesse puts his hand on his heart, which maybe is some tradition in his country, but I pull it down. I bow my head to show him what to do, hands clasped low in front of my belly.

He follows my lead, then, of course, I have to stop doing it. As a member of the royal family, my head is supposed to be up, gaze fixed upon the adoring citizens with pride and benevolence.

The royal children were taught this at age four, long before we could have even guessed what benevolence means.

Two rows of the King's Regiment follow the flag-keepers, then my father with my mother, then my sister.

There's another row of guards, then Leo with Sunny, and baby Lucy is on a cushion lifted by four guards. She's strapped in because every time they placed her on it, she would immediately crawl off.

I'm surprised she's not trying to wriggle her way out, but the sight of so many people has struck her momentarily still and silent. She wears a vivid yellow dress, a small crown on her head attached with a lacy band.

As she gets used to the spectacle, she seems to remember she has something attached to her head and reaches up to yank it off. It sails through the crowd. A woman catches it and hands it to a guard. No one titters, though. Not during the anthem.

They pass us and Octavia subtly tries to wave me over to the spot beside her. I pretend I don't see her. I'm not leaving Jesse quite yet.

The song ends, and the room politely claps. This time it's Father who catches my eye. Okay, *now* it's time to go.

I lean close to Jesse. "I should be with the family while they introduce Lucy."

"I'll be here."

As the family files onto the platform, I step in behind Octavia. Everyone's eyes are on baby Lucy. The guard with her crown passes the headpiece to Sunny, who tries to refasten it on Lucy's head. It lasts less than three seconds before it's flying through the air a second time.

Leo hefts the baby princess into the crook of his elbow and walks up the steps. Sunny follows, as well as Rosenthal, the Director of Culture. He's decked out head to foot in gold to bless the baby's first birthday.

The rest of the family is in the usual muted tones, Mother and Father in dove gray, Octavia in soft pink, Sunny in yellow, and Leo in the Crown Prince's slate blue. I must stand out like a flower in my red and purple gown. It's fine. It's proof that one of these things is not like the others.

Rosenthal recites a litany of blessings and proclamations about Lucy. She's having none of it, squirming nonstop to get down from Leo's arms. She took her first steps two weeks ago, and she's ready to *move*.

Leo looks like he's wrangling an octopus as he constantly moves about to keep her roughly in the vicinity of Rosenthal's raised hand, conveying the hope of a bright future for all Avalonians.

Finally, Lucy lets out a long, frustrated howl, and this time the crowd has a harder time holding back their laughter. Leo tries to set her down and hold her hand, but she manages to squirm away and toddle to the gold-enrobed table.

Sunny bends down to scoop her up, but it's too late, she's grabbed the end of the cloth and thrown herself off balance. Her chubby fingers have a death grip on the gold fabric and when she plops onto her diapered butt, the cloth slides off the table, covering her gold.

Laughter breaks out over the audience. Leo and Sunny try to drag the gold tablecloth off her, but she's gripping it with both hands.

Rosenthal realizes the solemnity of the moment is lost and closes his book, stepping aside.

Giggles erupt from below the cloth. Leo and Sunny pile wads of gold under their arms and finally unearth their child. When her cherubic laughing face is finally revealed, she says her only word, "Boo!"

And that's it. The room is filled with laughter and claps. Lucy looks out over the crowd, thrilled at the ruckus she's caused. She lifts the gold fabric in front of her face and then drops it down, calling out, "Boo!"

Leo kneels next to her, completely unable to hold it

together. Sunny presses the back of her hand to her lips, trying to control her laugh.

Mother is biting back a smile. Father, predictably, looks like he might murder someone. Sigh. There is literally no one more serious.

Rosenthal declares the birthday party has officially begun. Four chefs light the lines of candles on the cake. The room sings "Happy Birthday" to the baby while staff members extricate the gold cloth and spread it back over the table.

The cake is cut and the first piece is given to Leo and Sunny for Lucy.

And then there's a pause.

Leo looks over at me.

The orchestra plays a slow, gentle number, changing the mood of the room.

Here we go.

The set-up is perfect, like Leo predicted. Mother and Father and Octavia stand at one end of the dais. Leo, Sunny, and Lucy are at the other. Lucy licks frosting off her fist.

Rosenthal is present, which helps make this official.

I glance up at the microphone floating above the table, which had amplified Rosenthal's speech. Now it will do mine.

I clear my throat. "Jesse, can you come to the front?"

The crowd murmurs. It's not dark yet, and the early evening light streams in with bands of color through the stained glass windows lining the ballroom. Jesse walks through it, an artwork unto himself as his face reflects blue and green and yellow and red.

Then he's at the base of the platform.

I draw in a shaky breath. "One year ago, two amazing things happened. First, our sweet Lucy was born." I gesture to her, avoiding any glance toward my father. He's about to be so mad.

"The second is that I met someone incredibly important." I shift my arm forward. "The internationally renowned artist Jesse Adams."

My father takes a step forward, but Mother subtly takes his elbow, preventing him from going any farther.

Score one for Mom.

"There's a lot to a princess the world doesn't see." I look down at Jesse, who smiles up at me, his hands clasped like during the anthem. "Maybe we like riding the subway. Maybe we enjoy walking across a bridge with the wind messing up our hair. And maybe we sometimes fall in love with someone nobody expects." I glance at my sister. "Or maybe we do that a lot."

There's a gentle laugh across the crowd.

"I know poor Rosenthal hasn't gotten to do his usual pomp and circumstance for the betrothals of the first two Avalonian children of King Francisco. But today, I am rectifying that with the official transfer of the betrothal ring in a traditional Avalonian proposal."

Someone behind me sucks in a breath, but I don't look to see if it's my mother, or father, or sister. I keep going. "Rosenthal, I have the ring to be blessed." I pull it out of my pocket.

Rosenthal is momentarily frozen, looking from me to the King. I don't turn. I don't want to see my father's face. I hold out the ring. "Rosenthal?"

There is another hesitation, then he comes forward. He holds the ring high. "Let this moment be a renewal of all the sacred bonds of marriage in Avalonia."

He turns to me. "Please empty your pockets so that your beloved knows that all that you possess is now…" He hesitates. "Also *his*."

I flash him a smile. He's never done a reverse betrothal. The liturgy is intended for a man proposing to a woman. Good. Times are changing.

My fingers close around the first object in my pocket. I pull out a padlock and set it on the table. "This is a love lock. For decades, couples could leave a lock on the Brooklyn Bridge in New York, as well as several other bridges around the world, to declare the permanence of their unbreakable bond. This lock will be the first love lock to go onto the bridge over Lake Avalonia in the public park. We hope other happy couples will journey there to leave locks as proof of their commitment."

I reach into the opposite pocket for the second item and set it next to the lock. "This is a special art gum eraser, designed for artists. It reminds us that no mistake is so great that it can't be fixed."

Jesse nods. His eyes are shining, and for a moment, my throat tightens so much that I'm not sure I can speak. But then I reach for the last object in my pocket.

"This is a pin designed by the great jewel artist Arturo Felini. It depicts two flames merging into one. It represents the joining of our passions." I give him a wink. "Art and service."

He winks back. Like hell I'm talking about art and service.

I lay the pin on the gold table and turn to Rosenthal. "The ring?"

Rosenthal walks it forward, then gestures for Jesse to come up the steps to the platform.

He is pure grace as he ascends to the level of the royal family.

I come out from behind the table and give him a deep curtsy. "And now for your mother."

Jesse tilts his head. But from deep in the crowd, a tall woman in a jade-jeweled gown moves forward. I met her some months ago when she visited Jesse. Sensing I'm watching something important, Jesse turns his head.

"Mom?"

She ascends the steps with a grace that looks royal. Her hair is short, black and curly, long emerald earrings swinging to her shoulders. "My beautiful boy." She grasps his cheeks and kisses his forehead. His father was invited but had a shoot in Africa and this time, as always, chose his career over his son.

No matter. The important one is here.

Jesse and his mother stand side-by-side to face me. She holds Jesse's hand.

I draw in a breath. "Maggie Adams, mother of Jesse Adams, I present to you the betrothal ring of Avalonia, to be worn by those betrothed to a member of Avalonia's ruling family until the time of their marriage. If your son consents to our marriage, you will convey your blessing upon our union by placing the betrothal ring on his right hand."

Maggie nods.

"I do," Jesse says.

I laugh. "I haven't asked you yet."

"Oh." Jesse laughs nervously. I've never seen him this rattled. "Go on then."

I glance at my sister, who is beaming at us. Leo gives a thumbs-up.

"Jesse Adams, by the sworn authority of the crown of Avalonia, the jewel of Europa, and one of its heirs, fourth in line to the throne, I wish to bequeath upon you the title of Prince, as my bridegroom. Do you consent to this marriage?"

Jesse waits a moment to make sure I'm done this time. "Yes! Yes. I do."

"Maggie Adams, if your family agrees, you may convey your blessing with the ring."

His mother takes his right hand. She obviously knows her son well, or is practiced in eyeballing the girth of a finger versus the size of a ring, because she slides it on his fourth finger. It's a perfect fit.

Rosenthal steps before us. "As the Director of Culture for the Royal Family of Avalonia, I declare this betrothal officially begun."

Jesse leans in to kiss me, but Rosenthal steps between us. "As is customary, the non-familial betrothed will be guarded until he is escorted to the bridal, err, the wedding tower!"

I laugh. I didn't think Rosenthal would follow procedure to the letter of the law. But two royal guards come forward to stand on either side of Jesse.

"A tower?" Jesse asks.

I shrug. "It's sort of tradition. Don't worry. I'll come visit."

"Hope you know how to tie knots on a bedsheet," Leo calls.

Rosenthal gathers the items on the table. "Let the birthday and engagement party begin!"

I'm allowed to stand beside Jesse again, and I reach up to pull his face to mine. A great cheer goes up among the crowd, causing Lucy to let out another howl at the noise.

Everyone laughs and Leo feeds her more cake. The orchestra strikes up a lively song, and I drag Jesse and his mother onto the dance floor to turn in a circle. Soon the other guests are forming small circles to join in.

The music picks up speed, and the dizzying whirl makes me feel light. Jesse catches my gaze. Even as the other revelers blur as we turn in our frenzied circle, his features are clear.

And so is my future. Perhaps my escape from the castle was short-lived.

But the love I found in my two weeks on my own brought me the most important thing.

A love that will last my lifetime.

As the song ends, we break our joined hands and Jesse pulls me close. "Am I really going to have to stay in the tower?"

I wrap my arms around his waist. "Probably only for a few days."

"A few days trapped in a palace. Whatever will I do?"

I stand on my tiptoes to get closer to his ear. "You'll meet me somewhere extra special."

His grin is so wide that his cheek brushes mine. "And where is that?"

"This castle has an *actual* dungeon."

Thank you for reading *Royal Escape*!

If you missed Prince Leo's wild proposal to Sunny after only knowing her for five minutes, go back to the beginning of the trilogy for Royal Pickle!

And Princess Octavia had a seriously crazy start to her love life with a royal guard in the hilariously awkward Royal Rebel.

Curious about Axel and that spotlight operator? Axel is part of the Pickle family, and he's going to make his move in the hilarious *Tasty Pickle*. Sign up for JJ Knight's list to get an email or text message when it comes out!

Learn how the Colorado Castle came to be. Follow the incredibly funny and sexy billionaire romance between Donovan and Havannah in Tasty Mango.

Did Zerobia intrigue you? Meet her as Jo's best friend in the blockbuster bestselling first series by JJ Knight — Uncaged Love.

The Pickleverse is ten books strong! See the entire reading order!

BOOKS BY JJ KNIGHT

Romantic Comedies

Single Dad on Top

Big Pickle

Hot Pickle

Spicy Pickle

Royal Pickle

Royal Rebel

Royal Escape

Tasty Mango

Second Chance Santa

The Accidental Harem

MMA Fighters

Uncaged Love

Fight for Her

Reckless Attraction

Get emails or texts from JJ about her new releases:

JJ Knight's list

About JJ Knight

JJ Knight is one of the pen names of six-time *USA Today* bestselling author Deanna Roy. She lives in Austin, Texas, with her family.

To choose your next read from one of her sixty books, visit the web site **Read Laugh Swoon** to pick by book boyfriend, story line, heat level and more!

facebook.com/jjknightauthor

twitter.com/deannaroy

instagram.com/deannaroyauthor

bookbub.com/profile/jj-knight

tiktok.com/@deannaroy.author

www.ingramcontent.com/pod-product-compliance
Lightning Source LLC
Chambersburg PA
CBHW070437170726
48291CB00002B/545